SOUTHERN HEAT

SOUTHERN HEAT

DAVID BURNSWORTH

FIVE STAR

A part of Gale, Cengage Learning

GALE
CENGAGE Learning

Detroit • New York • San Francisco • New Haven, Conn • Waterville, Maine • London

LIBRARY OF CONGRESS CATALOGING-IN-PUBLICATION DATA

Burnsworth, David.
  Southern heat / David Burnsworth. — First edition.
    pages cm
  ISBN-13: 978-1-4328-2800-4 (hardcover)
  ISBN-10: 1-4328-2800-2 (hardcover)
    1. Veterans—Fiction. 2. Heirs—Fiction. 3. Charleston (S.C.)—
Fiction. I. Title.
  PS3602.U76755S68 2014
  813'.6—dc23   2013038371

First Edition. First Printing: February 2014
Find us on Facebook– https://www.facebook.com/FiveStarCengage
Visit our website– http://www.gale.cengage.com/fivestar/
Contact Five Star™ Publishing at FiveStar@cengage.com

Printed in Mexico
1 2 3 4 5 6 7 18 17 16 15 14

For Patty. Without you, this book could never
have been written.

ACKNOWLEDGMENTS

There are many people responsible for helping me with what eventually became *Southern Heat.* I'm sure I'm going to forget someone, but here goes. First and foremost is my wife, Patty. Not long after we married I mentioned I'd like to write a novel. Upon hearing that, she seized every opportunity to remind, encourage, push, pull, antagonize—the list could go on—me to do what I said I wanted to do. Her unending persistence helped me find my own.

Secondly, the past and present members of the South Carolina Writers Workshop, Greenville Chapter, are responsible for taking in this novice who showed up one day with a very rough draft. Phil Arnold, Susan Boyer, Mack Clarke, Roseilyn Clements, Kevin Coyle, Vickie Daily, Barbara Evers, Betsy Harris, Jim McFarlane, John Migacz, Marsha Migacz, Valerie Norris, Jim Saunders, Carole St. Laurent, Shaylene Scandale, Pat Stewart, Steve Stewart, Bob Strother, and Irena Tervo; thanks so much. Your honest critiques and support carried the day.

I had the pleasure of meeting Hank Phillippi Ryan at an SCWW conference after attending one of her courses. She is such a great lady and gave me much support and encouragement along the way. Through Hank, I connected with Editor Chris Roerden. Chris told me the truth. All I had to do was listen and make the changes, which included the entire ending.

Killer Nashville—what a great event. Thanks to Clay Stafford and Jaden Terrell and all of the people who help make that conference the benchmark it is. You guys rock!

My friends at Five Star: Gordon Aalborg, Deni Dietz, Marcia LaBrenz, Tracey Matthews, and Tiffany Schofield, have been great to work with. Thank you so much for this opportunity.

Thanks to my parents for instilling in me the love of reading. Mom, I'll get to those new authors after I finish the first twenty you recommended!

To my Men's Group brothers at Restoration: Tray, Mike, Danny, and Otis. You kept me on the right path.

Thanks to my agent, Jill Marr, who patiently answered every all-too-frequent email.

And, last but not least, Charleston, South Carolina. There is no other city like it. For those that know or don't, I took liberties with locations. Obvious ones like the Chinese brothel and the red light district, which, as far as I know, don't exist. Simmons Alley is named after Philip Simmons, a very talented Charleston blacksmith, but isn't on any city map. Neither are The Church of Redemption and Mutt's Bar. But I wish they were. Hagan Manor is what I pictured an antebellum home would be, but it isn't in Yemassee or anywhere else. The Isle of Palms thankfully doesn't have to deal with a dive like the Pirate's Cove, but it was fun to put it there. Station 10 on Sullivan's Island was my home for almost five years and it was the closest thing to paradise I've ever experienced.

CHAPTER ONE

"A man doesn't have the right to avoid reaping what he sows."

Brother Thomas

Saturday night in the holy city of Charleston, South Carolina, it was easier to find a cheap motel on the Battery than a parking space near the Market. Especially in July. I bounced over century-old bricks, made a big U on Meeting Street, and headed back.

My uncle wanted to meet for dinner, and I was late.

Three blocks over, a spot opened up on Chalmers Street, and I shoehorned my Mustang in. A birthday present to myself, the car had a screaming V-8, chrome wheels, and black paint. Its finish reflected the glow of the gaslights. I hadn't needed a new car. What I needed was something besides my dog to make me smile, and I was tired of double-shots of Beam.

To save a few steps, I cut down a darkened alley. A quick flash and a loud pop echoed off the surrounding walls. I hit the deck, rolled behind a dumpster, and reached for my Beretta. It hadn't been there in six months and wasn't now. The aroma of spoiled seafood from the garbage hit me harder than a bullet.

A voice in the alley shouted like my drill sergeant in boot camp. "Give me an answer!"

My eyes adjusted to the dim light. I peered around a corner

of the dumpster. A figure knelt over a body. To get a better view, I stood. My foot hit an empty bottle. It clanged across the cobblestones of the alley. The kneeling man raised his arm. The silhouette of a gun aimed in my direction. I dove back behind the dumpster. He fired. The bullet ricocheted off the steel frame. I needed an exit strategy.

Receding footsteps of someone running echoed in the alley. After a moment all I heard was labored breathing and I eased from my hiding spot. The figure with the gun was gone. The body on the ground wheezed. I got to my feet, hurried over to help, and found my uncle staring up at me with his one good eye, the other having been lost in Vietnam and now covered with an eye patch.

"Uncle Reggie!" I fell to my knees.

Blood trickled from his mouth as he said my name, "Brack." His voice was rough and muffled by the liquid filling his lungs.

Grabbing my phone, I punched nine-one-one.

"Brack," he whispered, and his uncovered eye closed.

The emergency line rang in my ear.

"I'm calling for an ambulance," I said.

"Ray." He coughed. "Ray shot me."

I let the phone drop a few inches. "Who's Ray?"

He swallowed hard.

A tinny female voice interrupted, "Nine-one-one. What's your emergency?"

The life went out of Uncle Reggie and I placed two fingers on his neck.

No pulse.

"Sir," said the operator. "What's your emergency?"

"My uncle's been shot. We're in Simmons Alley." I placed the phone on the ground next to me, raised my uncle's chin, and gave him CPR.

In the middle of my second round of chest compressions, the

howling intake noise and moaning exhaust of a car engine at full throttle made me look up. Flashing lights bounced off the dumpsters and trash lining the alley.

A patrol car headed for me, and I jerked my hands up in reaction. It skidded to a stop a few yards away. Doors swung open in unison. Two men stepped out and trained their weapons on me. "Police! Freeze!"

One of them moved out of my line of vision.

"He's not breathing," I said.

The officer by the cruiser said, "Get your hands up!"

Patience left me. "He's been shot! Make yourself useful and call an ambulance."

"Get down!" screamed a voice behind me. A hard shove made me hit the ground face-first next to my uncle. The officer jammed his knee into my back, frisked, and cuffed me.

I spit blood and dirt and tried to take a breath. "He's my uncle. Help him!"

The second officer knelt beside Uncle Reggie and checked for a pulse like I did. "He's gone."

It took both cops to lift all six-foot, two-hundred-and-ten pounds of me off the ground. I grunted at the strain on my joints from the handcuffs. They placed me in the backseat of a cruiser and shut the door. One of them rattled off something on the radio. I ran my tongue over a split in the middle of my lower lip. Blood on the front of my white T-shirt mixed with three-century-old soot from the cobblestones. Ten feet away my only family and best friend lay dead. I shook my head in disbelief. The moon cast everything in electric blue.

More vehicles showed up and the area erupted in activity. Gray uniforms and white-jacketed technicians crowded into the narrow passage between the old brick buildings. Cameras flashed. Two suits got out of an unmarked Crown Vic. One knelt beside my uncle. The other spoke with one of the uniforms, both of them glancing at me several times. After a few minutes, the suits teamed up and came at me like two sand crabs ready to make a meal out of a fish carcass washed up on the beach. I saw my wallet in one of the crab's claws and realized it was no longer in my back pocket.

The first one to the cruiser's door was slim and tall with stiff creases in his slacks and shirt. A silver Rolex flashed on his wrist. The second man, half a step behind, had a stocky build. His loosened tie exposed an unbuttoned collar. Both wore short sleeves, a necessity in the sweltering lowcountry.

The stiff-creased crab opened the door. "Brack Pelton?"

"Yes."

"I'm Detective Rogers." He pulled out a notepad and pen. "This is Detective Wilson. We're with Charleston P.D. and need to go over a few things with you." He looked at my face. "I see you're injured. We'll get someone to check you out in a minute."

"Thanks." I didn't feel the pain.

"Brack?" Detective Rogers paused. "Can I call you Brack?"

I grinned to show off my busted mouth. "Sure."

"How did that happen, Brack?"

"What?"

Rogers pointed at my mouth with the pen. "Your lip."

I gritted my teeth, knowing it wouldn't do me or my uncle any good to get on the bad side of the police. "I must have fallen. The officers were kind enough to help me up."

Detective Wilson spoke for the first time. "Good answer."

Rogers wrote something in his notepad. "So, what can you tell us about the deceased? You said he was . . ." He flipped a page. "Your uncle?"

"I was supposed to meet him at High Cotton."

"We can't seem to find any identification," said Wilson. "Can you give us his name?"

"Reggie—Reginald Sails." I spelled the last name.

Detective Rogers wrote it down. "Did he say anything before he died?"

I nodded. "He said Ray shot him."

Rogers and Wilson looked at each other.

"Did he say it exactly like that?" Wilson asked. "We need to know, word for word."

The cuffs dug into my wrists. I eased forward and exhaled. "He said 'Ray shot me.' I asked him who Ray was but he didn't answer."

Wilson said, "Any reason why someone might want to harm your uncle?"

"No. He owns a rundown dive on the Isle of Palms and spends his free time surfing."

Rogers asked, "Which dive? That pirate bar?"

"The Pirate's Cove." It was the only real dive left on the island.

"No kidding." Wilson's eyes focused on something past me, as if he was thinking.

I choked and cleared my throat. "No kidding."

"My nephews love the place," Wilson said. "All the pirate stuff and that big red and blue bird."

"Macaw," I said.

"Macaw, right." Wilson watched me. "What were you guys doing in this alley?"

"I couldn't find a parking spot close to High Cotton and ended up on Chalmers. I was late and turned through here to save time and that's when he was shot."

Wilson paused and scanned the area. "Where was Mr. Sails?"

"Already in the alley."

Rogers wrote more. "You didn't arrive together?"

"No. Like I said, I was on my way to meet him."

Without looking up, Rogers made another notation. "You see who shot him?"

"Can't tell you what he looks like. Maybe six feet and fairly stout."

Both detectives sized me up. Rogers said, "That could describe you."

I stood, forcing them to back up. "Look, you think I did it? Test me for gunshot residue. Otherwise, get these cuffs off me and go find who killed my uncle."

"Easy there." Wilson raised his hands in a calming gesture. "No one's accusing anyone of anything."

"At this point," Rogers added.

Wilson fished his keys out of his pocket and held them up. "Wanna turn around so I can unhook you?"

Murder in the tourist district was rare in Charleston and the TV news got wind of the shooting. Vans from three networks arrived from the opposite end of the street and set up camp. Their lights added to the intensity of the illumination used by the police and transformed the alley into a morbid scene from *High Noon*. Cameramen floated around along with reporters clutching microphones. Released from the confines of the cruiser's backseat, I sat on the rear chrome step-bumper of an ambulance within the safety of the police barrier. The detectives kept me company until the paramedics finished cleaning my face.

Detective Rogers said, "We'll need your T-shirt. For evidence."

I peeled off my shirt and threw it to him. "Take it."

Wilson got a green scrubs shirt from the back of the ambulance and handed it and a business card to me. "You're free to go. If you think of anything else, give me a call."

"Don't worry. You're going to hear a lot from me." I pocketed the card, slipped on the shirt, and walked through the alley to my car. At the police barricade, I found a spot with the fewest people loitering about and tried to cross the line.

A woman holding a microphone cut me off. "Are you

involved in the police investigation?"

I was ready to brush past her when a cameraman approached, flipped on the lights above the camera, and proceeded to film us. The woman stepped into the brightness and I caught a glimpse of my late wife, Jo, in the reporter's blond curls and pretty face. The momentary image of her almost made my knees buckle.

The reporter shifted on her feet, stood in front of me, and spoke into her microphone. "Darcy Wells, Channel Nine News. Are you with the police?"

She moved the microphone from her mouth to my face, but I said nothing. Channel Nine was supposed to mean something to me, I was sure, but all I could think about at the moment were the words I had wanted to say to Jo but didn't.

Darcy Wells aimed the microphone back at her mouth. "Can you tell us what's going on?" Her eyes did a good job of pleading as she stuck the microphone in my face for the second time.

I spit a glob of blood on the ground away from her, trying to get the taste out of my mouth, and didn't care it was on film. My forehead beaded with sweat from the sultry night air. "My uncle was killed tonight in this alley."

Detectives Rogers and Wilson pushed through the crowd and stood in my line of sight but out of view of the camera.

She said, "Did you see the killer? Was there more than one? Who was your uncle?"

I pointed to the investigating officers. "Ask those guys."

When her attention went to them, I stepped away. I heard her call, "Hey, wait!" But I turned the corner and hurried to my car, hoping the double-parked news trucks hadn't blocked me in.

The Mustang had just enough room to squeeze out.

★ ★ ★ ★ ★

Death followed me like a black cloud. I'd seen enough of it, caused enough of it, and hadn't planned on seeing any more for a while. Not like that. Not Uncle Reggie. I had to do something or I'd go nuts. The only place that might have some answers was the same place the police would be headed next, if they weren't there already.

As I wound the Mustang to a hundred and merged onto the Arthur J. Ravenel Bridge, my delayed reaction to what happened hit me. I thundered over the Cooper River and didn't let up on the accelerator until the descent on the other side into Mount Pleasant. If not for the patrol car usually parked at the end of the bridge, I wouldn't have let up at all.

The small beach-shack my uncle had called home for as long as I'd known him stood on the south side of the Isle of Palms. Sand covered the driveway—the entire yard, in fact. I swung around and parked, the high-intensity discharge headlights from my Mustang bouncing off palmetto trees. I got out of my car and walked to the house that mimicked my uncle's lifestyle. In the darkness, I opened the door to the screened-in porch, trimmed in rotten wood and white paint-flake, and eased my way between two old rocking chairs. At the front door I felt the top of the frame for the key, found it, and let myself in.

My uncle had left a light on in the living room. His prized surfboards leaned against one wall . . . vintage Hobies, Webers, and Nolls all waxed to perfection, unlike his car. A newer couch faced a big flatscreen TV. Two shot glasses and a tequila bottle sat on his glass-topped coffee table. Lipstick on one of the jiggers caught my attention.

He'd always said cell phones caused cancer. The one and only instrument for his landline sat in the kitchen. A calendar hung on the wall beside it. Ms. July stared at me with all her naked beauty. I pulled out the pushpin holding it to the wall and scanned the dates. Today, my birthday, had been marked in bold black marker. The previous week had a notation for a Mutt's Bar.

With the calendar in hand, I walked into the bedroom. My uncle had shown me his version of a safe-deposit box, a hole in the floor covered by loose boards, when I moved to town. He peered at me with his one blue-crystal eye and his trademark grin peeking through a graying beard. "If anything happens to me, here's some legal stuff."

"Uncle Reggie," I told him, "the next hurricane will blow this whole house and all your legal stuff to Columbia. It'll land on the front lawn of the capitol, right next to the confederate flag."

He said, "That'd be something, wouldn't it?"

I knelt beside the bed and lifted a couple flooring boards up and out of the way. In the hole I saw two bands of cash and a stack of papers on top of a moving carton. I picked up the papers and sat on the bed to read them. Nothing popped out at me other than the cash—ten grand in each band. I put the bills in my pocket and carried the carton and calendar out to my car. The police were about to get a whole lot of help to solve this murder. Probably more than they'd want. And I would make sure they found my uncle's killer . . . dead, if I got to him first.

CHAPTER TWO

The next morning I opened the front door of my bungalow to let my dog out. Shelby, my fifty-pound tan mixed-breed, headed for the bushes and afterwards roamed the yard while I made coffee. My two-bedroom house on Sullivan's Island was tiny compared to the McMansions surrounding it. Ten miles northeast of Charleston, the location gave me a short drive downtown and the crash of the Atlantic Ocean a hundred yards away from my back door. The view of the Intracoastal Waterway from my front porch was breathtaking. Jo had always wanted a place by the water. Three years after her death, I guess I was still hoping to please her.

Shelby looked at me, perked his ears, and barked.

"Ready to go?" A needless question.

He barked again, spun around, and ran into the living room to get his favorite possession, a worn tennis ball. I poured myself a large mug of coffee, snapped on his leash, and pocketed the ball. We took the long way to the water so he could sniff the Mallorys' mailbox and confirm it was still his turf. On the beach, we found our usual spot, a vacant stretch on the south side of the island where I wasn't likely to get a ticket for letting him rove freely. I tossed the ball a few times and he ran to retrieve it. Then I threw it in the water, he dove in after it, and we both went swimming. The warm water eased the tension from my muscles, which a sleepless night hadn't helped. Echoes of the recent gunshots made my hands ache for the M4 assault rifle I'd carried in Afghanistan. The image of blood trickling from the corner of my uncle's mouth parked on the edge of my sanity. I thought about the conversation I had with him on Friday, not realizing it was our last. I remembered every detail, starting with the time my cell phone vibrated and seeing his name in the caller I.D.

"What's up, Skipper?" I'd said. "Long time, no see."

"If I'm the Skipper, does that make you Gilligan?" He spoke with a deep tobacco voice, had for as long as I'd known him.

"Not if you're looking for some companionship on a secluded island."

"Got me there," he said. "Listen, don't make any plans for tomorrow night. You and me's going uptown for some good grub."

"What are you talking about?" I said. "And where have you been for the past week?"

"Don't try and sidetrack the issue, boy. I figured you'd forget, or pretend to forget. It's your birthday and I'm takin' you out whether you like it or not."

"Can't we just sit in the Cove and get drunk?"

"We can always do that," he said. "Let's do something different for a change. Like hang out with the socialites."

"Only if we can throw food at them."

Ignoring my comment, he said, "Besides, I've got important things to talk to you about, my good man."

"Yeah, like where you've been hiding."

"Like where I've been hiding."

At the time, I'd brushed what he said off as another one of his schemes. His business thrived on them. Unsubstantiated rumors of untaxed liquor and cigarettes kept him swimming in local and tourist patronage. Everybody wanted to take a shot at shafting the government, and alcohol and tobacco tax evasion seemed to be high on the list.

I was still running these thoughts over in my mind as Shelby and I headed home, passing the Schells' place on our way. The screen door screeched open like the gates of Sodom and Gomorrah, and Maxine Schell stumbled out onto the porch. Long, tan, slender legs stuck out of short shorts, and a tight halter top failed to cover the rest of her. A few years younger than me, she could have posed for my uncle's wall calendar.

"Hey, sugar. Wanna drink?" She tipped a sweating red plastic cup to her lips while watching me. Her porch greeting had become a routine, and not a good one.

I mentally kicked myself for forgetting to take a detour. "No thanks, Mrs. Schell."

Shelby wagged his tail like the dog he was.

Mrs. Schell flipped highlighted curls out of her face. "Maxine. Call me Maxine. How many times do I have to tell you, sugar?"

Her voice had a raspy, sensuous tone hinting at good things to come, but I'd already learned that cheap thrills only caused me to miss my wife that much more. "Sorry, Maxine. How're you doing today?"

"Fine. Just fine." She took another sip of her drink, batting long lashes as she swallowed.

"How's Bill?"

"Hmm. Still in Japan on business. I don't think he's ever coming home. Not tonight, anyway."

The screen door opened again and a little girl came out. "Mom? Sarah spilled her milk on the floor."

Maxine turned to face her. "I'll be there in a minute, honey. Now go back inside."

"Look at the doggie!" the little girl cried out and took a few running steps toward Shelby.

Maxine reacted sternly. "What did I tell you? Don't make me count to three."

The girl stopped and slowly retreated, giving Shelby a wave before easing the screen door closed.

I said, "Have a nice day, Maxine."

"Wait!" She held up her drink. "I saw you on the news this morning. I'm real sorry to hear about your uncle."

"I appreciate it."

"And someone was around your house while you were at the beach." She crooked her mouth. "Looked like that news girl from Channel Nine."

I slapped my forehead. Uncle Reggie's ex-wife owned the station. How could I have missed it? "Did you speak to her?"

Maxine put her free hand on a freer hip. "I tried. She got in her red convertible and drove away. Really kind of uppity, if you ask me."

I nodded, noting Maxine standing in front of her million-dollar house as she called someone else uppity. "Thanks, Mrs. Schell."

Shelby barked his goodbye and shot in front of me, taking up the slack in the leash and already sniffing for greener pastures.

Maxine waved. "You have a nice day, sugar. Come by later if you want to talk or have a drink . . . or whatever."

My wife was gone. Now my uncle. Nice days were in short supply.

I poured myself a glass of iced tea from a pitcher in the fridge and set the box from my uncle's hiding place on my kitchen table. The lid folded back easily. In it were photographs. Hundreds of them. I picked up a stack and flipped through them. Pictures of Uncle Reggie as a teenager. As a soldier with dolled-up Asian girls. Pictures of the Pirate's Cove before and after Hurricane Hugo came through in eighty-nine and ripped Charleston apart with its category five winds. Uncle Reggie had pictures of me during my dirt-track racing days standing on podiums with first-place trophies. Coming across wedding photos caused me to sit in a chair at the table. Jo was so beautiful in her long white dress. She'd gotten it custom-made and had talked about the dress and the flowers nonstop.

At the time, I'd been tired of listening to how white the material was and how pretty the flowers would be. But on this Sunday morning I would give anything to hear her tell it to me one more time. My world changed forever in the doctor's office when he gave Jo six months to live.

Mixed in with the other photos was a framed picture of me and Uncle Reggie taken the day I got off the plane after three years in Afghanistan, where I'd gone when Jo's time was up. I'd wanted my time to be up next, and the Marines seemed a good way to get there.

The bottom of the box was filled with pins from Uncle Reggie's service years and with his service history. Honorable discharge and medical forms went into a pile of their own. A page was labeled Air America. Uncle Reggie never talked about being in it. The paper was a commendation thanking him for five years of dutiful service. Of everything in the box, two things stood out—the name C. Connors printed at the bottom of a set of official-looking papers and an old stainless steel Zippo lighter.

At noon, I left with Shelby and drove to the Pirate's Cove. My uncle's dive, located on the beach on the Isle of Palms between two modern hotels, stuck out like a zit on a supermodel. The two-story wooden structure resembled a beached Spanish frigate. The first floor stood twelve feet off the sand thanks to the codes enforced after Hugo, the stilts covered by wood planks to resemble the sides of a ship. Its brown and green colors contrasted with the pinks and yellows of the other tourist traps.

Paige, the bar's manager, sat in my uncle's chair behind his desk going over what I guessed were last night's receipts. I walked in, inhaling the stale odor of my uncle's cheap cigars and missing him terribly. Shelby followed me in. To Paige's right hung a large Howard Pyle print depicting a pirate and his crew looking down on a bound magistrate. The bar's mascot, a blue and red Greenwing Macaw named Bonny, sat on a perch next to the desk. She flew to me and landed on my shoulder.

I stroked her neck feathers. "Hey, Bonny."

Bonny said, "What's up, Brack? *Squawk!*"

Paige's eyes were red and she was sniffling. Her brown hair was pulled back in a plastic clip and she wore a tight T-shirt with a picture on the front of the bar's flag. Uncle Reggie had redesigned the skull and crossbones of the Jolly Roger to show the pirate wearing a bandana made from a South Carolina state flag, sporting aviator shades, and smoking a cigar. Because the bar's air-conditioning unit was old and inefficient, Paige compensated by rolling the short sleeves of the shirt to her shoulders and knotting its hem above her stomach, which showed tan and flat. A top-forty station played on the overhead sound system. Bonny flew to her perch and I leaned against the doorway. Shelby laid his head in Paige's lap. She scratched behind his ears, and then wiped her cheeks.

I said, "Sorry I didn't call last night."

She nodded and bent down, kissing Shelby's head. He licked her face.

"I can't believe he's gone," she said. "I mean, it's like he was just in here complaining about how much the price of crab went up."

I walked to her and put my hand on her shoulder. A few seconds passed before she gave Shelby one last pat and stood. As soon as her eyes met mine, she put a hand to her mouth. Tears streamed down her face and a wail came out from deep within. She hugged me hard, her whole body shaking as she cried for the length of the song on the radio. When her tears subsided she let go and took a few deep breaths, wiping her eyes with the back of her hand. "How come you aren't crying?"

I handed her a tissue from a box on the desk. "I've become comfortably numb, as the song goes."

Paige laughed and wiped her face again. "I'm not sure why that's funny."

"Because it's not."

She wadded the tissue and threw it at me. "Jerk."

"As soon as I find out who did this, they won't have to worry about a trial."

I stood half a foot taller than Paige, but my height didn't stop her from pushing herself off the desk and giving me a shove. "Don't do anything stupid, Brack. He loved you. You know he wouldn't want you going to jail for doing something you'll regret later."

"First things first," I said. "Know anyone named Ray?"

"Why?"

I didn't answer.

"Come on, Brack. What's going on?"

"The police are going to ask you the same question."

"Why will police ask me if I know any Rays? What are you not telling me?"

Seconds ticked by as I thought about Uncle Reggie gasping for breath.

Paige shoved me again. "Tell me!"

"He died in my arms. He said Ray shot him."

Her hands covered her mouth again and she turned away. "Couldn't you do anything? Didn't you try to save him?"

"I was too late." I pulled an envelope out of my pocket with the twenty grand I'd found under Uncle Reggie's floorboards and held it up. "I need to put this in the safe."

I swung the Howard Pyle print to the right, revealing a wall safe. Besides me, only Uncle Reggie and Paige knew the combination. The safe door opened to an empty space, but I couldn't remember the last time I'd looked in it. I placed the twenty grand inside and closed it up.

Paige and I deliberated opening the Pirate's Cove for business, but both knew Uncle Reggie would not want something like his own death to interfere with the bar's operation. It was his soul. Before long, the place became packed—mostly with locals who scared away the tourists. I leaned against the railing on the upper of two large decks overlooking the Atlantic and sipped an iced tea loaded with two shots of Absolut, trying to clear my head. My dog lay at my side. I thought about how different the bar already felt without my uncle's presence. Someone put a hand on my shoulder, and I turned to see who it was.

Paige said, "We sold out of T-shirts, key chains, shot glasses, and every other trinket we had. I'm afraid people are going to start stealing the decorations. They must think we're going to close up shop."

"You've got to be kidding."

"I started selling the drink coasters and glassware. Anything with the bar's logo on it. Hope you don't mind."

"How much are you charging?"

"Five bucks for each coaster. They have to buy a drink to get a glass for ten bucks. I sent Mariel to the Piggly Wiggly to get all the plastic cups they had. We're going to need them."

Uncle Reggie promoted Paige to manager for good reason.

"By the way," she said, "I want to show you something."

She led me to the lower deck, Shelby following like the dog he was. I stopped twenty feet from the bar. People had enshrined the barstool my uncle always sat on. Taped to the stool, sitting on it, or hanging off it were a box of cheap cigars he smoked, a dive mask, a large conch shell, and other items like dollar bills with notes written on them. Some of these had already fallen and covered the floor, making a second pile. Shelby sniffed at a bronze plate leaning against one of the legs, probably something recovered from one of the shipwrecks around our harbor.

A man stood next to me and gave a sympathetic smile, his gray hair combed back and thinning at the peaks. His untucked white-linen shirt exposed the deep tan of a local. A big gold Cartier watch adorned his left wrist.

"People loved your uncle," he said, his voice dripping Charlestonian brogue.

I studied the mound. "It looks that way."

"My name's Chauncey Connors."

We shook hands.

"Brack Pelton."

"Mr. Pelton, I'm sorry for your loss."

"Thanks."

"He was a good man and he will surely be missed by a lot of people."

I nodded. "I've seen you in here before."

"My wife and I live on the island. We come in here about once a month."

"Connors," I said, thinking I'd seen the name before. "Your name is on some of my uncle's papers I found."

He handed me a card. "I was his attorney and his friend. I know this is all sudden and I don't want to keep you. When it's more convenient, I'd like to talk." We shook hands again. "In the meantime, if I can be of service, don't hesitate to call."

As the man walked away I looked at the card and put it in my pocket. Connors was the first name on the list of partners.

I went outside to get some air and encountered the same momentary vision of my wife from the night before, this time wearing a halter top, short skirt, and sandals.

"If it isn't Ms. Darcy Wells."

Shelby trotted to her and held out a paw.

She knelt and rubbed his head. "He's adorable."

I put my hands in my pockets. "I heard pets and their owners begin to look alike after a while."

"I hope not," she said, "for his sake. Buy me a drink?"

I leaned in close. "I think reporters with expense accounts can buy their own drinks. Even pretty ones probably not used to paying for anything."

"Okay," she said, "how about I buy you a drink? I'd like to finish our conversation from last night."

"That wasn't a conversation. That was an ambush. Tell Patricia I don't appreciate her network's tactics." Like using pretty reporters who look like my wife. "My uncle, your boss's ex-husband in case you didn't know, is dead. I really don't care about anything else."

I tried to walk away but the Channel Nine News girl kept up. "Patricia said you were a real piece of work."

A couple I recognized as regulars stopped me and I thanked them for coming. When they moved on, I turned back to Darcy. "Yet you came anyway."

She flashed perfect teeth. "I told her you'd like me."

I folded my arms across my chest. "Why's that?"

"I'm likable."

The similarities between this woman and my wife were many, from the blond curls pinned up to keep her neck cool in the summer to the relentless attitude. I said, "So where is your boss, anyway?"

Darcy motioned to the bar with one perfectly manicured hand.

Patricia Voyels had taken the stool next to the shrine and sipped a drink from a pink plastic cup. We must have run out of glasses already.

A few inches shorter than me, Patricia had stylish gray hair and a nice shape for a woman in her early sixties. Uncle Reggie had told me she hit the gym five nights a week. The lines in the skin around her eyes had grown deeper since the last time I'd seen her. She looked unhappy, but kept her emotions in check. She always kept her emotions in check.

Shelby, the traitor, ran and put his front paws on Patricia's lap in greeting. She scratched him underneath the bandana with the Pirate's Cove flag I'd tied around his neck and looked up at me. "Is there someplace we can talk?"

Chapter Three

When Patricia and Darcy followed Shelby and me past the entrance to the kitchen, Paige came out the swinging double doors. I stopped her and said I'd be in the office if she needed me.

Paige whispered, "What's Patricia doing here?"

"Not sure," I whispered back. "I'll let you know."

Shelby led us to the ten-by-twelve back room, Uncle Reggie's home away from home. The desk where Paige had been reviewing receipts earlier today was the first thing seen from the door. Neat stacks of paperwork told me she had spent time organizing things. Uncle Reggie would have left one big mess.

Patricia and Darcy sat on a couch taking up the other side of the room. After closing the door, I turned the desk chair to face them and sat. Shelby jumped on the couch between the women.

"All right, Patricia," I said. "Who's Ray?"

"What do you mean?"

"He said Ray shot him. Who is Ray?"

Patricia's eyes went to an old bookshelf in the corner, its shelves sagging from the weight of the Patrick O'Brian and Mickey Spillane novels crammed on them. She arranged her features to give the impression that she was thinking hard. "I'm sure I don't know any Ray. At least not any who would shoot Reggie."

I scratched the stubble under my chin. "The police will be coming by to ask so if I were you I'd have a list ready for them."

In addition to the TV station, Patricia owned the *Palmetto Pulse,* one of Charleston's daily newspapers. Both the station and the paper were big enough to make a tidy profit but small enough not to be considered too seriously. Thanks to hordes of unnamed sources, Patricia, the daughter of one of Charleston's exclusive Huguenot families, had the dirt on everyone in town. I wished Uncle Reggie had taken her for everything she was worth during the divorce, but he didn't. Couldn't, was more like it. He'd still loved her. I had to remember that.

Patricia said, "I'm not the one who's got to worry about being a suspect."

Before I could get a word out, Darcy said, "Okay. Truce."

Patricia said, "Did Reggie say anything to you about what he was involved in?"

I exhaled a long breath. "I was going to ask you the same thing. I hadn't seen him around in a week. My hunch is he was spending time with you again."

If Patricia sensed frustration in my voice, she let it pass. "He was, but he didn't tell me much. He came over at night and was gone by morning."

"The police are saying he was killed in a robbery attempt," Darcy said. "They couldn't find his wallet or I.D."

Patricia and I spoke in unison. "He didn't carry a wallet."

I asked Darcy, "Did the police find his necklace?"

"I don't know," she said, "but I'll check it out. If he didn't carry a wallet, what did he carry?"

Patricia said, "He had a money clip and a small pouch for change."

Monday morning, I woke after four hours of sleep on the couch in my uncle's office. Combined with no sleep the night before, I felt rough. Shelby nudged my arm, cocked an ear sideways, and opened his mouth, showing me his smile. He gave me a loud bark, kick-starting the hangover bulldozers in my head. They began to plow deep ruts, like giving me a lobotomy without anesthesia.

I rolled over and tried to catch a few more minutes of sleep, but the worn-out couch reeked of cigar smoke and felt as comfortable as cheap toilet paper. After staring at a large canvas sheet pinned to the ceiling with my uncle's interpretation of the Jolly Roger, I got up and let Shelby out.

The Pirate's Cove should have been trashed considering how many people had shown up, how much business we'd done, and how much alcohol we drank. But Paige had the staff stay late and help clean up. We filled the dumpster out back and had a truckload of plastic and glass in bags and boxes ready for recycling. Shelby and I reached my car. I spread his towel out on the rear seat and let him in before opening the driver's side door. An envelope stuck beneath the windshield wiper. The letter inside said:

Your uncle and I were working on something and it got him killed. I could be next. Meet me at Folly Pier today, 10 AM. I'll wait at the ocean end. Come alone. If I see anyone else, I will leave.

It was unsigned. I checked my watch. Five after nine. I had enough time to drop Shelby off at the bungalow, take a quick shower, and still make it to the pier at ten.

Folly was the runt of the nearby beaches. It faced the Atlantic from the south side of Charleston where the upper class hadn't yet come in with their stiff codes and big bank accounts. I parked and scanned the area. Nothing appeared out of place. Phish-Heads and surfers wandered the sidewalks. I got out of my car. The heat and humidity hit me like a warm, wet sponge. At a crosswalk, a black Chrysler with dark-tinted windows stopped and let me cross. Five Harleys idling nearby drowned out the sound of the surf.

By the time I made it up the steps to the wooden deck that extended a thousand feet out into the ocean, my clothes were soaked with sweat. At one of the shops, I bought the latest copy of the *Palmetto Pulse* because my uncle's picture was on the front page. The article was written by Ms. Darcy Wells, herself. I folded the paper and stuck it under my arm. Three black men fished over the railing, tackle boxes and catch coolers at their feet. An old couple sat on a bench watching the tide and holding hands. I walked the distance to the small pavilion at the end of the pier. Tourists were in full bloom, most of them wearing clothing with Charleston or local bars they had visited written across their chests. A lot of ball caps and wicker hats and bright bags.

Someone said, "Excuse me."

I turned and saw a man half a foot shorter than me wearing a white Charleston ball cap and a T-shirt with the logo of the biggest tourist trap in the city, the one the locals avoided. He looked to be a few years younger than me, maybe thirty.

I said, "Yeah?"

"My wife's shopping in one of the stores," he said. "I was wondering if you could take my picture. The sun's reflection on the water is perfect. By the time she gets out here, it may be too late."

"Um," I said. "Sure."

He came closer and handed me the camera.

I asked, "Where y'all from?"

"Right here," he said in a low voice. "I left the note on your car. Thanks for coming."

I stared at him a few seconds. Under the ball cap I saw a face partially hidden by glasses with clip-on sunshades.

"This will do," he said, louder, resting a hand on the railing. Behind him was the ocean. "Go ahead, take the picture."

I raised the camera and centered the man in the viewing window. He was sweating. I snapped the shutter.

"Good," he said. "Take a few more."

I did as he asked.

"Thanks," he said. When he approached me, he knocked the newspaper out from under my arm.

"Sorry." He bent down and picked it up, handing me the paper and another envelope, smaller than the one he left on my windshield. "Thanks for taking the pictures. I think I just spotted my wife." In a lower voice, he added, "Don't follow me."

I watched him walk up the pier and lost him in the crowd at the shops. After I returned to the car and started it to get the AC going, I looked at the envelope. It had a phone number written on it with instructions to call at five PM. Inside I found a jump drive. I placed the envelope and jump drive in the Mustang's glove box and headed downtown.

CHAPTER FOUR

Uncle Reggie did not live in the twenty-first century. Paige had threatened to quit if he didn't buy a laptop for her to run the business. Last night at the Cove, I used her Apple to find Mutt's Bar, the place noted on my uncle's calendar for a week ago. The bar wasn't listed in any phone book. My Internet search came up with one hit in the city, but not because Mutt's had a listing anywhere. Someone had gotten stabbed on the sidewalk in front of the place last month.

The East Bay exit off Highway Seventeen looped through Charleston's depressed area. Across from a dilapidated brown building with a neon-lit beer advertisement in the window, I found a parking spot. The outside temperature according to the gauge in my car showed one hundred, so I checked out the scene from the driver's seat with the AC blowing hard.

Formosan termites had decorated the outer face of the structure with their elaborate tunnels, like veins, entwined in what was left of the wood. The neon flickered against years of soot caked on the window. Next to it hung a rusty screen door. I'd been in places like this before, but not without an automatic weapon.

The hands on my watch pointed to noon. I got out of my car with the newspaper I'd bought at the pier and pressed the alarm remote. It acknowledged me with a quick blow of the horn.

The street was a different world. Black kids played on the cracked and broken sidewalks. Clothes hung on lines strung across the front porches of shotgun homes, most of which leaned to one side or the other. Daylight, I truly believed, was the one thing keeping me from becoming a missing person file. This same scene twelve hours later would be bad news.

Sour bar-wash and stale cigarette smoke permeated the air escaping through the rusty screen door. I grabbed the handle and pressed the old latch. The door's corroded springs squealed like Ned Beatty in *Deliverance* as I pulled it open. While my eyes adjusted to the dark room, I heard B.B. King's "The Thrill Is Gone" blaring from somewhere. A bar stretching the width of the room came into focus. Several men sat on mismatched stools, elbows riding the worn wood of the bar. A window unit protruding from the wall failed to condition what passed for air. A ribbon tied to the vent on the front of it fluttered in the tepid breeze. My eyes spotted an old Wurlitzer jukebox straight out of the fifties, its neon lights fighting to shine through decades of grime. I walked past two men posturing at a pool table with ripped green felt. At the bar, I eased out a stool two spots down from the other guys and sat.

The barkeep held a dirty towel. "You lookin' for directions?"

I gave him my best smile. "This Mutt's place?"

"Yep."

"Then I don't need directions. How about a Coke?" I placed both hands on the bar and nodded at the men seated next to me. "How you guys doing?"

Their manners weren't available, apparently. Much like my Coke. The bartender hadn't moved.

He put a cigarette in his mouth and lit it. "What you want, Opie?"

His boxed afro and lamb-chop sideburns were a few decades off but I didn't feel like offering any styling tips. He was taller than me, and I counted six others in the room who most likely wouldn't end up on my side if a fight broke out.

"I'm looking for Mutt," I said. "And a Coke." I pulled folded bills from my front pocket, peeled away a five, and set it on the bar.

The bartender blew out a stream of smoke in my direction. "Just 'cause Lincoln freed the slaves don't mean he's that popular here."

"Huh?" I was genuinely puzzled.

He pointed to the face of the bill.

I felt a bunch of eyes on me so I held up a twenty.

"Jackson's more like it," he said.

I dropped it on the five and the bartender scooped up both bills. He went to a rusty cooler, reached in through the ice, and pulled out my drink. With an opener tied to a long leather strap around his neck, he popped the top and placed the bottle in front of me.

I said, "You Mutt?"

"Who wants to know?"

"Jackson." I wasn't about to give him anything.

He wiped the bar with his grungy towel. "Mutt's on break. What can I help you wit?"

A Muddy Waters tune started and the bartender straightened up, cocked his head, and snapped his fingers. "How!" He forgot about wiping the bar and danced around.

I sat there watching him groove.

Chuckles came from somewhere in the room. The tension in the air felt like a hot landing zone, and I was unarmed. I opened the paper and pointed to the picture of my uncle. It was a good one Patricia must have taken a few years ago. His hair was tied back in a ponytail, his beard neatly trimmed, and the black patch covered his left eye.

The bartender stopped moving, picked it up, and looked at it for a long time. His dark face lightened a few shades.

He said, "What about it?"

I didn't know what to say next.

He laid the paper on the bar. "I asked you a question, boy."

A voice came from behind me. "You want us to take this cracker out back, Mutt?"

Sweat dripped down my back from the heat.

Mutt took a long drag from his Kool as if to ponder the offer and exhaled a cloud of smoke toward the ceiling. "Naw."

I realized my hands had the Coke bottle in a white-knuckled death grip.

The creaking of the screen door broke the tension.

A big voice boomed, "Everything okay up in here?"

The bartender looked past me to the doorway and nodded. "Brother."

After a moment, a man pulled out the stool beside me and sat. "Got any root beer, Mutt?" His minister's collar complimented a black suit hanging on a large frame. He was dark-skinned like the others and didn't seem uncomfortable being in a bar. A large belly strained the buttons of a black shirt and hid his belt buckle. His gray-speckled hair and mustache were neatly trimmed.

He turned toward me. "How you doing?"

"It's been one of those days," I said.

The bartender went to the cooler while the minister picked up the newspaper from the bar and looked at it. His eyes turned to me and he held out his hand. "Reverend Thomas Brown. People around here call me Brother Thomas. It mean Brother-in-Christ, mm-hmm."

I tried to match his meaty hold. "Brack Pelton."

Mutt sat the bottle of root beer in front of Brother Thomas and leaned on the bar. "This is all nice and cozy-like. I just got a few questions for the white boy, here."

Brother Thomas held up a hand. "No disrespect, Mutt, but I'd like to give Brother Brack a tour of our community." He looked at me. "How about it?"

What could I say to an offer like that? No thanks, I'd rather stay here and take my chances? "I'd appreciate it."

We pushed our stools back from the bar, took our soft drinks, and turned toward the exit. One of the patrons, a bald man with a gray beard, held the door open when we approached.

"Thank you, Clovis," Brother Thomas said. "I sure hope to see you in church next Sunday."

The man grinned. "I'll sure try, Brother. I'll sure try." Clovis's stained shirt had a "City Garage" patch over the pocket. Once Brother Thomas and I reached the sidewalk, Clovis waved at us with a cigarette and eased the squealing door closed.

Down the block, Brother Thomas stopped and turned to me. "What you did back there was either brave or stupid. I can't tell which."

I forced a smile.

"I seen you drive by," he said. "The whole street seen you. A white man like you parks his nice new car up in here and walks into that bar? Oh, Lord."

He walked. I kept up.

His mouth formed a grin and he shook his head. "Heh-heh. It'll keep that bunch back there busy talkin' for a while, mm-hmm."

I looked at the leaning houses we passed wondering if a pattern accounted for their off-centeredness. "You knew the man on the front page of the paper, didn't you?"

"I did. He was a good man."

"He was my uncle and I wanna know why Mutt's Bar was written in his calendar."

"I guess you'll have to ask Mutt," Brother Thomas said.

"You know my uncle was murdered, right?"

He nodded.

I said, "Anything you can tell me about him?"

"Not much you don't already know yourself."

"I'm having a hard time seeing a connection. My uncle owned a rundown bar on the Isle of Palms and sold overpriced drinks and shrimp cocktails to tourists. As far as I knew, he didn't attend church and wasn't the volunteering type. The only thing he enjoyed doing was wreaking havoc with the town council."

Brother Thomas gave me an "mm-hmm," but nothing else.

After a few moments of silence, I said, "I guess I'm wasting your time, Brother Thomas. I'm sorry to have bothered you and your community. Please extend my apologies to Mutt and everyone else."

I held out my hand.

The large preacher took it. "No bother. Come any time. Church service is at ten every Sunday morning. Sometimes Wednesday nights, too."

I carried a Swiss Army knife that had every tool imaginable including a small pen. With it, I wrote my cell number on the back of an old receipt and handed it to Brother Thomas. "If you think of anything I can add to the obituary, please give me a call."

He took the number. "Thank you, young man. I surely will."

I left him there and headed back the two blocks alone, thinking this was a big waste of my time, if not his. At the Mustang, I pressed the alarm remote and reached for the door handle. Someone grabbed my shoulder. On instinct, I dropped my keys to free my hands. Something stiff pressed against the back of my head.

Mutt's voice was low and serious. "You better tell me why you here axing questions before I blow your brains all over this shiny ride."

"Mutt!" Brother Thomas yelled from a distance. "Don't do it!"

"Stay outta this, Brother," Mutt shot back.

I kept calm and formulated a plan.

"It's . . . not . . ." Brother Thomas huffed from a closer distance, "what you . . . think." He must have been running.

Mutt moved closer to my ear. His breath felt like a bad fog. Spittle sprayed the side of my face when he spoke. "I smoked a lot of camel jockeys in Desert Storm. One white boy ain't gonna make a big splash on the list."

He tried to spin me around and I decided his one chance at me was over. I jammed an elbow in his face. The blow caught him off guard and he staggered backwards a step. I followed with a fast uppercut. My fist made solid contact with the underside of his chin. His head jerked back like a Pez dispenser followed by the rest of him. When he landed on the ground, the gun dropped from his hand. I picked up the pistol and my keys and scanned the area. A small crowd had gathered. Brother Thomas stood facing me, stooped over with hands on his beefy thighs and gasping from his run. Mutt was out cold.

In Afghanistan, I'd been assigned to Recon and volunteered for point every chance I got. With my wife gone, getting blown up seemed like a good idea. The commanding officers mistook my suicidal tendencies for leadership ability and promoted me. The problem with my military plan turned out to be quick reflexes—real quick reflexes. The kind that won car races. And fights.

"Brother Thomas," I said, "you wanna revise your story?"

CHAPTER FIVE

Elmore James's voice filled Mutt's Bar from the speakers of the vintage jukebox. As the old blues master sang about swinging a broom, Brother Thomas asked the bar patrons to leave. The ones who'd seen me take the gun from Mutt made a few threats.

To the exiting crowd, Brother Thomas said, "If Mr. Pelton or his car leaves here any different than they arrived, there will be hell to pay." He locked the door behind them.

Brother Thomas and I had found an old first-aid kit underneath the bar, and after we dragged Mutt inside took smelling salts from the kit to wake him.

Mutt stood unsteadily behind the bar and wrapped ice in a towel. He put it to his swelling nose, groaned, and said, "You one fast white boy, Opie."

Brother Thomas watched the bartender. "Not the smartest move you could've made, mm-hmm."

Mutt said, "Reggie was killed, man. You think we ain't next?"

I sat on the same stool as before. The gun was still in my possession, stuffed down the front of my shorts. Its handle stuck out the top of my waistband and jabbed me in the stomach. I said, "What did you do in Desert Storm, wash dishes?"

Mutt jutted out his chin. "Fifty-first infantry. You?"

"In Afghanistan, Recon, among other things."

Mutt repositioned the icepack. "I heard it was crazy over there. You don't know who you should be shooting at."

"I got out just in time."

"Brother Brack," Brother Thomas said.

"Just Brack."

"Brother Brack, what do you want from us?"

"The truth would be nice," I said. "You did a lot of nodding on our walk and not much talking."

The fat preacher sat on one of the stools and looked at Mutt, then at me. Mutt went to the other end of the bar, stooped down, and came up with a shoebox that he sat on the counter. He took the lid off, flipped through it until he found what he was looking for, and walked back.

"You big on pictures," Mutt said. "Here's one for you."

I took the black and white photograph. In the dimly lit bar, I could make out two soldiers standing arm in arm like best friends. One of the men was my uncle. Though he looked a lot younger when the picture was taken and had no eye patch, his crooked nose was the same. The man with him was black and I didn't recognize him. "Who's my uncle with?"

Mutt said, "My daddy, Sergeant Willie B. Tucker."

Another snapshot of history.

I said, "Who's Ray?"

At two-thirty, I skidded into the parking spot of the Pirate's Cove and killed the motor. The speeding ticket I had acquired lay crumpled in my hand as I gripped the steering wheel. Eighty in a fifty-five. At least the Highway Patrol hadn't been around when I hit one-twenty on an open stretch. A Mustang five-point-oh *moved*. The cop didn't ask if I had any weapons and I didn't offer Mutt's pistol stashed in the glove box. I threw the ticket onto the passenger floorboard and picked up the jump drive the tourist had given me.

Inside my uncle's office, I pulled the jump drive out of my pocket, sat in the chair, and turned on the Mac. Three spreadsheet files came up: Jameson Refining, Chromicorp, and

Cooper River Chemicals. I opened one of them and an expense sheet took up the screen.

Five PM, when I would phone the man from the Folly Pier, could not get here fast enough. I forced myself to focus. All three files had lines of data and a summary tab with "reported" and "actual" columns. Every figure in the "reported" column of each file was greater than the "actual." I printed out the summary sheets and copied the files onto another stick. When I finished, I put the drive in the safe and locked up.

At five o'clock, I phoned the number written across the envelope from the tourist on Folly Pier.

After a few rings, the voice of the same tourist answered. "Mr. Pelton, thanks for calling."

"You said in your note my uncle was murdered because of something you and he were working on. You want to tell me what that was?"

"Did you look at the files yet?"

"Yes, but I'm not sure what you've given me."

"Come on. Your uncle said you were smart."

Maybe I was reading more into it than was there. I decided to speak the obvious. "Looks to me like the companies were misrepresenting expenses or something."

"You could say that."

This conversation wasn't getting me anywhere. "You want to meet?"

"I'm not sure I can trust you yet," he said. "Take what you've got so far and run with it. Reggie already paid for the files. I'll call you in a few days. Be ready with twenty grand for the rest."

I planned to ask him about Ray but he broke the connection. My call back to him went straight to a generic mailbox. I didn't leave a message. All I could think about was two stacks of bills, ten grand each, sitting in the safe.

★ ★ ★ ★ ★

Paige had the evening shift covered at the bar so I left about six. At home, I emptied the pockets of my work jeans from a long Monday. Out came the all-in-one pocket knife that Uncle Reggie had given me. Every time I handled it, my thoughts filled with him. Like the knife, he was a Jack-of-all-trades. I put it inside a wooden box on my dresser where I kept my watch.

After spending time with Shelby on the beach to unwind, I took a second shower and, because I wasn't hungry, had a glass of iced tea for dinner. TV gave me an escape and I barely remembered to catch the eleven o'clock news. Uncle Reggie's picture filled the screen, the same shot used in the paper.

Shelby padded to me.

I scratched his ears. "I can't get a break, can I?"

Darcy Wells appeared onscreen, standing in front of the Pirate's Cove bar on the Isle of Palms. She looked cool and collected in her business garb and perfect blond curls.

"The search continues for those responsible for the death of local bar owner Reggie Sails. Police are interviewing suspects all over the greater Charleston area."

Her image segued into the clip of her ambush interview with me, and the camera panned to Detectives Rogers and Wilson. I turned off the TV, noticed the message light blinking on the answering machine, and pressed play.

"Mr. Pelton," said a familiar upper-class Charlestonian voice, "this is Chauncey Connors, your uncle's attorney. I am calling to see how you are doing. Please contact me at your earliest convenience."

Tuesday morning, from my front porch rocker, I called the police to see when they might release my uncle's body. All I got was Wilson's voicemail. After leaving a message, I next dialed the man who said he was my uncle's attorney and friend. A

44

perky receptionist's voice answered for "Connors, Matheson, and Gooding Law Firm." She put me on hold and forced me to listen to Muzak's version of "Stairway to Heaven." Maybe it was me, but Zeppelin did a better job.

A voice interrupted the music. "Mr. Pelton, this is Chauncey Connors. How are you holding up, son?"

"I'm okay. Thanks for checking in on me."

"My pleasure. You need anything?"

"I need advice," I said.

"Counsel is my vocation."

"The reason I'm calling is I'm wondering if I should be keeping the bar open."

"Well," he said, "you are named as the executor of your uncle's estate. Why don't you come in and we'll start the process. I happen to be free today at four if that works for you."

"Where's your office?"

He gave me a street number on Lower King, meaning old Charleston money passed down over centuries and currently resident in the antebellum homes along the Battery and Tradd Street. I had trouble picturing Uncle Reggie park his rusted-out bomb in front of Connors, Matheson, and Whoever's law offices, stepping out in his best cutoffs, wife-beater undershirt, and flip-flops, and strolling in to any King Street address to make a will—friend or no friend.

"Four o'clock in your office," I said.

My uncle and I had been estranged from the family for different reasons a long time ago so I wasn't surprised he had named me executor. There wasn't anyone else.

In my college years, I'd spent summers part-time bartending for Uncle Reggie at the Pirate's Cove. One day, two drunks decided it was time to settle an old score. I stepped in the middle of them and caught a fist in the mouth, the only other time I'd gotten a split lip. The Saturday night beauty the Charleston cops gave me was healing, but not quickly enough.

For my appointment with Chauncey, I dressed in khakis and a heavily starched blue oxford, and slid into polished loafers. My dad's old Heuer watch said half-past-three. The cell vibrated in my pocket. I checked the caller I.D. but didn't recognize the number and answered the call. "Pelton."

"Brother Brack," a baritone voice boomed. "This is Brother Thomas, mm-hmm. How you doing today?"

Everybody seemed interested in how I'm doing.

"Not very well, all things considered. The police haven't told me when they're going to release my uncle."

"We don't have much luck with them around here, either," he said.

I tried to think of something funny to say but thought better of it.

He said, "I was wondering if you had any plans for dinner."

"Dinner?"

"Tonight."

I pulled the phone away, not sure what to do. Our motto in Afghanistan—when in doubt, full steam ahead. I said, "What time and where?"

"Meet me at the Church of Redemption on Sheppard Street at seven. No need to bring anything, Mr. Pelton. Just yourself, mm-hmm. Just yourself." He hung up.

The gun I had taken from Mutt rested innocently on my kitchen counter. Brother Thomas's suggestion I didn't need to bring anything meant, I decided, it wasn't potluck and I wouldn't have to contribute a dish. But watches and rings and smart phones—and personal protection—fell into an entirely different category. I slipped the gun into my pocket, prudently and properly accessorized.

Shelby gave me a final look, circled his cushion a few times, and plopped down. I patted his head and walked out.

CHAPTER SIX

The large oak door to Connors, Matheson, and Gooding Law Firm opened to the scent of wood polish and leather. The smells, along with original paintings and sculptures, conspired to make me feel out of place, and I hated feeling out of place. An attractive receptionist sat behind a curved hardwood desk. Sun-bleached hair framed a pretty face and tan skin. Early twenties, I guessed, although the business suit and blouse were a little misleading. Her eyes started at my Italian shoes and stopped at my hair. She smiled big, apparently not concerned with my bruised mouth. "May I help you?"

"I'm here to see Chauncey Connors," I said. "I have a four o'clock appointment."

She typed something into the computer and said, "He'll be with you shortly, Mr. Pelton. Can I get you something to drink while you wait?"

"No thanks."

"I'll let him know you're here. Have a seat." She motioned to the waiting area, giving me the big smile again.

I needed something to brighten my mood and her pretty grin did the trick. The leather couch in the waiting area engulfed me. Magazines lined a coffee table and I snatched an *Architectural Digest* and flipped through it.

The man who'd introduced himself as my uncle's lawyer appeared from a door behind the receptionist and spoke with the parlance of an old southern plantation owner. "Mr. Pelton.

Good to see you."

Only someone named Chauncey could pull off wearing a bow tie. His blue one complimented a light-gray wool two-button suit and white oxford shirt. As I rose from the cocooning leather and shook hands with the lawyer, I wondered how much this meeting would set me back. The attorney's wardrobe suggested more than several hundred bucks an hour. Maybe a thousand.

Chauncey led me up creaking wooden stairs to the second floor of the turn-of-the-preceding-century building. The windows of his walnut and book-lined corner office overlooked palmetto trees flanking King Street and were too free of distortions to be originals. I took a seat in a leather chair.

Chauncey sat facing me behind the large mahogany desk. "Mr. Pelton," he said, "this isn't easy for me. I've known your uncle for a long time. Since Vietnam."

"Uncle Reggie never talked about the war much," I said. "I knew it was where he lost his eye."

He nodded, saying nothing.

"I found discharge papers in with his stuff. Was he really in Air America?"

Chauncey laced his fingers on top of his desk. "He was. One of the best pilots we had. What we called an ace."

"You were in with him?"

"I was his copilot. Still fly when I get the time."

"My uncle said Ray shot him," I said. "You know any Rays who might have had something against him?"

"I can't think of anyone who would do such a thing. Of course, I've never represented anyone brought up on murder charges."

"Were you there when he lost his eye?"

"I was. We were in the air carrying a load of medicine when the North Vietnamese opened up on us. Tore the plane all to

49

hell. I got hit in the chest, arm, and leg and could not move." He sighed. "Your uncle took two bullets. A piece of metal from the plane got his eye. But he kept flying and landed us safely. He should have gotten a medal. He saved my life by getting me back to the base, and many other lives with the medicine in the shipment. When the barometer drops, my leg reminds me how much I owe him."

"He never even told me he could fly," I said.

"He quit. The government cut him a check for losing his eye and he used the money to buy the bar. As far as I know, he hasn't flown since."

It was my turn to nod.

He said, "So, are you ready for me to read your uncle's will?"

I felt my chest tighten. "Yes."

Chauncey picked up papers in front of him and read. "Upon my death, I, Reginald Austin Sails, hereby leave my estate in its entirety to my nephew, Brack Edward Pelton."

The words hit me like a freight train. I sat in the leather chair in Chauncey's office, put my head in my hands, and closed my eyes.

Chauncey said, "Do you need a minute?"

I didn't move. "Keep going if there's anything else."

"Your uncle had a formidable estate."

I looked up. "What? He owned a rundown bar and a Cadillac held together by Bondo."

Chauncey sat back and folded his arms across his chest. "You don't know, do you?"

"Know what?"

"After Hurricane Hugo, your uncle purchased a hundred acres of undeveloped prime riverfront property from a speculator selling out. He called it Sumter Point. His intention had always been to preserve it. The recent oil rig disaster in the Gulf Coast made him all the more protective."

Chauncey's words bounced off the walls of his office and peeled open my mind like a grappling hook.

He continued, "He has been offered exorbitant amounts of money by developers for the land and turned them all down." The lawyer set the papers on his desk, removed his glasses, and rubbed his eyes. "Unfortunately, the ownership has not been without problems. Current laws require land to be taxed at fair market value. So, while Mr. Sails was able to buy the land at a much reduced price in the aftermath of Hugo, the value has gone up considerably."

I said, "Okay, so the obvious question is how much does he owe the county?"

Chauncey read the sheet from the file. "A hundred and forty thousand, to be settled with proceeds from the sale of items and/or property of Mr. Sails's estate. Of course, as the executor and sole beneficiary, and, assuming you proceed with liquidating the estate, you would be entitled to a large sum of money even after Dorchester County got its share."

An hour later I stood outside the building on the uneven brick sidewalk lining King Street. With power-of-attorney papers in my pocket, I rested my hand on a palmetto tree as if it could provide moral support. Sweat dripped down my back. I looked at the sun and took a deep breath before making my way to the parking garage.

When I stepped from the stairwell and into the parking area I saw two men standing next to my car. One of them leaned against the right fender, leaving fingerprints on the polished black paint. Each wore khaki pants and a polo shirt. The one touching my Mustang had huge biceps and a chiseled frame. His youthful face was outlined by bleached hair blow-dried in place. He pushed away from the car, revealing his height, or lack of it. His beady eyes would have been menacing on someone taller. The other man was closer to my six-foot height, his goatee starting to gray. In the dimly lit garage, their bright orange polo shirts, the words "Palmetto Properties" embroidered over their hearts, glowed like neon.

"It's about time," said the younger man, his chest stretching his shirt. "We been waiting long enough."

Twenty feet away, I said, "Get away from my car."

The kid looked at his buddy. "You believe this guy?"

"I'm talking to you, Shorty," I said.

His eyes sighted on me. "Who you calling Shorty?"

More than a little jumpy, I reached into my pocket for Mutt's gun and remembered it was in the car.

The man with the goatee held up his hands. "Whoa, there. Easy now."

I kept my hand in my pocket and hoped he'd continue to think I was armed.

"Never mess with a man's ride," I said. "Get out of here before someone gets hurt."

A Cadillac Escalade stopped a couple yards away from me and idled. The dark-tinted rear-seat window slid down, and a bald, shiny head the size of a large melon wearing wraparound sunglasses jutted from the opening. "Sorry to disturb you, Mr. Pelton. I wonder if I might borrow a moment of your time."

I looked at the man inside the Escalade and then at the guys in the bright shirts. "You have got to be kidding."

The rear door of the SUV opened and the man shambled out. His body shape could best be described as a pear in summer wear and his white shirt bore the same logo as the two idiots in front of me.

"I don't kid, Mr. Pelton," the fat man said, holding the SUV's rear door open for me. "Just a few minutes . . . an hour at most. I promise we aren't here to harm you. In fact, you could say it might be worth your while."

I eased my hand out of my pocket and held it up to show I wasn't holding anything. "I've read a lot about you and your business ventures in the paper, Mr. Galston."

A large grin stretched across the bald man's face. "I'd like to take you on a little tour of the town."

"I've already seen it," I said. "I live here."

"I know, Mr. Pelton. I want to show you the future of our way of life. And by the way, I am so sorry to hear about your uncle."

I looked at Shorty. "We're going to finish this later."

Shorty patted the fender of my car where his hand had been. "Looking forward to it."

My curiosity was too high to let a little thing like personal safety get in the way. I climbed into the backseat of the SUV and slid to the other side so Galston's rotund body could fit. The two goons in the neon shirts walked to a black Chrysler 300 and got in.

"Sorry about my security," Galston said. "They're just overprotective of me. Sometimes they get a little too carried away."

"They were certainly about to be," I said.

The driver of the Escalade was a Latino with a thick head of hair. He glanced at me in the rearview mirror through dark sunglasses as he maneuvered us down the levels of the garage. At the exit, he waited for a break in traffic big enough to squeeze through and gunned it.

Galston smiled, as if what he was ready to say was rehearsed. "People come to Charleston from all over. Women come for the shopping, carriage rides, and the beaches. Men come for golf and deep-sea fishing."

We merged onto I-26 and headed out of the downtown area.

"Tourists," he said. "They're the lifeblood of our city."

"They're something, all right," I said.

"Exactly. Your uncle's bar benefits from them like the rest of us do. But preservation is what it's all about, these days. What I'm trying to do is protect our city. Make sure if it's going to be developed, it's done the right way."

"That's great, but why does any of this concern me?" I already knew why it concerned me because Chauncey had told me. To let the fat man finish his pitch was more fun.

"Mr. Pelton, for the past twenty years, your uncle has been trying to do what I'm doing, which is to defend Charleston from outsiders coming in and turning it into an amusement park."

"I'm glad he wasn't working alone," I said.

At an exit five miles down the road, the driver exited the interstate toward the Ashley River. Through the window as we got closer to the water I saw housing developments and strip malls fade away. The road ended and the driver pulled to a stop. A makeshift sign read:

Sumter Point
Keep Out

I'd never been here before, but I wouldn't let this guy know. "What are we doing at my uncle's property?"

Galston said, "Mr. Pelton, I'll be frank with you. I want it."

"No kidding," I said.

"As I said, I never kid. And I promise to safeguard it so that others will get to enjoy it."

I looked away from what I knew were a hundred acres covered in trees. "How would you do that?"

Galston held out his hands, palms up, and opened them in a gesture reminiscent of pictures of Jesus I'd seen. "Create a preservation neighborhood," he said. "I'm not talking about bulldozing it flat and putting up houses six inches apart along the water, either. I'm talking real codes, stiff ones that make the owners sign over a kidney before they plant a flower. Elevated houses barely touching the ground. Minimum one-acre lots to keep the number of houses down. The whole thing wrapped up tight with wetland offset credits. It'll be like we're getting two-for-one on the preservation side of things."

I nodded as if in agreement.

"For the privilege," he said, "I'm willing to offer two million dollars. Payable today."

He grinned big, showing me a mouthful of white-capped teeth.

Galston certainly wasn't any protector of Charleston. And he wasn't the only one doing damage, just the biggest one at the moment.

I let out a long sigh. "A lot to think about."

The fat man bobbed his head up and down like a used car salesman about to offload a lemon. "Sure, sure. I understand. Take some time, but not too much. I've got to get this deal rolling. You know how it is."

On the ride back to my car, I thought about Uncle Reggie. I'd learned more about him in the two days following his death than my lifetime of knowing him alive. An expression Galston used played in my mind: "You know how it is."

I surely did.

CHAPTER SEVEN

The Church of Redemption was easy enough to find—a good thing because I was running behind in meeting Brother Thomas for dinner. In the middle of the projects, the tall steeple stood out like a beacon of hope. I parked next to a rough, early-eighties Buick. The alarm chirp from my car was slightly comforting. Brother Thomas held the large vestibule door open as I walked toward it.

"I see you found us all right, mm-hmm." He extended a hand. "Want a tour before we head out?"

It had been a long time since I'd been inside a church, and I was still too angry with God to kneel. "Um . . . Okay."

The setting sun projected a kaleidoscope of colors from the tall stained-glass windows across old folding chairs and ragged linoleum flooring. We passed a battered podium facing the seats.

"We're a small congregation," Brother Thomas said, "but the Lord provides, mm-hmm. The Lord provides."

I'd been raised a Catholic—chandeliers hanging from vaulted ceilings, stiff wooden pews, and burning incense.

The aroma in this place was strong soap. "How long y'all been here?"

"We built this church in 1983. The community was different then. The shipyard ran twenty-four hours and all the black men around here had jobs and homes and new Oldsmobiles. Now nothing and nobody's working."

We walked through a hallway with peeling beige paint to a

large office. On the walls hung black and white photos of Civil Rights protestors getting hosed by redneck cops. A desk stood somewhere underneath piles of papers and books in the middle of the office. A phone rang but I couldn't see where it was. Brother Thomas dug beneath the mound, pulled out an old black receiver connected by a spiral cord to a base with a rotary dial. He answered, "Church of Redemption." His voice lost its baritone when he spoke again. "Hey, Cassie." A smile brightened his face as he listened, holding the receiver away from his ear. I could hear an irate woman on the other end, though not her words. When she stopped the tirade, he put the receiver back to his head and said, "Heh-heh. We ain't lost. We was on our way, mm-hmm. Thanks for checking." He hung up the phone without waiting for a reply and looked at me. "Um, our dinner's waiting."

We strolled outside into the lowcountry pressure cooker and down the sidewalk. Brother Thomas hadn't bothered to lock the door to his church. I felt embarrassed turning on the alarm in my car until I spotted shops closed long ago with plywood for windows. The boards were spray-painted with multicolored names and symbols.

Brother Thomas gestured to the graffiti. "Those are tags."

"Tags?"

"Gangs aren't only in Los Angeles, mm-hmm. They use tags to mark their turf."

Two blocks later we arrived at a restaurant. Every parking spot was full and a line formed out the door. The crowd parted like the Red Sea when we approached.

"Come on in, Brother," said a man standing in the doorway.

The woman with him said, "You eatin' out tonight, Brother?"

Brother Thomas greeted many of the people in line and shook many hands as we walked through. I got more stares than the bearded lady at the freak show and absently touched the small of my back where the gun was. Any of the guys who had seen me take Mutt down might be around and want to make up for it. After driving away from Chauncey's office, I'd untucked my shirt and stuck Mutt's pistol inside the waistband of my trousers.

A light-skinned black woman in a flowing purple dress came out from behind a counter supporting an old cash register. Short and round, she wore her dark hair pulled back in a bun. Her face beamed. She shook a chubby index finger at us. "I told you not to be late, Brother."

Brother Thomas gave her a grin and a peck on the cheek. "I'm sorry for our delay, Cassie. This is Mr. Pelton."

"My name's Brack."

She offered her hand and I took it, finding the firm and calloused handshake of someone who worked hard.

Her stern expression melted. "Oh, he's a cute one, Brother. Don't leave him alone at the table is all I'm gonna say. Yes, sir."

Brother Thomas looked at me. "Mm-hmm."

Cassie led us through a small room with crowded tables and steaming plates of food. Loud voices, laughter, and the clatter of knives and forks overcame the sound from a TV in the corner. We stopped at a booth in the back.

Cassie said, "Hope this'll do."

Once we were seated, she had our food brought out, a mixture of lowcountry and soul. I was hungry, and, after Brother Thomas said grace, shoveled food into my mouth.

He pointed his fork at me. "Boy, you got some appetite on you."

"It's been a while since I've had home cooking," I managed to say around a mouthful of cornbread.

"We come to the right place, then."

I swallowed and nodded, selecting a fried dill pickle from a small wax-paper-lined basket full of them.

He chuckled. "Cassie's single, too."

A piece of the fried dill pickle lodged in my throat and I struggled to wash it down with iced tea. Brother Thomas tilted his head back and laughed harder, one of those open-mouthed cackles that went on for days.

Cassie appeared next to me and put a plump hand on my back. "Everything all right over here, gentlemen?"

My muscles tensed, but Cassie worked her fingers into my shoulder in a massaging motion and I immediately loosened up. Since my wife died, I hadn't exactly chosen the best female companions. Most of them had been as lonely and hopeless as I was. And none of them had rubbed my shoulders.

The grin on Brother Thomas's face took up the whole room.

Cassie said, "Let me know if you need anything else, and I mean anything." She gave my shoulder a final squeeze before departing in a sea of lavender.

Brother Thomas wiped his face with a paper napkin. "Poor Cassie's been looking for a suitor a long time. I'm afraid she might be desperate enough to take anyone."

I closed my eyes and rolled my shoulders a couple times. "She's selling herself short."

"Mm-hmm," he said and eyeballed me for a moment.

"You trying to play matchmaker or are we here to talk about something else?"

"Sorry, Brother Brack," he said. "You right. We're not here for that. I 'membered you say Reggie had something about Mutt in a calendar."

I decided Brother Thomas didn't need to know what kind of calendar it was. "All it said was Mutt's Bar. Why'd he pull the gun?"

"I've known Mutt a long time," Brother Thomas said. "Been jumpy since he come back from Kuwait."

"No kidding."

He said, "How you holding up?"

"Fantastic," I said. "I just need to find out who murdered my uncle."

Brother Thomas took a long drink of his tea and put the glass down. "Don't you think the po-lice should be handling it? I mean, it's not as if your uncle was from this part of town."

I felt my face flush with anger. "They're not going to get very far."

Brother Thomas said, "Are you a man of faith?"

"What's that got to do with anything?"

"Don't mean to pry," he said, "but if someone in my congregation was to come to me with this problem, I'd say sometimes you got to wait on God."

"I haven't had much luck with Him, lately." I forked greens into my mouth.

Brother Thomas nodded as if he knew something I didn't. "A man doesn't have the right to avoid reaping what he sows."

I chewed on what he said and swallowed my greens. "Meaning?"

"Whoever killed your uncle will have to answer for it. And you don't get a free pass just 'cause you think revenge is the right thing to do. They don't and you don't."

To prevent my foot from going down my throat, I took a swig of tea. The break gave me clarity. "So tell me how you knew my uncle."

The pastor worked on the pile of potatoes smothered in gravy covering half his plate. "Your uncle would come by to see Mutt a lot. I think he was helping him."

"Helping him how?"

Brother Thomas stopped his loaded fork an inch short of his mouth. "I didn't ask."

"Okay, then," I said. "Why?"

He swallowed his food before answering. "None of my business. I might be wrong, but Mutt never asked me or the church for anything and I know the few customers he does get ain't big spenders. He's gotta pay his bills somehow."

"That's no reason for Mutt to be paranoid."

"You right as far as I'm concerned. But that stunt yesterday sure didn't win you any friends around here, mm-hmm."

I tossed a cleaned chicken bone onto my plate and selected another piece. "He can't go pulling guns on people."

Brother Thomas signaled one of the waitresses for another napkin.

I kept talking. "I was in the alley when my uncle was killed. It put me back in the war."

"Why'd you go to Afghanistan, anyway?" he said. "You seem smarter than that. Educated."

"My wife died of cancer," I said. "I didn't want to deal with it so I left. I thought eating sand for a couple years might clear my head." And maybe catch a bullet or two.

Brother Thomas opened his eyes wide. "With people shooting at you?"

"You'd be surprised how effectively that works."

"I never thought of it that way."

I took another drink from my tea. "When my tour was up, I was given the opportunity to re-enlist. My uncle talked me into coming to Charleston instead. Saved my life. Now that he's gone, I don't have any friends except the young woman running his bar."

Brother Thomas nodded. "You don't think your uncle was killed for his wallet?"

"No. He's got valuable real estate. I'm going to check out that angle." A two-million-dollar offer, and Uncle Reggie isn't cold yet. I was definitely going to check that angle.

Brother Thomas cleared his throat. "I, um, called him a month before this all happened."

Finished, I pushed my plate forward. "Yeah?"

"I knew about the land," he said. "It's what fired your uncle up more than anything. People trying to ruin the land. He was one of them, what do they call? En-vi-ro-mentalists?"

I didn't say anything because I didn't know what to say. My uncle never showed me that side of him. Maybe I hadn't paid enough attention.

Brother Thomas said, "There's this old factory not too far from here. Neighborhood kids go there to play during the day. Junkies go there at night. It's awful. Rundown. Got these pools of water look like they'd glow in the dark." He held my gaze. "I asked him to check it out. See if the city could do something about it."

The names of the companies on the memory stick flashed across my mind. "You happen to know the name of this place?"

"No," he said. "But I can show you where it is."

Brother Thomas squeezed himself into the front seat of my car and said, "Sure you want to check this place out tonight?"

The four-cam engine barked to life and settled into a low rumble. I said, "I got nothing else to do. You?"

"The Lord always keeps me busy."

When he shut his door, I drove, using a light foot on the gas so as not to frighten my passenger. We passed under the new bridge heading away from the city, and East Bay Street turned into Morrison Drive. Brother Thomas directed me to a right turn. My headlights reflected off broken bottles and trash littering the street, and I did my best to dodge the debris. Homeless people scattered when I turned on the brights. I leaned forward and pulled out Mutt's gun from the small of my back and tucked it between my legs.

Brother Thomas said, "You the one insisted we come out here tonight. I tried to tell you."

A locked gate loomed ahead attached to a chain-link fence

stretching in both directions, prohibiting us from going any farther. I braked to a stop. Kudzu took over the front landscaping and I couldn't make out the name of the company. The place was thirty minutes from Sumter Point, but a world away.

Because it wasn't mine, I left Mutt's gun with Brother Thomas at his church and went home. In bed, whenever I closed my eyes the faces of my wife and uncle kept me awake. A full moon made the white-planked ceiling glow. I sat up and threw a pillow across the room. It hit the dresser below the clock and bounced on top of Shelby, who grunted and rolled over.

"Sorry, fella," I said.

The clock showed three AM. I pulled on a pair of shorts over my boxers, slipped on a T-shirt and sandals, and walked onto my back porch. The decaying smell of the marsh hit me as fast as the mosquitoes. I swatted at them and ran to my car.

Uncle Reggie's driveway was empty when I pulled onto the sand. A shiny Lincoln Navigator with a big brush guard was parked illegally in a neighbor's yard. I couldn't believe the old man living there let anyone park on his property. My uncle had kept to himself and spent most of his time at the Pirate's Cove or on the water, but the old geezer across the street always found a reason to report him to the police for something.

I looked at the Navigator one last time, opened my trunk, and retrieved a police issue Maglite. The black aluminum shell housing three D-cell batteries felt perfectly weighted in my hand. It reminded me of my friend Jimmy as I walked to my uncle's house. Before Jimmy got busted for letting the prostitutes on his route slide for rides, he'd been a patrolman.

"The proper way to hold a Maglite," he said one night after too many beers, "is like this." He stumbled to his feet, a mug of beer in one hand and a bottle in the other. The bottle, his prop, spilled its contents down his back as he lifted it to demonstrate, holding it like a spear he was ready to throw.

"See, this way it becomes a club if you need it." He swung it in the same motion a football was thrown and showered us.

I opened the door to the small screened-in porch and found the front door to the house ajar. A voice in my head, the one that got me through Afghanistan in one piece, said there might be a problem. I gave the cracked-open front door a shove and aimed my light into Uncle Reggie's shack of a house. The light reflected off a shiny object held by a figure heading for me. I swung the flashlight as hard as I could. It struck with a thud. The metallic smell of blood filled the still night air. A body crashed into me at full speed. I fell backwards to the porch and hit the floor hard. It knocked the wind out of my lungs. What felt like two hundred pounds fell on me. The flashlight bounced across the porch and clicked off. I kicked and punched and got out from underneath the weight and managed to get to my knees. I could hear a man shuffling and groaning as I gained my breath. In the darkness, estimating where the figure's face was, I balled my fist and hit as hard as I could. The figure grunted again and stopped moving.

I struggled to my feet, grabbing the door jamb leading into the house. When I felt for the switch to turn a light on, something smashed into the back of my head. I collided into blackness.

CHAPTER EIGHT

"Brack!"

The sound of my name brought me out of the black hole.

Someone shook me. "Brack!"

I coughed and opened my eyes and realized I lay facedown on the floor. The lights were on and I blinked a few times. Paige came into focus.

Her mouth dropped and her eyes opened wide. "What happened? Are you okay?"

I coughed again. "Yeah."

"Yeah, what?"

I tried to push myself up and felt Paige's arms helping me. A sharp pain in my head made me squint. My hand searched and found a lump. "Ouch."

Paige helped me sit and lean against the doorway. "What are you doing here?"

"Couldn't sleep, so I came here to see if I could find out anything else." I examined the hand I had touched my head with. There were flakes of dried blood on it. "How's my head?"

She brushed my hair aside. "You got a nice bruise. Let's get you to the hospital."

"I'm fine." I tried to stand to show her I was all right, but the floor moved and I fell.

She tugged at my arm. "Come on, let's go. Good thing I came by to get the mail."

"Mail?"

"Reggie got his addresses mixed up all the time and had the bar's mail delivered here and his home mail delivered there. The guys in the kitchen really like his taste in magazines."

The centerfold calendar I'd taken came to mind. We stood in the screened-in porch and saw, through the open front door, debris littering the house. The legs of an upside-down chair stuck up in a defenseless position, reminding me a little too much of myself.

"Oh my God," she said.

Anger was my first emotion. Followed by rage. We did a quick check but couldn't tell if anything was missing. At least the valuable surf boards were still there, all of them lying on the floor instead of against the wall. I finally calmed down as Paige helped me into her Honda Civic. Like Paige, it was neat and clean. A child's seat sat in the back.

I said, "How old is Simon now?"

"He's five," she said, "going on ten."

"Did you tell him what happened to Reggie?"

She nodded. "The G version. He still cried."

Uncle Reggie loved Simon as if he was his own son. A week after Paige started working at the Cove, Simon's father walked out on them. Simon was a year old. Since that happened, my uncle made sure they were taken care of. Paige became the best thing that ever happened to the Pirate's Cove.

Despite the doctor's protests, I walked out of the clinic under my own power, feeling better thanks to what amounted to expensive aspirin. Aside from a bandage on the back of my head to cover what the doctor described—after seeing a CAT scan—as a mild concussion, I was the same. Except, I wasn't. Deep inside, in a part of me reserved for thoughts and emotions I shared with no one, a blue-hot flame burned. After Jo died I'd tried to douse it with Corona long necks, shots of tequila, and easy women. When that didn't work, I added the War in Afghanistan to the mix. Now, in the warm wind of the lowcountry city I'd grown to love, the city that survived the war for independence, the Civil War, fires, earthquakes, and hurricanes, I stood by Paige's car and laughed.

Paige looked up from fumbling in her purse for her keys. "What's so funny?"

"Pouring alcohol on a fire."

She creased her forehead. "Huh?"

"Never mind. I need to get home to let Shelby out."

"Don't you want to report this to the police?"

I thought for a moment. "You need to do it, but leave me out. If they knew I was there, they might think I broke in."

"But it's your house."

"Whoever knocked me out cut the strip of evidence tape across the door to get in. I'm not sure, but I think that's illegal."

Paige drove me to my car, which was still at my uncle's. When I pulled into my driveway, Shelby stood outside in the yard waiting for me. The front door was wide open. Those two points all but distracted me from the red Infiniti convertible I'd parked next to.

Shelby came to me when I got out of the Mustang. I knelt and scratched his fur, checking to make sure he was okay.

"He's fine," a female voice said.

I recognized the voice immediately. "If it isn't our favorite weather girl."

Darcy said, "Very funny, Jack. I heard you were at the hospital so I came by to check on your dog. If you're going to continue to do stupid things, you need to get him a doggie door."

Shelby turned to her, his attention span as good as mine.

"The name's Brack, not Jack," I said, still kneeling in the driveway. "How'd you hear I was at the hospital? I didn't tell anyone."

Darcy lifted her right hand and examined red fingernails. "I have my sources."

I stood and felt the blood rushing to my head, messing with my equilibrium. "My door was locked." I put a hand on the fender of the convertible to steady myself. "How'd you get in?"

"I picked the lock."

"No kidding." I didn't know what irritated me more, my lock being picked or not being able to stand on my own two feet. Sizing the situation, I came up short. When that happened, I switched topics. "Shelby likes the beach."

Darcy held a large green bag. A strap of her dress fell off her shoulder and she slipped it back in place. "Me too."

Shelby barked and nudged her leg.

"Lemme change first." I went for the door but stopped and turned. "Thanks for letting him out."

"You're welcome. Now hurry up."

Inside, the spreadsheets I'd printed at work covered the table along with the naked women calendar and the memory stick. My balance returned slowly. I swapped shorts for swimwear and removed the bandage. Aside from the bruise, it only covered minor scratches anyway. On my way out, I relocked the front door. "Find anything interesting in my house?"

Darcy said, "Nice calendar. I'm guessing it isn't yours unless you needed to remind yourself when your own birthday was. You want to tell me about the spreadsheets?"

I had to remember this girl packed more brain cells than her blond hair suggested. "Not much to tell at this point. I'm trying to figure them out."

The path led to a small beach and one of the best views of the Charleston harbor. Some of the first shots of the Civil War had been fired at Fort Sumter, which lay a half-mile across the harbor directly in front of us. I removed my shirt and kicked off my flops. When I pulled Shelby's tennis ball out of my pocket, he saw it and ran down the beach as I let it fly. He jumped and caught it in midair and pranced back, proudly.

"Good boy." I scratched his head when he released the ball in my hands. He took off running and I threw it again.

Shelby caught the ball and came back, this time going to Darcy. He dropped the ball in her hand and sprinted down the beach. I guess she met with his approval.

When Darcy threw the ball, it went farther than I could've sent it. I whistled.

"I played softball through college," she said. "Outfield. I could help you with your throw, if you want."

I frowned. Beautiful and feisty. A bad combination. Shelby returned and gave me the ball. I threw it out to the water and he barreled in after it.

I said, "We usually take a swim next."

"It's about time." Darcy peeled off her dress, revealing a well-toned figure wrapped in a bikini.

We waded in together. I was older than her by a decade but still too young for a midlife crisis. At least, I thought so.

"You're going to have trouble getting rid of me," said Darcy. "I can tell."

"If you're looking into your uncle's murder, I can help."

"Rumor is your family owns Wells Shipping."

If something was shipped into or out of Charleston, chances were good the family business brokered the freight. The Wells name was everywhere, and Darcy's career as a news correspondent had been thoroughly documented, both good and bad.

Darcy said, "My grandfather started it from nothing."

"Why aren't you working there?"

Shelby dog-paddled to her and gave her the ball. Again she lobbed it, but not as far as before. "I'm not good at sitting in an office."

"That makes two of us." I thought about what she'd said, "Okay, how can you help?"

She gave me her made-for-TV smile and said, "I told you, I've got informants all over this town."

When we returned from the beach, the front door to my house was wide open again.

"What is this, break-into-my-house day?" To Darcy, I said, "Stay here."

Shelby growled and darted into the house and I ran after him, not caring who was in there. Either they would die or I might, but the intruder wasn't walking away. I reached my doorway and stopped. My furniture was in pieces. The drawers and cabinets were open and my stuff littered the floor. Shelby worked the house with his nose. No one was waiting.

"Brack?" Darcy called from the front porch. "Is everything all right?"

"Someone was nice enough to redecorate for me." I looked down and saw the old watch my father had given me ground into the floorboards. Someone would pay.

Darcy walked into the living room. "Wow."

I said, "This wouldn't happen to be the work of friends of yours, would it? You make nice in the thong while your boys ransack my house?"

"I already looked through your stuff. I didn't need to trash the place to do it." She put her hands on her hips. "And I don't wear thongs."

The papers, memory stick, and calendar Darcy had left on the kitchen table were gone. I chose a T-shirt from a busted drawer and pulled it on. The slight sunburn on my back stung. I didn't bother to lock up this time as I walked out. Shelby came when I called and we turned toward my car. The trunk lid on my Mustang was open and its four tires were flat. Deep scratches glinted in the sunlight along the fender where Shorty's hand had been. Darcy's car appeared untouched.

I said, "You better get out of here."

"I'm not going anywhere."

"Whoever did this might still be around. Give me a number where I can reach you."

"Yeah, right, you'll call me later. I've heard that one before." She dug into her purse and pulled out a card. "My cell's on the back, but you don't have to worry about calling. I'll find you." She walked to her car, threw her bag in the backseat, and drove away.

It occurred to me whoever trashed my house knew her car from mine. My guess was Shorty and his buddy, but I couldn't figure out why Galston would be behind this. Underneath a ragged tarp in what made up my backyard sat a ten-year-old Jeep Wrangler bought when I first got back from the war. I packed a bag while we waited for the flatbed to come for my Mustang, then Shelby and I piled in the Jeep. We drove south on Seventeen to the other side of town.

At the Folly Beach Pier, I called Detective Wilson. "My uncle's house was trashed last night. Mine was broken into this afternoon. Check them out for yourself if you like. I'm not staying home tonight. What I am going to do is find out what's going on."

"I wouldn't do anything stupid if I were you," he said.

"How's the investigation coming?"

Silence.

"I thought so." I hung up and walked next door to a vacation rental office. They had one place available that allowed pets, a recent cancellation. The agent said the place was eccentric. When I opened the door, I realized eccentric meant dive. The Pirate's Cove had been described in a similar fashion. And, like the Cove, this one had an ocean view.

Chapter Nine

Thursday morning I awoke in an Adirondack chair on the back deck of my rental. The sun filled the horizon with a bright orange glow. Shelby was playing with the sand crabs in the dunes and ran to me when I whistled. I groaned as I got out of the chair, feeling every hour I'd slept in it. Stretching didn't help. Neither did a walk on the beach with Shelby.

After a shower, I examined my head. It was tender but healing. I wished I could say that about the rest of me.

My phone said I'd missed a call. Checking voicemail, I learned from Paige's message that we now had a new problem. Apparently, the bar's checks were bouncing.

Just great.

Shelby barked through the thin walls of the unfamiliar house, upset he wasn't going with me. I jumped into the Jeep and hit the starter. The straight six fired up like it always had, but it lacked the power of the Mustang, and I wanted it back, bad. The Ford dealer had told me the replacement tires would take a day or two. Same with the repaint. I asked them to check the car for anything out of the ordinary—like explosives. The service manager laughed, but I didn't.

At a gas station, I filled the Jeep's tank and bought a ball cap, sunglasses, and a roll of breath mints. The counter displayed the kind of cigars Uncle Reggie smoked. So for old time's sake, I bought a pack and lit one with matches the cashier gave me. I hadn't smoked a cigarette since Afghanistan. These plastic-tipped stogies weren't much better and would probably affect my jogging. The smoke turned over in my mouth as I hopped into the Jeep. I put on the sunglasses and hat and checked myself out in the rearview mirror. They were the best I could do at incognito.

A mile down the road, a digital sign showed the temperature of eighty-three degrees and it wasn't ten o'clock yet. A Bob Seger tune belted from the speakers wired to the roll bar behind my head.

While I stood in line at the bank watching the flatscreen TV mounted on the wall, Channel Four's *News at Noon,* one of Patricia's competitors, ran an interesting clip. On it, they accused my uncle of tax evasion and mentioned rumors of his controlling an underworld gambling ring from the bar.

When it was my turn with the teller, I pulled out the power-of-attorney papers Chauncey had given me so I could get a look at Uncle Reggie's bank statement. Chauncey said my uncle reluctantly opened a checking account when he couldn't pay certain bills in cash anymore because of the changes in banking and accounting. Now, we couldn't pay for anything.

The teller was an older woman with thick glasses, gray hair, and a figure shaped like a Weeble-Wobble. She typed in my uncle's information and waited. When the account details came up, her wide-eyed stare at the computer screen told me something was not right.

"Excuse me," she said, "I'll be right back."

Her rotund physique bobbled past the other tellers and headed into an office. The title beside the door she entered said Branch Manager. It had no windows so I couldn't see what was going on.

I tapped my fingers on the counter to an old Stevie Wonder song playing on the sound system and smiled at a young black girl with a pretty face working at the next counter. Her name tag said Wendi. No other customers were in the lobby.

Wendi said, "Marge will be back in a moment."

I nodded and chose a sucker from a candy dish sitting on the counter, peeling off the plastic wrapping before sticking the grape flavored treat in my mouth. More finger tapping followed to the end of the song. A short, skinny man with a bad comb-over came out of the Branch Manager's office. Marge wobbled close behind.

He spoke in a nasal voice. "Mr. Pelton, I'm George Wiggins, the manager of this branch. I'm sorry for your loss."

I shook his offered hand. "Nice to meet ya."

"I'll be happy to review your uncle's accounts with you in my office." He motioned me toward the door.

As I followed him, I caught Marge watching me. Her eyes darted away. Wendi waved.

Once we were seated in his office, Wiggins explained my uncle had three accounts—a personal checking account, a business account for the bar, and a third account. The first two had balances of roughly five thousand each. The third was the one that must have triggered Marge's initial reaction because I couldn't believe the balance, either.

"Two million, one-hundred fifty-eight thousand, nine hundred and twenty-seven dollars, and eighty-three cents."

I swallowed hard. "Huh?"

"Two million—"

I held up a hand and sat back. The office had no intra-office windows but a nice-sized one overlooking the parking lot.

"Mr. Sails took out a mortgage on his restaurant property on the Isle of Palms a month ago. I remember him doing it."

I asked, "How much is the mortgage for?"

"Two million, five hundred thousand. Unfortunately, Mr. Pelton, the police have put a freeze on his accounts during their investigation."

I nodded. "When is the next mortgage payment due?"

"It's past due by a week. Seventy-five hundred dollars, give or take."

The bigger question was what happened in a month's time to the difference between the current balance of two point one million and the mortgage amount of two point five. And I couldn't cover the difference.

Outside the bank, I dialed Wilson's cell. He, of course, didn't answer and I left a message, making no mention of the freeze on the accounts, deciding to let it slide for the moment. Instead, I called Paige and told her I'd cover the costs until things were resolved. As I hung up, I realized I should have asked her how much we needed before going all in.

My dog deserved better than being cooped up. And I wanted the company. I stopped by the beach house and got him.

Before Reggie was killed, I could not have imagined going to the place I headed next. Thankfully, even after purchasing the Mustang, I still had a decent balance of my combat pay left over in the bank. After I made another withdrawal, I parked in the lot of a strip mall and walked to the entrance of one of the local businesses. At the door to Big Al's Pawn, I poked my head in and spoke to a huge man sitting behind the counter. Big Al, I presumed.

I said, "Is it okay if my dog comes in with me?"

"Sure, as long as you buy something," he said. "Otherwise, I'm gonna have to charge you a pet fee."

"Fair enough."

I opened the door wider so Shelby could enter. His nose went into overdrive, leading him around the room like the dog he was.

Big Al said, "What can I help you with today?"

"Pistols."

"Target shooting or personal protection?"

"A little of both, I'd say."

Big Al rolled his stool sideways to the handgun section. "I've got a nice Beretta nine-millimeter and a Colt nineteen-eleven. Personally, I prefer the Colt, but Nines are more popular these days. Six hundred will get you either."

In Afghanistan, my M4 assault rifle boomed in my hands and I always hit what I aimed at. If my uncle hadn't been shot in front of me, I wouldn't be here looking at a gun. But he was. I peeled four hundreds from my wallet and laid them on the glass counter.

The big man looked at the money and at me. "Five and I'll throw in a nice nylon case."

"And a box of shells."

"Don't carry 'em. But I know a place where you can get a good deal."

The watches in the display case caused me to think of my crushed timepiece.

Big Al scooted along, keeping up with the wallet in my hand like Shelby did when I carried one of his bones. A bead of sweat formed around the big man's receding hairline from the exertion—or from anticipation.

After I passed the background check, Shelby and I walked out of Big Al's with the Colt and a pristine vintage Monaco watch like the one Steve McQueen wore in *Le Mans*. Eight hundred bucks for both and the big man still threw in the gun case. All of it probably hot. Uncle Reggie would've been proud.

It was a ten-minute drive to *Plug It and Stuff It*, the place Big Al had suggested I could buy ammunition. I parked next to an old Ford F-150 with faded "W" stickers on the tailgate along with less-than-flattering statements about the current administration. On a wooden sign in front of the business, someone had painted:

We can help you load it and shoot it. If your pistol still don't fire right, see a doctor.

The owner greeted us with a lined, white face. He held my Colt in wrinkled hands poking out of a long-sleeved flannel shirt. "You say Big Al sold you this?" He racked the slide. "Nice action."

I nodded.

A little girl dropped to her knees on the floor beside Shelby and scratched his back. He licked her face in appreciation.

The man said, "That's my granddaughter."

Her naturally brown skin and African features complimented a thick black mound of beautiful curls. The rebel flag patch on the man's ball cap had me picturing him in a white hood. Reunions in his family must be interesting.

I said, "Do you have any lanes open? I haven't shot in a while."

He raised his eyebrows, picked up a burning cigarette from an overflowing ashtray, and took a drag. "Why didn't you start with something a little tamer? Forty-fives have kick, ya know." Smoke trailed out of his large nostrils.

He'd probably love to hear about my time in the war, but I didn't want to talk about it. Back then, all the anger of losing Jo had come out as the carnage I inflicted on everything in my path. My uncle had taken it upon himself to bring me back to reality, and he did. But he wasn't here anymore.

I left Shelby with the girl, his new friend, and followed the man to the shooting stalls. Half the lanes were occupied and he set me up at the end, away from the others. He pulled a box of shells from his pocket and two extra clips he'd sold me.

"I had one of these in 'Nam," he said loud so I could hear over the shooters. "I was there in sixty-five." The slide clicked shut when he shoved the clip in and thumbed the release. "Mind if I try it out first? I'll replace the ammo."

"Be my guest." I stepped back and slipped on ear protection.

He aimed down the lane at a silhouette of a bad guy with a turban on his head hanging twenty feet away and unloaded the entire clip. The shots were grouped in the center of the torso.

He handed me the empty weapon. "You got a good one. Army surplus, most likely. Not too old, either. But anything under forty's new to me."

I changed clips, thumbed the release, and walked to the tape line on the floor. The Marines had taught me everything. How to sight. How to breathe. Squeeze slowly. Ride the recoil.

With the safety off, I put three shots in the center of the paper terrorist's forehead. I took a few silent breaths and pulled the trigger four more times. The slide locked back.

The old man said, "Haven't shot in a while, my shorts. That camel jockey ain't got no brains and no testicles left." His look was one of admiration.

With nothing but revenge on my mind, I didn't feel all that admirable.

He slapped my shoulder. "I'd love to be over there in the Middle East picking off what's left of them Al Qaeda. Wouldn't you?"

Chapter Ten

In the parking lot of the shooting range, I propped a foot on the front bumper of my Jeep while I checked my cell. The message symbol showed I had a voicemail from Detective Wilson, asking me to give him a call.

This time he answered. "I'm sitting in your living room, Pelton. Nice view. You left your door unlocked."

I watched the traffic pass by on the four-lane. "There wasn't anything left to break or steal."

"You're lucky they didn't do worse," he said, "and you really need to file a complaint with Sullivan's Island P.D."

"Yeah. I'll get right on that."

"I'm not sure why you want me here. Unless it's for my health. You know, the beach air and all."

I felt myself get rigid. "You don't see a connection? What do you want, a map?"

"Look, Pelton, I've got some news."

I had a bad feeling.

"All the evidence in your uncle's case points to a mugging."

"He knew the killer," I said, my voice getting louder. "Remember? Ray?"

"I wish there were something else I could do. Just isn't enough for us to go on. The coroner's office is ready to release your uncle's remains."

"Isn't it a crime to slice through the evidence tape you guys put on his door?"

The detective said, "It could be you got a jealous family member or friend looking for some precious heirloom."

"You've got to be kidding." My standard response to news. "You've seen the bar and his house. Does it look to you like he had any precious heirlooms?"

Silence.

I said, "What about the gambling connection reported on the news?"

"We didn't find anything to support that. If a TV station wants to go a certain direction on a story, it's not our concern."

I couldn't control myself anymore. "Seems to me the only concern you got is how quickly you can get the file shut on this one. But it's not going to happen. I'll let you in on a little secret you probably already know. My uncle was back with his ex-wife. You know who she is, don't you? You say it's not your concern if a station decides to go a certain way on a story? Then you better be ready for World War Three in the media 'cause it's coming to a Channel Nine broadcast near you."

I hung up and called Chauncey Connors to tell him about the police releasing Uncle Reggie's body. It was a harder conversation than I'd anticipated. The whole concept of talking about Uncle Reggie as "remains" was too much.

I stood in the parking lot for at least ten minutes after these calls to shake off the anger.

Three teenage girls arrived in a yellow Beetle convertible and parked by the curb to the convenience store next to the shooting range. The aroma of suntan lotion and cigarettes wafted my way. When the girls spotted Shelby, he barked and wagged his tail and they surrounded him. He rolled over on the sidewalk and let them scratch his belly, his tongue hanging out.

"You've got a sweet dog," one of the girls said.

"Thanks."

My dog received attention from every female in close proximity. I couldn't even get the police to pursue a murderer in the middle of the tourist district. The girls went inside the store and Shelby perked his ears, curled his tail high, and danced around in victory.

"Go ahead and gloat," I said. "They're nothing but heartache." Sometimes forever.

Unlike the natural surf of Sullivan's Island, Folly Beach had empty beer cans and the occasional used condom washing on shore to uphold its reputation. The warm ocean breeze blew inland as Shelby and I walked the sand. I thought about the arrangements for the wake. Chauncey told me my uncle's wishes were cremation and no funeral. Typical Uncle Reggie to make it easier for me.

I wore the ball cap and sunglasses I'd bought and led Shelby to Folly's main drag to find lunch. The gun rested under a folded stack of boxer shorts at the rental because I wasn't sure I'd need it just yet. At a food joint with an outside counter, whose health code score I purposely didn't look at, I bought a couple of chili dogs and a root beer and sat on a bench close by. The teenage girl who served us had a cheery personality. She slid over the counter, got down to pet Shelby, and gave him a bowl of water, talking nonstop the whole time. With my hunger satisfied, listening to how a younger person views the world made me realize there might still be hope. I gave the girl a ten-dollar tip and walked away. My phone chimed and I checked the caller I.D.

"Hello, Darcy." I put a King Edward cigar in my mouth.

"Got your message about the police putting the case on the back burner," she said. "I did some checking and couldn't find out anything new. My sources said they'd get back to me. Where are you?"

"Tell you what. I'll meet you at the news office."

"You holding out on me?"

"You're the reporter."

"Maybe so, but there's one thing I know for sure."

I said, "What's that?"

"Your fly's open."

Without thinking, I looked down to see if she was right. A car horn blew. Across the street sat a shiny red Infiniti convertible, with Darcy waving from the driver's seat. She held a phone to her ear. "Gotcha."

I pressed End on my phone as she made a U-turn and pulled to the curb in front of me. The grin on her face said it all.

"Nice," I said. "Real nice."

"I spotted your dog as I was driving by a while ago. At first, I couldn't tell for sure if it was you with him."

So much for low profile.

She said, "I went by your house and it was roped off with crime-scene tape like your uncle's. By the way, your neighbor is crazy. She told me to stay off your property and away from you. Eleven in the morning and she was sucking down highballs." Darcy shook her head. "Reminded me of a drunk Daisy Duke."

"Everybody likes Daisy," I said.

Darcy rested her elbow on the top edge of her car door. "I'll bet."

Darcy, Shelby, and I sat on the back deck of the beach rental. A flock of pelicans flew over the vast expanse of ocean in front of us, their V-formation reminding me of fighter ships in a *Star Wars* movie. A school of dolphins cut through the surf fifty yards out, their silver-gray bodies arching in and out of the water as they swam.

"You've got a killer view," she said, "but this place is a dump. How'd you get it on short notice?"

"Cancellation. You'd think they would give me a reduced rate for filling it."

She laughed and I caught another glimpse of Jo and felt the need to change the subject.

I asked, "You own a handgun?"

"What kind of question is that?"

"An important one."

She pulled a thirty-two semiautomatic out of her purse. "Of course. Why?"

"Know how to use it?"

"My father taught me."

"Good," I said. "I'd like to check out a property downtown, but it's not exactly on the Battery."

Notorious for summer afternoon downpours between four and five o'clock, Charleston apparently enjoyed drenching her residents as they dashed to their cars after a long day at work. Lowcountry inhabitants learned early to plan around this meteorological practical joke. Unfortunately for me, my arrangements weren't planned as skillfully as others. The sole protection for my Jeep was an old strip of canvas strung from the windshield to the roll bar. Called a bikini top, it functioned like the apparel—it barely covered anything. The top worked except when the wind blew the rain sideways.

I parked underneath an overpass and waited out the monsoon. Darcy had decided to give up a little control and let me drive. She stayed busy in the passenger seat making phone calls. Shelby stretched out in the back, oblivious. My gun was locked in the glove box.

Inactivity gave me time to contemplate my life. Until a week ago, I was content to work at the Cove with my uncle and let thoughts of Jo consume me. Before that my goal consisted of suicide missions in Afghanistan, so I'd made improvement. But unlike my wife's death, someone was responsible for Uncle

Reggie's, and I had the feeling the cops thought it was me. They wouldn't have frozen his accounts otherwise.

Someone tore up the houses looking for something. If it wasn't to find and take the jump drive and files, I was in trouble because I hadn't a clue what else it could be. I pulled the pack of cigars out of my soaked shirt pocket and pressed the Jeep's cigarette lighter. The cigar lit nicely. Darcy coughed and fanned at the smoke with her free hand. I blew a ring in her direction.

Forty-five minutes later, Darcy and I arrived at the property Brother Thomas and I had checked out Tuesday night. On the rusted chain-link fence in front of the place hung a white sign with green lettering obscured by kudzu. I got out and brushed away the invasive vine and read: U.S. EPA SUPERFUND CLEANUP SITE. Back in the Jeep, we bounced over a rough and muddy drive on the side of the property I'd missed before. A faded business placard could still be read: CHEMCON. Using a pen and scratch pad I found in the glove box, I wrote down the company name and what the white sign out front stated. Darcy used her phone to take pictures of everything. Busted windows lined the sides of a large steel and brick building near the roofline. Weeds poked through cracks in the asphalt of the parking lot. The landscaping had long ago been taken over by undergrowth. We walked the fence line. The ground still damp from the rain, my sandals had trouble finding traction as we traced the property—at least ten acres by my estimate. Shelby had a field day marking the turf.

Along the rear of the building, the wood around the truck docks had rotted away. One of the roll-up doors had been pushed in. Two large pools of stagnant brown water took up the back corner of the property. With the Cooper River two blocks from this chemical plant, I understood why EPA signs were posted.

We drove I-26 West toward the Ashley River and my land inheritance. This place reminded me of one of the last missions I'd taken in Afghanistan. My company escorted an Army Corps of Engineers team to a wastewater treatment facility. With insurgents all around, we took a lot of gunfire but held our ground. Hindsight being twenty-twenty and all, we risked our lives for one big septic tank, and I wasn't sure which side was crazier.

From the driver's seat of my Jeep and under a curtain of bug spray, I took in the sight of Sumter Point. The sulfur smell of the marsh penetrated everything. I pulled out another cigar, and pressed the lighter.

Darcy swatted at a mosquito. "I say sell it."

Two more bloodsuckers circled my feet, trying to find a break in the repellant.

The Jeep lighter popped out and I lit the stogie, my third of the day. Darcy didn't mind this time once the mosquitoes vanished with the first whiff of cheap cigar. I blew out a cloud of the pollutant. "There has to be more to this than riverfront property."

Darcy's cell phone chimed. She said, "Patricia sent me a text. She's got someone for you to meet."

The *Palmetto Pulse* office was all business. Scarred desks furnished a large open room occupied by people working on laptops. Darcy greeted a few coworkers as she led me to an office in the back and rapped on the jamb of the open door.

"Come in," Patricia said.

Shelby entered first and Darcy and I followed. Patricia's personal office had nicer furniture than the outer room. She sat at a large antique mahogany desk I guessed was two-hundred years old. Unrestored, it had a perfectly aged patina of nicks and scratches. Patricia kept it gleaming. I would've bet big bucks the Tiffany lamp on its corner was also original.

Shelby walked around the desk and poked Patricia's leg with his nose.

Patricia scratched behind his ears. "Hello there, sweetheart."

"Hello, yourself," I said.

"I was talking to your dog," she said.

In one of the chairs facing Patricia sat a white-haired woman with a squat figure and big glasses. She turned slightly to get a look at us.

Darcy patted the woman on the shoulder. "Hello, Mrs. Calhoun."

The woman's face lit up. "Hello, dear. It's so nice to see you."

Darcy asked, "How did you get here? You didn't drive yourself, again, did you?"

"Oh, heavens no. My driver is picking up a few things at the store for me. He'll be along soon enough."

"Mrs. Calhoun," Patricia said, "this is Brack Pelton."

The old woman reached and took my hand. "I'm so sorry to hear about your uncle."

"Thank you, ma'am," I said. "Did you know him?"

She let go of my hand. "I was telling Patricia here about the time my daughter and son-in-law brought the grandchildren to see me. We took them to the beach and afterwards went to your uncle's pirate place. The kids loved it."

I looked at Patricia and wondered what this had to do with anything.

"Mrs. Calhoun is on the Isle of Palms Town Council," Patricia said. "She wanted to meet you and talk about what your plans were for Pirate's Cove, since you've inherited it."

The town council had been trying to get rid of the bar for years. It occurred to me the rich old bat sitting here was a little less than sincere. Probably not too sorry to hear about Uncle Reggie's demise, either.

Darcy pulled a chair for herself from the conference room across the hall.

I took the seat next to Mrs. Calhoun. "Well, ma'am, I haven't thought that far ahead."

She nodded. "Oh, I understand, dear. I don't mean to pry, but through the years the Isle of Palms has developed a good reputation. People who visit our island expect things a certain way. Our beaches are clean, and alcohol is not allowed on them. Our businesses have certain codes to be met. All these things have been put in place to make sure people want to keep coming back to our little paradise."

"What can I do to help?" I hoped I sounded convincing.

"That's why I'm here," she said. "I want to make sure you know you have the town council's support. Several people have come forward inquiring as to the future of your restaurant and I believe a generous offer will be delivered to your lawyer's office before the end of the week."

"And what would the members of the council deem a good future for the place?" I wanted to hear her say the answer I knew she was going to give.

Her face became one big grin and her eyes sparkled behind her Coke-bottle glasses. "Oh, it would be in good hands. The last phase of the shops and restaurants on Ocean Avenue would be complete."

"What changes could make that a reality?"

She touched my arm again. "You are such a dear. We'd rebuild it to match the Charleston theme we've been using on the other shops and cafés and create a more family-friendly atmosphere."

I rubbed my chin. "You'd have it torn down."

"Oh yes. Especially that scary cigar-smoking skull flag."

Patricia chimed in. "What would you call it?"

The old woman sat up in her chair and clasped her hands

together as if in prayer. "We have several names in mind. Um, let's see . . . Pelican Bay is one of them, and we'd put in those observation viewers so families could watch the birds in their natural habitat. Another is Dolphin Swimmer. We'd create a mini-museum and education center so kids could learn all about the ocean wildlife."

Patricia's tightened smirk softened at the edges.

I turned my attention to Mrs. Calhoun. "You guys have this all planned out, don't you? It's a good thing my uncle wants to be cremated because he'd turn over in his grave if I let any of that happen."

Mrs. Calhoun's high-spirited disposition dropped back to reality. "Now listen here, young man."

"No. You listen. If the good members of the town council were so interested in educating the public to save our local wildlife, they never would have allowed all those hotels and shops to be built in the first place. You know how fragile the sand dunes are because you post signs everywhere to stop people from walking on them. Though I guess it's okay to bulldoze them flat and pour concrete foundations there."

Mrs. Calhoun abruptly stood up, gave Patricia a curt nod, and marched out of the room. Patricia, Darcy, and I stared at the doorway a few seconds.

Patricia broke the silence. "I think that is one of the funniest things I have ever seen."

I said, "Dolphin Swimmer?"

CHAPTER ELEVEN

Patricia pushed away from her desk and stood. "Where have you two been?"

We described our trip to the Chemcon site.

Patricia said, "He never told me. In fact, I was thinking about last Saturday morning. He took me out in his boat."

"His boat." I'd forgotten he had one.

Patricia said, "We dropped crab pots in the I.C.W. just north of the Isle of Palms."

"Paige said he complained about the price of crab. I never knew he fished for his own."

"It was the first time I know of."

"Can you show me where he dropped the pots?"

Patricia nodded and pointed at the pack of cigars sticking out of my pocket. "Don't tell me you're smoking those awful things. Are you paying homage or something?"

"Something like that."

Darcy said, "They smell like the monkey cage at the zoo."

Patricia left the room for a moment and returned with a wooden box. "Try these. I bought them for Reggie but he wouldn't take them."

I examined the box. "Cubans."

"Yes," Patricia said. "He told me Castro was just another Ho Chi Minh."

★ ★ ★ ★ ★

I called ahead and had the marina prep my uncle's boat. Patricia, Darcy, Shelby, and I stopped at a convenience store with a sandwich shop and bought a cooler, ice, several bottles of water, and subs. The Isle of Palms Marina docked several hundred boats at any given time. The hundred-fifteen-horse Suzuki outboard on Uncle Reggie's nineteen-foot Twin Vee fired up and I eased it around the other vessels. Patricia finished applying a layer of sunblock. She wore Jackie-O sunglasses and a straw hat. Both women looked good in their shorts and tank tops.

Still, I asked Darcy, "Where's the bikini?"

She squeezed SPF 15 out of a bottle into her palm and said, "Thought I'd give you a break."

I could feel embarrassment color my face and tried to mask it with a smile. Smooth, Brack, real smooth. The lanes around the marina were designated a no-wake zone, which meant no speeding. The slow pace gave me time to light one of the Cubans Patricia had given me. After a few drags, I said, "Not bad." As if a few days of smoking cheap cigars made me an expert.

Once we hit the open water of the I.C.W., I pushed the throttle down and we sped off. Nothing in the world was like riding the water. I hadn't been on it in a while and it felt good to be back. Salt spray peppered our faces. The women's hair blew in the ocean wind. Uncle Reggie's twin-hull cruiser smoothed the naturally rough water. We followed the channel north. The homes lining the waterway, much like the ones facing the Atlantic Ocean, went for seven figures. If my house were on a bigger lot, I might have had to pay more than the four-hundred-thousand I'd coughed up—a big chunk of Jo's life insurance gone with one stroke of the pen.

My favorite Eagles song belted from the speakers when I turned on the FM radio in the instrument panel. I turned up the volume and tapped my bare feet on the fiberglass hull.

Boat traffic on the waterway was light. Darcy sat at the bow with Shelby while Patricia remained at the stern next to the cooler. Across the blue-green water the miniature fiddler crabs scrambled up the mud banks sideways. Pelicans and cranes perched on broken pilings jutting out of the water.

Over the wind's noise, I yelled, "So where's the spot you dropped the pots?"

"Ten more minutes up the channel," Patricia shouted.

I slipped off my shirt and tightened the adjustment on my ball cap so it wouldn't fly off. Darcy scratched Shelby's ears and he licked her face. The heat of the sun baked my skin so I lathered up with sunscreen as I managed the wheel. After three years in the Middle East and six months at the beach here in Charleston, I didn't need a lot of sun protection.

Patricia was right. It took us ten minutes. She pointed out a trio of buoys in a cove to our right. On each flew the flag Uncle Reggie had created for the Pirate's Cove. I idled closer. Twenty feet away, I cut the motor and rotated the prop out of the water. It was low tide and I didn't want to get bogged in the pluff mud where the water was shallow.

I was about to throw my cigar butt over the side when Darcy said, "I don't think the fish like smoking any more than I do."

"I knew there was a reason I brought you along," I said, and put it in the ashtray.

Darcy smiled and helped Patricia drop the anchor. Uncle Reggie's old deck shoes lay in one of the compartments under the seats. I slipped off flip-flops for the deck shoes to avoid cutting my feet on the oyster shells embedded in the mud, then jumped into the water. It was three-feet deep and I sank another couple of inches when my feet hit bottom. Shelby tried to come in with me but I stopped him. The water was too muddy and the current moved at a swift pace. He looked at me like I had just snatched a steak out of his mouth.

"I'll make it up to you, boy."

I could tell he wasn't buying it as I turned and plodded toward the buoys. My feet squished and crunched like I was walking in cookie dough, with jagged shells instead of chocolate chips. The water level dropped below my waist as I got closer. The tops of the crab cages were barely submerged. I picked one up by the handles. Empty. The cage was a cylinder of wire mesh two-feet high with a diameter of a foot, attached to a square wooden base. I carried it to the boat. Darcy and Patricia grabbed the handles and hauled it on board.

"It's empty," Darcy said.

"Look at the bottom," I said, holding onto the edge of the boat. The bottom section of the pot was at least four inches thick.

Patricia looked at me. "I didn't notice it when we set these out."

The three pots had the same false bottom and none had trapped any crabs. We worked for ten minutes trying to find an opening before I pulled up the anchor and used it as a hammer. Two good licks and the base of the first pot broke into pieces. Inside we found something wrapped in black plastic. I took out my Swiss Army knife and sliced through it.

"Hello!" said Darcy.

Patricia's eyes were wide. "Money."

The second pot held the same thing.

The third one came apart after three blows. The package it contained was wrapped in the same black plastic but was larger than the money bricks. Patricia opened it with my knife.

"Papers," she said.

We sorted through them. They were pictures of old industrial sites. I recognized the names as those on the memory stick.

Patricia pointed to one. "I'm pretty sure this place is in

Charleston."

On a note stuck on one of the sheets, I saw a name, Ken Graves, and a phone number, written in my uncle's handwriting. At the bottom of the note were three underlined initials: EPA.

"I guess we know who to call," I said. "If we're being watched, we can't be seen hauling these things to the dock."

"Uh, Brack?" Patricia said. "Look at this."

She handed me a folded sheet of paper. I read my uncle's handwriting.

Brack,

If you're reading this, I'm surfin' a mondo tube with both eyes open. I just hope it's not on fire. In Nam, I flew with a buddy named Chauncey Connors. He looks like one of those Charleston High Society types and his office is on King Street. He's got my will. Things are going down connected with Sumter Point and other properties. I made copies of what I could find out so far and I've put them here. It all revolves around Galston. Don't trust him. With me gone, he's going to offer you millions for Sumter Point. If you take his money, I'll haunt you the rest of your life. You hear me? Use the money here for whatever you need. The bar will take care of itself as long as Paige is running the show. Just don't screw it up. I love you but don't mope around for me. You've already done enough of that. It's time to get on with your life.

Reggie

PS: Tell Patricia I—tell her she was always the one.

Patricia read the last sentence and put her hand to her mouth. Her eyes welled with tears.

Darcy said, "Let me see that." She read it and put her arm around Patricia's shoulders.

My head swirled with thoughts of revenge. "We don't have

time for this right now," I said. "Let's go get the fat bastard."

Darcy said, "Have a heart, Brack."

Patricia leaned forward, her face in her hands and her shoulders shaking, and cried. Probably something I should have done when Jo died. I removed the buoys and put the busted pots underwater close to the shore, so other boats would not hit them. Darcy rewrapped the money and papers in plastic and hid it in the bottom of the cooler underneath the ice. We headed to the marina. On the way, Patricia kept wiping her eyes with a tissue. I didn't ask because she would have said it was the salt water spray. Shelby licked her face and pawed at her hand.

In a large meeting room at the *Palmetto Pulse,* Patricia set up a conference phone. We had decided to speak with the EPA contact, but we didn't want to spook him with press credentials. I was to do the talking while the women listened in and took notes. If they wanted me to ask a specific question, they were to write a note and hand it to me. As Darcy dialed the long distance number, I held up one of the cigars.

Patricia pointed to a No Smoking sign.

A man answered. "Graves."

I cleared my throat. "Mr. Graves, this is Brack Pelton. Reggie Sails was my uncle. I believe he had been in contact with you."

"Yes," he said. "I spoke with him a week ago. You said Reggie Sails 'was' your uncle? What does that mean?"

"He was killed Saturday night."

Graves didn't say anything.

I said, "Mr. Graves?"

"I'm here. Just a little surprised. I'm very sorry for your loss. What can I do for you?"

"Your name was found along with pictures of industrial sites. In fact, I think he might have called you about one in particular."

"He did. I don't have the name of the site in front of me. Do you have it?"

"Chemcon." I gave him the address.

"Hold on," Graves said.

The reception was sketchy but I thought I heard him typing on a keyboard.

He said, "Yes, that's the one. Site was closed in 1985 and declared a Superfund site in ninety."

"What's a Superfund site?"

"They are the nation's worst toxic waste sites."

"Mr. Graves," I said, measuring my words carefully, "is there any reason someone would be murdered because of one of these sites?"

"I never heard of that happening before, but it's possible. The government supplies funds to help clean them up. But seventy percent of the cleanup cost is usually absorbed by the responsible polluters, if they can be located."

I said, "How dangerous is the Chemcon site?"

More tapping followed before Graves spoke. "Okay, here it is. It's listed as having furnace dust, sulfuric acid, phosphate, and other materials. Overall, pretty nasty stuff."

"It's near a neighborhood," I said. "I'm guessing it isn't the healthiest place in town."

"Typically, people living near one of these sites are at the lower levels of income and don't vote."

"My uncle must have known something was up. I just don't know what."

Graves said, "The Chemcon site is past due on the reconstruction phase. The last entry I have lists it as an ER3 site with a PPA."

I said, "Do all you government types speak in initials?"

He chuckled and said, "Sorry, my wife has the same complaint. ER3 stands for Environmentally Responsible Redevelopment and Reuse. In a nutshell it means the owner has a plan for the site after the cleanup so it doesn't just sit there. It's probably past due on the reconstruction phase because there hasn't been much cleanup done."

"And the P-P-something?"

"PPA stands for Prospective Purchaser Agreement. In this case, it means the EPA was in negotiation with an individual or corporation for the site."

Patricia handed me a note with a question she wanted me to ask.

I read it and said, "Can you tell me if my uncle was the individual?"

"Not with the information I have in front of me. Since this is in my neck of the woods, you'd think I'd know more about it. I will when I talk to you again, you can bet on it. Give me a number where I can reach you."

I gave him my cell number and we hung up.

Darcy said, "Holy cow."

Patricia stood and paced. "My ex-husband was a real piece of work. He never told me he had a tax problem. And he certainly never told me about any of this."

"I'm glad I'm not the only one," I said.

After securing the cash from the crab pots in a safe at the *Palmetto Pulse,* I called Uncle Reggie's lawyer, now mine.

CHAPTER TWELVE

A bath for Shelby and a quick shower for me, and we were new men. At least I felt like a new man. As Shelby and I walked into the law firm's reception area a little before seven PM, my dog was busy sniffing everything his leash would let him reach. When the same young receptionist from my first visit saw Shelby, she removed her phone earpiece, came around the desk, and knelt to pet him. Shelby raised his eyebrows and lifted a paw to shake hands.

As if talking to a baby, the receptionist addressed him in the third person. "He's such a pretty boy, yes he is."

I said, "It's okay if he's in here, right?"

"Are you kidding? Do you know how many desperate housewives of Charleston stroll in here with a Gucci purse in one hand and a miniature Chihuahua in the other? If we had a pet ban, our clients would find another law firm."

The phone rang. I expected her to go answer it but she didn't. Thanks to my dog, the master-manipulator of females, I found out her name was Jane and she was Chauncey's granddaughter. Chauncey came out and waved me into his office, saying, "Sorry it took so long. I was on a phone conference with another client."

Shelby didn't want to follow us into the office and I couldn't blame him. Jane happily took the leash from me. In his office, Chauncey motioned to the sitting area by a big bay window overlooking King Street.

I said, "You bill phone time too?"

He took a chair to my right. "Sometimes."

"What about for a client sitting in your waiting area?"

He crossed his legs. "Real sharks prefer the big kill of a settlement. So what's up?"

"Patricia and my uncle dropped crab pots in the I.C.W. last week. Turns out they were fake." I handed Chauncey the papers from the pots. "We found these in them along with bricks of cash."

Chauncey leaned forward and read the papers. After a few minutes he said, "Government-subsidized environmental cleanup. I don't believe it." He sat back in his chair. "Do you know what this means?"

I shrugged.

He said, "I'll tell you what it means. It means hundreds of millions in untaxed income. It means you don't know who your friends are."

"Except for you," I said.

Chauncey smiled and said, "I work for you. There's a difference."

"Say, that brings up another point. If the cops don't release my uncle's funds, I'm going to have to start selling. That is, assuming I can't use the cash we found."

"We have to first establish it was claimed income," Chauncey said. "In the meantime I happen to have received an offer on the bar."

"I heard. How much?"

"Three-point-five million," he said. "How'd you find out about it?"

"A little old lady told me. A little old lady who'd probably sell her own children."

Chauncey squinted as if in thought. "Mrs. Calhoun?"

I nodded. "Who's the buyer?"

My hired shark selected a file from the bureau behind him. "Trans World Unlimited."

"Trans what?"

He opened the folder, pulled out a sheet of paper, and turned it so I could see the company logo. "Trans World Unlimited. They're a conglomerate. Among other things, they own franchises. Weekends Bar and Grill, O'Malley's Pub, and Surf's Up Nightclub."

"They want to turn the Pirate's Cove into one of those cheesy pickup bars with that stupid blue neon wave hanging over the liquor bottles? I don't know what's worse. That or what Mrs. Calhoun said."

"Which was?"

"Dolphin Swimmer."

He said, "Three million, five-hundred-thousand dollars."

I slouched in the seat. "If I sold out, Uncle Reggie said he'd come back to haunt me."

"The tax situation isn't going away," he said. "You got any other money?"

"Not that kind. The old bat is probably getting a kickback in all this."

Chauncey grinned and said, "On the bright side, the police can't freeze the accounts forever. I can probably stall the bidder while I see what I can do about releasing your funds."

An hour later, I decided to take another run at Mutt. Since his place was a mile from the Chemcon property, maybe he could tell me why my uncle wanted to get involved. In front of the bar, I stepped out of my Jeep and, in case anyone was watching, stuck the barrel of the forty-five down the back of my shorts. Shelby jumped out and sniffed the sidewalk, inhaling the scents and smells of the projects. I didn't bother with his leash. The rusty screen door creaked when I opened it and Shelby padded in ahead of me.

John Lee Hooker's "Boom Boom" rumbled out of the juke.

Several African American men stood around the pool table. Two perched at the bar. Mutt, facing them from behind the bar, cleaned a glass with what looked like the same dirty rag from my previous visit. The swollen nose my fist had given him appeared to have deepened in color, which meant it was healing. I walked to the bar and took a seat. Shelby growled and went behind the bar to Mutt.

Mutt stepped backward. "He don't bite, do he?"

"Not usually," I said. "Just don't let him think you're scared." In the six months I'd had him, Shelby never bit anyone. Of course, he'd never been provoked. Women loved him and the feeling was obviously mutual. But men were a different story. My dog had a curious way of greeting them, and I could hang my hat on his judgment of their worth.

Every man in the dump crowded the bar and peered over the top to watch Mutt lower a finger-twitching hand to my dog. With a snarl and show of teeth, Shelby moved in closer. Extra sweat beads formed on the bartender's forehead. Shelby jerked his head up and gave a sharp bark. Mutt yanked his hand back. I eased my hand around the butt of the forty-five just in case my dog needed backup. After another bark, Shelby grabbed one end of the dirty towel hanging from Mutt's hand, and tugged and grunted like he wanted to play. The men crowded around the bar hooted and howled. I released my grip on the forty-five and let out a long breath.

Mutt looked like he was about to need a diaper. "Good doggie." He rubbed Shelby's head. "Good doggie."

Shelby released the towel and licked Mutt's hand.

With the towel, Mutt wiped the sweat from his forehead. Shelby barked again and Mutt held the towel out as an offering. My dog snatched it out of his hand and ran around the bar with the filthy rag in his mouth. He was current on his shots but I wasn't sure they covered this place. I took the rag from him. Shelby whimpered until one of the patrons held out a cheese puff. Obedience school had taught Shelby to eat only what I gave him, so he looked at the treat, sat on his hindquarters, and stared at me.

"Thanks for the offer," I said to the man, "but he's been trained not to take food from strangers."

The man offering the cheese puff said, "That's all right." He took three more out of a bag he was eating from, set them on a napkin, and slid them to me. "He deserve something for putting Mutt in his place."

I fed them to Shelby.

Mutt propped himself on a stool. "Who were you gonna shoot, me or the dog?"

"I'd never shoot my own dog."

That Mutt had seen me reach for my gun while Shelby terrorized him genuinely impressed me.

"Real funny, Opie. So what can I do you outta?"

I pulled two Cuban cigars from my pocket, clipped the ends, and offered one to him. "What do you say we smoke a peace offering?"

Charleston bars and restaurants had been forced to go smoke-free a few years ago. Judging from the smoke clouds hovering in the room, Mutt must not have gotten the memo. My uncle's stainless Zippo snapped open in my fingers and I lit Mutt's first.

After a few puffs, he examined the cigar. "Not bad." He took a long drag and blew a few rings toward the ceiling. They danced around one of the exposed bulbs hanging on a dusty cord. "You want a beer or something?"

"Trying to quit."

Mutt reached into the cooler, pulled out a Sun Drop, and

opened it for me. The pool players went back to racking shots. The other men returned to their conversation.

I lit my cigar.

A voice boomed behind me. "You shouldda called and told me you was coming back to town, mm-hmm." Brother Thomas pulled out a barstool next to me, sat, and slapped my knee.

I exhaled a cloud of smoke. "I'm sure glad we're all friends, now."

"A lot happened in the past few days," Brother Thomas said.

"You sure right," Mutt said. "Archie over there hit the daily on Monday. He was so happy he come in here and bought rounds 'til it was all gone. Someone told his wife and she throwed him out. He staying wit me 'til she takes him back."

Brother Thomas wiped his face and neck with a handkerchief. "You think she will?"

Mutt nodded. "She always take him back. I figure another day."

I said, "So, what did my uncle have going with the EPA cleanup site?"

"Neighborhood kids sneak over there to play," Mutt said. "Reggie was trying to make sure it got cleaned up."

"How was he going to do that?"

Brother Thomas said, "He talk like he was gonna buy it."

I thought about the money in his accounts, thanks to the loan against the bar. "Did he say what he was going to do with it?"

"Naw," Mutt said. "He said he was gonna look into it is all."

Chauncey made arrangements with a funeral home for the viewing of Uncle Reggie, and that's where Brother Thomas gave a bold eulogy Friday morning. Paige and I closed the Pirate's Cove for four hours so the staff could attend. Most of the crowd came to the Cove afterward, and out of deference to Uncle

Reggie and his inherent need for the Cove to make a profit, Paige and I kept it a cash bar.

The crowd that showed up could have come together only in a place like Charleston. And could have only my uncle as the common denominator. The owner of a million-dollar beachfront house traded vodka shots with a man from Brother Thomas's congregation in the projects. Three Folly Beach surfers cornered several state legislators and demanded they fix beach erosion. My personal favorite encounter occurred when Mutt asked Detectives Rogers and Wilson if they had any weed. They pulled out their badges and pretty much cleared the room, which was okay with me. It was late. Good thing I'd left the gun in the safe.

At two in the morning, a small group of us relaxed in chairs on the upper deck of the Cove and listened to the crash of the ocean. Shelby sat at the legs of Patricia's chair. Brother Thomas dozed in a lounge chair.

Even though Chauncey's wife had gone home to bed a few hours ago, he was still hanging around. I knew he missed my uncle. He stooped to pet Shelby. "Trish and I have two Labs. I think she treats them better than the grandkids. Or me, for that matter."

Darcy stood by the railing, her blond wisps gently blowing in the wind. "You blame her?"

The lawyer laughed. "Not really."

Mutt lit a cigarette. "There sure was a lot of people here."

Bonny, the bar mascot, landed on the railing beside Darcy.

I said, "You're right about that."

Patricia held a glass of red wine by the stem, her legs tucked underneath her. "The police never did find Reggie's necklace or his other things."

My late wife had bought Uncle Reggie a white shell necklace on our honeymoon. He wore it every day. I couldn't remember

103

if he had it on when I was giving him CPR. Holding a mug of root beer, I propped my feet on the deck railing and rocked my chair back. "We've got a lot of work to do when the sun comes up."

Sleep did not come easily and seeing Uncle Reggie for the last time didn't help. It was compelling to think he'd risked it all for his friends in the projects, and I didn't want to shortchange his good name, but there had to be more to it. His last words were not "Save the black kids." And so far I had no idea who Ray was.

My cell phone rang. I looked at the clock as I picked up. Five AM.

The voice from Folly Beach Pier said, "So, what have you found out?"

Still lying on my back, I said, "Who's Ray?"

"Ray who?"

"That's what I'm asking. Before my uncle died, he said Ray shot him."

The man took his time answering. "I don't know any Ray."

I sat up. "All this cloak and dagger and you don't know any Rays. That's great. What else don't you know?"

"Look, there's enough information in the files to bury some people."

I gripped the phone tight. "If you've got something, give it to the police. Give it to the IRS. Better yet, give it to me and I'll make sure it gets out there."

"I'm not giving anything away. I'm selling it. To you if you're buying."

I said, "Someone trashed my uncle's house and mine looking for something. They got a copy of the memory stick."

"It can't be traced to me," he said, "but your uncle was probably killed for it. Who did he talk to? Who turned on him?"

I swung my feet onto the floor. "How do I know you aren't on their side?"

"You don't. Just like I don't know if you're the one who sold your uncle out. I heard he left you everything."

"Yeah, and after running the bar for the next twenty years I can probably retire."

"Ah, but what about the land? It's a hundred acres, isn't it? Lots of river frontage. A couple million, easy."

"You sound like you're making me an offer."

"Your uncle agreed to pay twenty grand for more information. You get the same price."

I inhaled deeply and blew it out like smoke. "So, do you have a name, or do I call you Deep Throat?"

"Clever, but it's still twenty grand. I'll let you pick the location. Someplace with a crowd. It's easier to hide."

"It's not like we live in New York City, you know."

"What do you suggest?"

After a few seconds of thinking, I said, "The opposite. Sullivan's Island, past Fort Moultrie toward the harbor. The shore's pretty narrow. There's beach access. Not many people. Lines of rocks stretch out to the water."

He said, "Meet you in two hours."

The line went dead. So much for any sleep now.

Chapter Thirteen

When I pulled into the beach access parking area not far from my house, the sun was coming up over the ocean, coloring the sky a bright crimson. The old saying about a red sky in the morning came to mind.

A new gray Volvo sedan was already parked in the sand lot. By my watch, I was five minutes late. A stop at the Pirate's Cove had put me behind. I took a bottle of bug spray from the glove box along with the gun and stuck them in my pocket. Shelby and I walked the path to the ocean and cut left.

My source from the pier stood on the narrow beach. He held a briefcase in one hand and used the other to swat at his head and neck. "You didn't say anything about the no-see-ums."

Shelby ran past us into the water.

I let the man smack his bald head a few more times before I took out the spray and threw it to him. The no-see-ums he referred to were gnats living in the marsh. As irritating as mosquitoes—maybe worse. The man set his briefcase in the sand and doused himself from head to toe, probably ruining his suit. When he threw back the bottle, it was close to empty.

"Nice suit." I sprayed myself. "You working on a Saturday?"

"You got my twenty thousand?"

"You got the goods?"

He took one step back. "Not on me."

I finished with the carcinogenic shower and stuck the bottle in my pocket. "Then I don't have the twenty grand."

He gave me a long look before he opened his briefcase and pulled out a file folder, waving it at me. "You sure you don't have the money?"

I showed him the envelope with the cash I'd picked up from the safe in the Pirate's Cove. He took the envelope and thumbed each brick like he was checking to see if I'd stuck blank sheets in the middle.

"It's all there," I said.

He put the bundles in his suitcase. "One man is behind the companies on the file. Did you do the math? It's like ten million dollars and that's just last year."

"Did he kill my uncle?"

"I'm not sure. But Sails was going to expose him."

"Galston?"

"Yes."

Shelby swam in circles as the waves charged the shore.

I said, "If you had the evidence, why was my uncle going to expose him? Why weren't you?"

"Because I can't afford to lose my job. It's where the information's coming from."

"So it's stolen. Great."

"You think information like that is available to the general public?"

I took out a cigar, clipped the end, and lit it with my uncle's Zippo. The lighter snapped shut with a loud metallic click. After two long pulls on the cigar, I said, "I don't know much about the IRS, but something tells me they won't use illegally obtained information."

"Yeah, but the EPA will. All they need to do is send someone there—look at what's not getting done. Call it a surprise audit or whatever. Then the fines start. You don't mess with the IRS and you don't mess with the EPA. They've shut corporations down for less."

"Why didn't my uncle report what he had?"

"Because what we were digging up would be so much more damaging. Think about it—defrauding the government of millions and taking a tax deduction on it. Michael Galston's a thief who should be in jail for what he's been getting away with."

Said the one selling confidential information.

"If he killed my uncle, he won't make it that far."

"That file has copies of all the receipts. My fingerprints aren't on them." He put the money in his briefcase.

I flipped through the papers, folded the file and stuck it in my waistband next to my gun, and held out my hand. "Brack Pelton."

He hesitated, looking at my hand as if it belonged to a portal leading to a whole new dimension, before he took it. "My name is David Fisher."

"I've got some people you need to meet," I said.

Fisher shook his head. "Patricia Voyels and her news girl? No thanks. I've seen you with them already and I don't want my face on TV or in the paper."

"Are you ready to talk?"

"Only to you, and the price goes up to a hundred thousand. What you do with what I tell you is your business. If my name gets out, I'll know exactly who did it and, rest assured, you won't survive either."

I stepped closer and grinned at the small bald man. "We all think we're tough until someone starts shooting. I know I can handle it. The question is, can you?"

Fisher poked me in the chest with his right index finger. "If you keep your mouth closed, I won't have to find out."

I grabbed his finger and wrenched it up. He squealed like a little girl and tried to pry my hold loose with his free hand. His desk job didn't do him any favors in the strength department.

"How did the murdering bastard find out about my uncle?"

"I-I'm not sure. Let go you—"

I bent his hand a little more. "What did you give him that gave him away?"

"N-not much more than what you have, okay? Now let go!"

I released my grip. "How did my uncle find you, anyway?"

He rubbed his hand. "I found him. I knew Galston wanted the Sumter property and I knew your uncle was having trouble paying the taxes on it."

"How did you know?"

"Galston has his fingers in a lot of pies. He knows what's going on everywhere. You think your ex-aunt has dirt on people? Galston is like J. Edgar Hoover. Only thing missing is the lipstick and boyfriends. He's probably got something on you, too."

"Nothing to get. What did he have on my uncle besides the taxes?"

Fisher shook his head. "Zilch as far as I know. Your uncle mortgaged the bar and I assumed he was going to pay the taxes. Galston will probably use his clout to force you to do the same. Why was your uncle so adamant about keeping the Sumter property, anyway?"

Shelby came out of the water and ran to me. I checked my pocket and realized I'd forgotten his ball. He whined and shook water and sand all over Fisher.

"Ahh!" Fisher tried to move away and tripped and fell over a tree limb that had washed up on the beach. "Stupid dog!"

Shelby licked Fisher's face, getting his glasses wet in the process. Fisher got to his feet and tried to wipe his glasses with his shirt, grumbling. When he put them back on, he looked down at himself and saw he was coated with sand. He scowled and brushed himself off. "All I'm saying is to be ready. It's coming." He grabbed the handle of his briefcase and walked unsteadily on the loose sand path to where our vehicles were parked. Halfway up the trail, he stopped and turned toward me. "Remember, it's a hundred thousand."

On the way to my Folly Beach hideout, Shelby and I stopped and picked up breakfast at McDonald's. As we sat eating on the back porch of the beach rental, my cell phone vibrated. I looked at the caller I.D. before I answered. "Hey, Chauncey."

"Good morning, Brack. I hope I didn't wake you."

"Already up. But I was thinking of going back to bed."

"I see," he said. "The reason I'm calling is I've got some not-so-good news from a reliable source."

"I'm being forced to settle the issue of the back taxes."

"How'd you know?"

"Lucky guess?" I forked the last of the Big Breakfast eggs into my mouth.

"It would take a lot more than luck to nail that one."

Steam escaped from the large coffee once I popped the lid off. I thumbed my nose at the "Contents very hot" warning, took a gulp, and rinsed the breakfast residue from my teeth before swallowing. "I'm getting some help."

Chauncey's voice lost all lightness when he said, "Nothing illegal, I hope."

"Not as far as you know."

"Let's keep it that way."

I decided not to ask if he meant for me to stay away from anything illegal or to just keep him from knowing about it.

Shelby and I drove to the *Palmetto Pulse*. Patricia and Darcy hovered over the antique desk and flipped through the file Fisher had given me. My dog slept in the corner, still damp from the shower I'd given him to get the rest of the sand out of his fur before we'd left.

Patricia said, "How did you say you came by this?"

Exhausted, I stretched out on the floor next to Shelby and closed my eyes. "I didn't."

Darcy said, "Army boy's got skills."

I crossed an ankle over the other. "Very funny. And it's Marine."

"You might make a reporter, yet," Patricia said.

"Strictly off-camera, I hope," Darcy said.

"Are you going to read the file or am I here for your entertainment?"

"Seeing your busted-up face on the news was funny enough," Darcy replied.

"Thanks to you."

"This is good stuff, Brack," Patricia said. "I think we can use it."

I said, "Without receiving any collateral damage?"

"That's the idea." Patricia drank some of her coffee. "First, we have to flush him out a little bit."

I said, "What did you have in mind?"

She said, "How quickly can you get a tux?"

The Ford dealer called and said the Mustang was ready. On a Saturday, even. I left Shelby at the Cove with Paige, parked the Jeep at my house on Sullivan's Island, and took a cab to get my car. The gun was tucked in my waistband under my shirt.

The dealer had detailed my Mustang and the new paint was brilliant. Almost made the five-thousand-dollar bill worth it. Almost. Like the difference between losing three fingers instead of the whole hand. Luckily, the insurance company was footing the extremities. Everything but the deductible.

When I walked out of the service department, a black Chrysler 300 with tinted windows faced me from across the busy five-lane of Charleston's motor mile. Galston's goon squad. Just great. I opened the door to my car, got in, and pulled the forty-five, keeping it below the window line. The warm metal felt slick from sweat as I laid it on my lap.

The Mustang's starter made the familiar whir before the engine turned over. I sat there and goosed the gas. The motor roared in anticipation. The Hurst gearshift I'd installed slid smoothly into first. The rear tires chirped as the clutch engaged and shot the car onto the street ahead of traffic. I caught second and third gears, keeping one eye on the rearview mirror as I ran two yellow lights before getting stopped by a red a mile up the road. No black 300s in sight.

At a men's store downtown, I found a forty-four long Armani tux on a discount rack. With shoes and all the accessories, I still had to fork over a thousand bucks, plus another fifty to a local seamstress to get the pants hemmed on the spot.

CHAPTER FOURTEEN

The reason I needed the tux, Patricia informed me, was for a fundraiser being held that night in the Old Exchange Building. Located at the corner of East Bay and Broad Streets, the structure had been constructed in the late eighteenth century. The price of admission to the event was a tax-deductible fifteen-hundred bucks per couple. Patricia could have gotten me in free and clear, but I decided the Pirate's Cove needed a presence in Charleston high society. Its members might view the bar's attendance as they would a skid mark on a pair of tighty-whities, but I didn't care. I had Paige cut a business check from a new account established from my now rapidly diminishing personal funds to the Preservation Society, the organizers of the shindig.

Darcy answered the door to her condo in a slinky black cocktail dress. Jo had worn something similar to get a rise out of me. Both succeeded.

"You clean up nicely," she said. "Give me a couple more minutes and I'll be ready."

She vanished down a hallway, leaving me to close the door. Her condo overlooked the Cooper River. The shades were open and I enjoyed watching the water flow by, making its way to the harbor and out to sea. I turned and took in the small room decorated with a lot of glass and chrome. A medium-sized flatscreen hung on one wall flanked by several journalism and broadcasting awards. A minibar stood against the other wall with nothing but top-shelf spirits. The rest of the vertical surfaces were windows. A couch and coffee table occupied the center of the room, with the kitchen to the right. I guessed her bedroom lay to the left. Aside from the awards, I saw nothing personal. No framed pictures of family or friends. No paintings or prints.

The Old Exchange was a five-minute walk from her place. Darcy went barefoot, carrying her heels. The heat forced me to remove my jacket, making me glad to have left the gun in the car's glove box. We each donned sunglasses. The only thing missing was Shelby, who'd curled up on the couch at the Folly Beach rental when I left.

Patricia, also wearing black, met us at the entrance escorted by her ninety-year-old father, Mr. Gordon Voyels. As soon as he learned I'd been in Afghanistan, Mr. Voyels became my new best friend. Patricia and Darcy, the local celebrities, worked the crowd. Mr. Voyels and I found a table near the windows and I helped the elderly World War Two veteran into a chair.

He said, "Thank you, Lieutenant."

Patricia must have told him my rank. I took a guess at his. "My pleasure, Captain."

He nodded. I had guessed right. We traded stories through most of the hors d'oeuvres.

Galston appeared at our table, his round head gleaming. "I thought I saw your name on the guest list."

Mr. Voyels said, "What are you tearing up now, Michael?"

Galston feigned insult. "Why, ol' Gordo, despite what your daughter prints about me, rest assured I've got this city's best interest at heart."

Mr. Voyels said, "The only thing I ever heard your father say you got was a good case of crabs. And he didn't say which sailor you got 'em from."

Galston's face turned red but he kept his composure. "Indeed. Well, I was wondering if I might have a private word with Mr. Pelton."

"It's a free country," Mr. Voyels said, "despite what yahoos like you are trying to do with it."

I excused myself from Mr. Voyels and followed Galston to the bar, where he ordered a double scotch. I had the bartender refill my tonic and give me a fresh lime.

Galston said, "I was wondering if you'd thought about my offer."

"I did and I to have to pass. I'll let you know if I need my house redecorated or another paint job on my car."

He put his drink to his mouth and took a pull, smacking his lips slightly. Without looking at me, he said, "I've got a lot riding on this project. To help you reconsider, I'll double my offer. That should cover any inconveniences."

Four million dollars. I think I blinked, but I couldn't say for sure.

"There are things in motion I would like to keep in motion. Any delay could jeopardize my plans." He put his hand on my shoulder. "I'll have my lawyer contact yours."

A man approached us, slapping Galston on the shoulder. "How's it going, Mike?"

Against my better judgment, I said, "I'll think about it."

"Good." He turned his attention to the other man.

I made my way toward the restrooms, passing Patricia who was talking to two women. She called me over.

"Brack," Patricia said, "I'd like you to meet Muffie Cromwell and her sister, Jackie."

I smiled, not sure if I should offer a hand or not. A closer inspection of the women told me they'd had alterations. Compared to Patricia, who held onto her beauty naturally, the faces of these women looked a little too tight. They nodded, probably afraid any facial expression would undo the work their plastic surgeons charged a small fortune for.

"Sorry to hear about your uncle," Muffie said.

"It was just awful," Jackie said. "I didn't think crime was that bad here. I mean, it isn't as if we live in New York City."

Exactly what I told Fisher.

Muffie asked, "Have the police found who did it?"

"No," I said.

"They've closed the case," Patricia said. "Can you believe it?"

"Closed the case?" Jackie said. "Can they do that?"

Patricia nodded. "They're saying it was a random mugging. They're not even going to look for the man who did it."

A couple from across the room waved at Muffie and her sister. They waved back.

"We must speak with the Andersons." Jackie squeezed my arm. "It was nice meeting you, Brack."

Muffie touched Patricia's shoulder. "Let's do lunch tomorrow."

I watched the two women walk away.

Patricia signaled a man carrying a tray of wine glasses and took one.

I asked her, "Who exactly are they?"

She swirled the red wine in the glass. "Muffie is married to the mayor's brother."

"Not bad," I said. "And the other one?"

"She married into a family that owns hotels."

I thought for a moment. "So neither of them would want a story getting out of a crazy mugger killing people in our fair city?"

Patricia said, "I'll bet the chief of police gets a call tonight."

"Thanks."

"By the way," Patricia said, "you and Darcy look good together."

I slipped my wallet from my back pocket, opened it, and took out a weathered photo, a wedding portrait. Jo's smile really was out of this world. I handed the picture to Patricia. "Notice anything familiar?"

She looked at it. "I didn't see the similarity before. They do look a lot alike. Did you show this to Darcy?"

I shook my head. "No."

She returned the picture. "Don't."

I felt Patricia's eyes on me as I replaced the photo in my wallet.

She said, "I would have sent someone else if I'd realized."

"It's okay. I like being reminded of her. Pretty disturbing, huh?"

My aunt brushed her hand gently across my cheek.

After the fundraiser, Darcy and I walked to one of the downtown bars and took a table outside. A waiter came over. Darcy ordered wine and I got a Coke.

When we were alone, I asked her, "How is it you can spend all your time on this story?"

She crossed her legs. "I'm a reporter. It's my job."

"Don't you have a boyfriend or a fiancé, or . . . something?"

"I have a cat. And an automatic feeder."

"He must have been hiding when I was there," I said.

"Must have been."

Our drinks arrived. When we were alone again, I continued. "No boyfriend?"

"Fiancé. He's at Emory in Atlanta," she said. "PhD program. I don't wear my ring when I'm working."

"He's probably named Thurston Howell the third," I said and took a drink of my Coke, crunching ice.

Darcy teased a strand of curls. "Actually, his name is Roger. I've known him forever. Our families are close friends."

Of course they were.

"He doesn't care if you go out with strange men to fundraisers?"

"Not as long as it's work-related."

Which is what this had to be because she didn't have the ring on.

The next morning, Sunday—a full week from my uncle's murder—the Tom Petty ringtone I'd programmed into my cell rescued me from a nightmare. Two dimwits in a Chrysler were chasing me and gaining. With my eyes still closed I answered.

"Mornin'," said a familiar voice.

"Darcy?" I forced open my eyes, let them focus, and reached for my watch from the night table. The little hand was on the eight and the big hand on the twelve. A simple calculation told me five hours had passed since I'd walked her back to her condo. "You don't sleep, do you?"

"Get dressed," she said. "No tux required this time."

When I walked out the door thirty minutes later, Shelby gave me a look telling me how he felt about being left behind again. With my freshly painted Mustang hiding under a car cover behind the beach rental, Darcy picked me up in the convertible. She drove and I rode shotgun. Top down, sun shining, and so hot my thighs stuck to the leather. I reclined the seat and stretched out, the forty-five in the waistband of my shorts jabbed into my side.

I said, "Mind if we get java? I'll even buy you a cup."

"A man after my own heart."

"We all have our moments," I said.

She stopped at a local donut shop and I paid for two large coffees and a mixed half-dozen.

When she saw the box she said, "You plan on eating all those yourself?"

I took a bite out of one with chocolate icing and rainbow sprinkles and offered her the box. "Where we headed?"

She chose a French cruller and pulled out of the parking lot.

"I put the word out I'd pay for information."

"You think someone's gonna tell you they murdered my uncle?"

She blew by all the churchgoing cars on the road. "No, but they might know who did. They also know I reward any good leads."

We merged onto the Mark Clark Expressway and headed toward the airport, her foot hard on the gas.

A half hour later, we pulled into the parking lot of a strip mall in a part of North Charleston I'd never seen before. This section specialized in pawn shops, used car lots, and cheap motels giving deep discounts to senior citizens. A black Chrysler loomed in a handicap spot in a lot across the street.

I took the forty-five and chambered a round. "Wheel it around to the back."

Darcy stared at me but didn't argue. We parked next to a dumpster behind a vacant store.

"Calm down and tell me what's going on," she said.

"Galston's morons are in the black car across the street. It's time they stopped following me around." I got out and ran.

Darcy yelled behind me. "Brack!"

At the end of the building, I stopped and peered around the corner. All clear. The front of the strip mall lay a hundred feet ahead. I made it in seconds and peered again. The 300 was still there.

Jacked up on sugar, caffeine, and adrenaline, I ran across the street and ducked behind a parked car, peering one more time. Nothing moved.

I sprang to my feet, covered the distance to the driver's door, yanked it open, grabbed the driver, and stuck the forty-five in his face. The old man I held stared bug-eyed at me. He wasn't Shorty or his buddy. His hat fell off. Before I could say anything, something crashed into the side of my face and knocked me into the open door. I looked up in time to see a handbag in midair on its way to strike again.

"Leave my husband alone!" An old lady with blue hair and a bluer dress blocked me in and tagged me one more time. She yelled, "Help!" and raised the bag for another shot.

I darted past her and across the street.

Darcy had moved the Infiniti to the front lot to watch the show and was eating another donut when I ran up. I was surprised she didn't applaud my performance.

"There's only a few left, Soldier," she said. "You want the Boston or the Bavarian Cream?"

The 300 screeched out of the parking lot, mooning me with its Ohio license plate.

CHAPTER FIFTEEN

Darcy's paid-for information was to come in the form of a young Chinese prostitute who sold her wares in an underground massage parlor.

Darcy put on a brown wig.

I said, "You work here too?"

"Very funny. No, I don't work here. But if they find out I'm a reporter, I'm dead. And so are you."

"Why are they even letting you in?"

"You don't want to know."

I grabbed her arm, probably a little harder than I intended. "I want to know what I'm walking into."

She shook me off. "Fine. They're running a blackmail operation on certain customers. I've been helping them identify targets."

"No kidding?"

"No kidding." She opened the door and stood.

I did the same. "How'd you get hooked up with that?"

"A lead. The people running the parlor found me sneaking around and I had to do some fast talking. Now I'm what you might call their 'consultant.' "

She walked and I followed.

"What do you get for it?"

"From them? Nothing. They figure I'm running my own scam, which I guess I am. I've got full access behind the scenes. And some cheating husbands get what's coming to them."

I said, "I know a guy who might not agree with your revenge theory."

She didn't reply.

We walked to the backside of the rundown strip mall and Darcy rapped on an unmarked door. An Asian girl opened it. Not much more than sixteen, she wore not much more than a teddy. Black silk hair fell over her shoulders. Her eyes bounced from Darcy to me and back to Darcy.

Darcy flashed several hundred-dollar bills.

The girl turned her head and said something in Chinese.

An older Asian woman came forward. The Madame, if I had to guess. Deep lines made an evil frown. "Who this? You bring me someone to take care of?"

Before I could answer, Darcy said, "Maybe, but not now. Remember our arrangement?"

The Madame waved us inside and barked an order to the girl, whose short teddy rode up as she closed the door. I forced my attention to Darcy in time to see her hand the Madame five fanned-out hundreds.

The woman took the money, pointed at the girl in the teddy, and said to Darcy, "You follow Crystal." To me, she said, "Let me know if you see something you like."

I gave her a grin.

Crystal led us through a steel door into another room. Dim lighting made the room and furniture appear maroon. A few men were being entertained by girls in what must have been the reception area, an interesting place to spend a Sunday morning. A red banner hung above the bar with gold letters spelling out *The Red Curtain*. The fifty bucks in my wallet probably wouldn't have been enough to get me this far.

We went through the lounge to a closed door in the back. Crystal knocked. A twenty-year-old Asian kid wearing sunglasses, a thick silver chain around his neck, and spiked hair opened it. A cigarette hung from his lower lip. Crystal said something to him. The kid pulled the cigarette out, yawned, and opened the door wide enough to let us in. His shoulder holster held a nine millimeter. Faint lighting gave everything a black-and-white feel. Five kids a lot like the one who answered the door sat at a table staring at me and Darcy. They all had cigarettes hanging out of their mouths, shoulder holsters, and heaters. Half-full forty-ounce bottles, dice, and a pile of cash lay splayed across the table. Behind them was a door. The volume of smoke in the room would have taken all night to produce, which is probably how long they had been playing their game.

The kid in front of us pointed to another door. "Suzy in there." He gripped the butt of his gun, still in the holster. "No funny business or you die."

I nodded, thinking one grenade could take care of the security detail in this place, and followed Darcy through the door. It closed behind us.

A small Asian girl, a child, really, sat on a massage table smoking a man's pipe. The smell that nearly overcame me was sweet and pungent. Definitely not tobacco. The skin around her right eye was black and purple and did not mask the vacant stare she had. I pulled out a stogie and lit up to counteract what I knew from too many hot spots in Afghanistan as opium. Darcy handed the girl a folded bill, probably another hundred. The girl took the money and put it in the pocket of tight red shorts, which, together with a yellow shirt, made her look like pedophile bait.

Darcy said, "Tell us about the man who hurt you."

"He come in last week Saturday night. Say he want a rubdown." She took a hit of her pipe.

"Go on," Darcy said.

On the exhale, she said, "He want *full service.*"

I said, "Meaning?"

"E-v-er-y-ting." She drew out the word, breaking up the syllables and adding a few extras.

Darcy nodded.

"He say he want a young girl. *Fresh,* he say." Her shoulders shook when she said it, like she had a chill.

Darcy said, "And you were . . . with him?"

Suzy moved her head from side to side like a metronome. "I didn't want to. He look scary."

I said, "What was scary about him?"

"Eyes," Suzy hissed. "The way he look at me. Eyes tell me go with him or else. So I go."

Darcy asked, "What happened next?"

Suzy blinked. "He hold gun to my head. Tell me take his clothes off. He hold my hair and shove my head down. All the time, he keep gun in my face." She took another hit of her pipe. "He pull me up and whisper in my ear. He whisper he just kill a man. I so scared. Then he throw me on the table. He say he like gook girl after he kill. He say I no gook girl but I do."

I watched her smoke her pipe. She inhaled deeply and shut her eyes before exhaling. When she opened them again, her irises had transformed into impenetrable black orbs.

"He hurt me bad," she said. "I can't work all week. It hurts when I work."

"There's a bunch of guys out there with guns," I said. "How come they didn't stop it?"

"I not here. I work in village. He pay a lot of money," she said. "Nobody care what happens when door is closed."

The kid with the cigarette that pointed us into the room had said "no funny business or you die." Maybe five hundred wasn't enough for full service *and* roughing up the talent.

Darcy said, "What village? On Harmon Street?"

The girl nodded.

I said, "You mean the owners of this place operate more than this?"

Darcy said, "A lot more."

Outside, in the palmetto heat, Darcy and I got in her Infiniti convertible. I had a hard time focusing. It could have been the secondhand opium in the air. The more the girl reloaded and smoked her pipe, the more she'd talked. She was sixteen. Her mother had been a prostitute in China and her father a customer . . . some tourist. He was long gone. To pay for a heroin habit, her mother sold her into the life and later died from an overdose.

Then she told us how the man who'd killed last Saturday night hurt her. How he tied her and forced himself on her, over and over. By the time she reached this part of her tale, she was so high she giggled.

As we drove to Folly Beach, I said, "I breathed my opium quota for the week."

Darcy said, "We need to come back and show Suzy photographs. See if she can I.D. the guy."

"You must have one serious expense account. It will probably cost you another five bills to go back inside and another C-note to get anything else from that girl. I say we report the whole bunch to I.C.E."

I.C.E., pronounced *ice,* was the acronym for Immigration and Customs Enforcement.

Darcy took a breath. "Look, you're right, okay? The truth is I've been investigating the place since I found out about it two months ago. I know most of the players in Charleston. As soon as I have the rest, I'm going to expose the whole operation."

"Did you get a look at what was printed on the banner above the bar?"

Darcy nodded.

"I guess the Chinese found another commodity to import."

In Afghanistan, I'd been known for handling problems a lot hairier than six Chinese kids with pistols. And when I finished, there were no more problems.

Darcy dropped me at the Folly Beach rental and I played with my dog on the beach and gathered my thoughts. War hardened me. I'd seen innocent women and children blown to bits. Men in my unit, barely out of high school, gutted from land mines. Medevac helicopters full of wounded on their way to the hospital shot down out of the air. What bothered me about the massage parlor? I'd seen it all before, just not in my own backyard.

After a late lunch, I went on a little field trip. The cops hadn't found Reggie's Cadillac. With nothing else to do at the moment, I cruised through the parking garage closest to the alley where Uncle Reggie was shot. My hunch was the car had not disappeared like the cops would have me believe. I idled up the levels of the garage in second gear with the windows open, partly to listen to the rumble of the engine, and partly to get a good view of the cars. On the last level before the roof, I spotted Uncle Reggie's bomb and parked. At least it sat in the shade.

My uncle rarely put the top up on his clapped-out Eldorado convertible. The factory brown paint was faded where it wasn't rusty, and the leather seats were torn. The carpeting couldn't be seen through the mound of junk on the floor. The surfboard Reggie always carried with him still stuck out of the backseat.

I sat in the driver's side and opened the glove box. It contained the registration, a bottle of aspirin, and surf wax. The door pocket treasures included a dead flashlight, a wrench, and cassettes. Bob Dylan and Crosby, Stills, Nash and Young. Uncle Reggie stopped keeping up with trends around the time this Cadillac was built so I was surprised he made the switch from eight-tracks.

I rummaged through the stuff on the floor, scaring several crickets, but found nothing interesting. My uncle kept the Caddy's keys in the ashtray, and they were there when I opened it. With the newfound keys, the trunk lid popped open and another pile emerged. Before long, *Playboys,* a bowling ball, and wet gear made a pile of sorts behind the car in the middle of the drive lane. When the trunk was empty, I pulled the spare tire cover off, leaving nothing unchecked.

After I put the stuff back in the trunk, neater than I'd found it, I sat in the driver's seat. The sun visor fell down and something dropped into my lap. Another key. The ring had a plastic tab that read "U-Store It" and included a website.

"It couldn't be that easy," I said aloud.

I phoned Detective Wilson and told him where I was. He said he and his partner would meet me within the hour but didn't sound too happy. While I waited for them, I lit a Cuban cigar.

My phone belted out Ozzy Osborne's *Ai Ai Ai* from "Crazy Train." I'd assigned that ringtone to a particular number.

I said, "Hello, Patricia."

"I had lunch with Muffie today," she said.

"Yeah? How'd it go?"

"I think you'll find the police have become more receptive to the investigation."

I blew out a cloud of smoke. "Great. Instead of disinterested detectives, I get to work with uncooperative ones."

"It's a start. Anyway, I made an appointment for us to meet someone tomorrow. You can thank me later. Be at my office in the morning and wear something nice."

"You never told my uncle what to wear."

"You're still salvageable. Not as set in your ways."

Detectives Rogers and Wilson arrived forty minutes after my call. Rogers pulled the cruiser into an open parking spot and they joined me behind the Cadillac.

Wilson said, "I suppose you already went through the car."

I sat on the trunk and puffed on my Cuban cigar. "What would give you that idea?"

"We have to tow it to the station," Rogers said. "It won't look good if your prints are all over it."

"He was my uncle. I've driven this car and ridden in it many times. You will find my prints all over it." I threw him the keys.

The detectives declined my offer of cigars.

Wilson snapped on gloves. "Did anything look out of place?"

"Not to me," I said. "I think he parked it here sometime Saturday evening. I doubt if anyone's messed with it since."

Rogers said, "You find the parking ticket?"

"How much more work do I have to do for you guys? Can't you flash your badge or something to get it out?"

Wilson said, "It will tell us the time he parked here. Might not be much, but you never know where something like that could lead. If nothing else, it could tie up a loose end."

Rogers put on a pair of gloves as he walked to the front of the Caddy. The look on my face must have told him I hadn't thought to check under the hood. He gave me a sneer and popped it open. I had to exercise a lot of self-control to keep from running to join him. Instead, I went to my car and took out the Maglite baton. To show I wasn't a complete jerk, I handed Rogers the light. He turned it on and scanned the entire engine compartment. Aside from years of oil-soaked dirt and duct tape, the five-hundred-cubic-inch V-8 and accessories were more or less as they were when they left the GM plant in 1976.

"By the way," Wilson said. "Thanks for getting us reinstated on the case. We were looking for more work."

"Finish what you start."

Rogers slammed the hood shut. "Yeah, right." He poked me in the chest with the flashlight. "You and the woman that runs the paper got us in a lot of trouble."

I grabbed the light out of his hand but stopped myself from beating him senseless with it.

Rogers put his hands in his pockets. "I'm betting it was her idea. Guess you're not wearing the pants here, are you, Pelton?"

"Sounds like you're a man of experience, detective." I walked to my car, passing Detective Wilson. It almost looked like he was grinning.

I left the detectives and rolled across the new Cooper River Bridge into Mount Pleasant. Directory Assistance had given me the number for U-Store It and I'd called and gotten an address. The kid in the office could have been a poster boy for the "Wanted" flyers at the post office. He must have had a hundred piercings in his face. Tattoos colored his exposed biceps and his shaved head reflected the overhead lighting. Doc Martin boots were laced up his shins, Nazi SS style. Overall, a good candidate for a meth lab bust. I wanted to tell him the skinhead thing was a bad idea twenty-five years ago and hadn't improved much since. Instead, I tried to explain my intention.

The kid said, "You're not Reggie Sails?"

"He's my uncle," I said. The green paneling in the office dated to the time I'd been born, and the linoleum flooring was worn through in places.

"Sorry, our policy states only the renter can have access."

I showed him the papers Chauncey had given me. Interpreting the legalese would have been a long shot on someone with half a brain. With this kid, I'd be more realistic asking for Moses to come and part the harbor. I tried anyway. "He died and left me his estate."

"How I know these are for real?"

I folded the papers. "What else do you need to let me in?"

"I guess I need Reggie Sails to come in here and add you to the list."

"He was cremated, but I have his ashes in an urn if that will help." I leaned in. "Look, kid, you've probably seen the news coverage of the murder. Reggie was the local bar owner killed last week."

A small glimmer of recognition appeared underneath the metal ornamentation jutting out from his face. "He was your uncle?"

"Yeah. So, can I check out the unit, or not?"

He gave me a dopey face. "I guess so. It ain't like it's my lot, anyway, ya know."

I wanted to throw the punk out the window but didn't. He gave me a diagram of the complex and pointed me in the right direction. I found the unit and approached its roll-up door, pulling the key out of my pocket. The padlock was new and snapped open when I inserted the key. The door rolled more easily than I expected. But the escaping dust sent me into a sneezing fit. When I recovered, I took stock of what the sunlight exposed. Boxes filled the space, which went back twenty feet. "Oh, great. More junk."

I spotted a canvas cover and realized the boxes were stacked on top of something else. I moved a couple and peeled the cover back, exposing a car fender. Uncle Reggie's old Mustang!

When I was a teenager he had the baddest car on the island, a sixty-eight Shelby GT500 convertible. Chrome wheels and a four speed. I wondered what happened to this thing. My memory flashed on how he used to take me for joyrides, catching the gears, a grin pasted around the plastic tip of the ever-present cigar sticking out of his mouth. This car was the reason I bought my new Mustang and the reason I named my dog Shelby. My uncle, the old coot, never told me he still had it.

The boxes would require a truck. Mostly Civil War relics Uncle Reggie collected before he got into pirates. I left them where they sat.

The drive to the beach rental had me thinking of the old Mustang. Out of everything I'd inherited, it was the one thing I'd always wanted. He'd hidden everything else from me for some reason, and I wasn't sure why. The hundred acres of wetlands. The EPA sites. Fisher. Everything. Maybe he was protecting me because he recognized the danger, but I think it was more because he was worried about me. I didn't have myself together when I returned from Afghanistan and I still had to deal with Jo's death. The pain nearly killed me, but I worked through a lot of it.

When I eventually came out of my funk, Uncle Reggie went into one. He spent more time away from the Cove and wouldn't tell me or Paige anything.

The key to the storage unit was where he'd know I'd find it. And he made sure Patricia knew about the crab pots. Something told me those weren't the only clues he'd left.

Chapter Sixteen

Spanish moss hung from the branches of live oaks along the sides of the road and glistened like garlands in the Monday morning sunshine. Outside Charleston County, the speed limit increased to the double-nickel and four lanes became two. Patricia blasted along at eighty in her SL550 Mercedes, one hand on the wheel, the other holding an iced triple-shot latte.

The sweet tea with extra lemon in my own hand suggested a slightly less exotic palate. I said, "I think it's time you tell me where we're going."

"I told you at the office. It's a surprise."

"I don't like surprises." Especially when my gun was locked in the glove box of the Mustang and not on my person.

"We're going to meet the most influential environmentalist in the lowcountry."

The trees gave way to marsh. Bridges crisscrossed muddy banks. For the next thirty miles, fields of grass over the wetland danced in the hot breeze, changing colors with the reflected sunlight bouncing off the shoots. Halfway to Beaufort, our coffee and tea long gone, Patricia switched on the right turn signal and dropped to sixty. We were in the middle of nowhere, and I was ready to ask what she was doing when a county sign appeared.

"Yemassee? You're telling me the king of environmentalism lives in Yemassee?"

Patricia said, "No, but the queen does."

We took the turn at speed, the sport suspension of her new SL absorbing the sudden change in direction with state-of-the-art precision. Patricia pushed the accelerator hard and we rocketed down a rough road. The windshield filled with blind curves and tight switchbacks. By the time she slowed again, I'd been wishing myself back in the brothel inhaling the secondhand opium smoke and being threatened by Asian mafia punks. Any place other than the passenger seat of this fearless woman's car.

We turned into a heavily overgrown drive and stopped at the gated entrance of what I guessed was a large estate. The tropical vegetation and local wildflowers were someone's interpretation of planned chaos. Large palmetto trees grew here and there. Patricia lowered her window. A muscular black man stepped out of a modest guard hut protecting him from the elements. It occurred to me that the guard, like the rest of the world, was relegated to the peasant side of the walled fortress.

He tipped his uniform hat to Patricia. His biceps flexed as he raised a clipboard. "Can I help you?"

"We're here to see Ms. Hagan," Patricia said. "She's expecting us."

The guard looked at his clipboard. "Name, please."

Patricia gave our names and I wondered if this routine was for show or if so many visitors actually came on a Monday to warrant a list for keeping them straight.

After a brief moment he said, "Here you are." He stepped inside the hut and pressed a button. The large metal gates ahead swung reluctantly outward. "Follow the drive around. It will take you to the house. You can park by the fountain."

"Thank you," Patricia said.

"I'll call ahead and let them know you're here. Have a nice day."

As we drove through, I watched the side mirror to see how fast the gates closed. I half-expected them to spring shut before anyone else could sneak through, especially the banished guard.

I asked, "So who's Constance Hagan?"

"Michael Galston's sister," she said.

Crushed shells popped and cracked under the tires as we cruised between monstrous, centuries-old live oaks. Beyond them loomed an imposing antebellum mansion complete with the large white columns out front. An impeccable lawn flanked the residence, each pass from the lawnmower leaving opposing diagonal lanes.

The drive circled a large running fountain next to the porte-cochere. Patricia eased to a stop and we got out. Another black man greeted us. Smaller than the guard at the gate, he wore a neatly pressed butler's uniform. His white jacket was buttoned to the top.

"Welcome to Hagan Manor," he said. "Ms. Hagan is expecting you. Please follow me."

We were escorted up the front stairs and into a large entryway. Staircases with mahogany balustrades anchored each side of the large room, the grandeur of the Old South. A large crystal chandelier hung from the center of a high ceiling. The butler led us through a doorway to the right and into a much larger room. Lined with patterned crown-molding, the ceiling soared at least another six feet above my head. Portraits of people whom I assumed were dead family members hung on the walls. Thanks to my wife's influence, I recognized the artist's name.

A very large woman filled a couch in the center of the room, her legs stretched out over the cushions. Her light-blue cotton summer dress draped over her full figure like the tarp I covered my Mustang with. A small table to her left held a little silver bell with a handle, a cup and saucer, and a dish with pastry crumbs on it.

The woman held out a hand in greeting but did not get up

from the couch, undoubtedly because the task couldn't be handled easily. "It is so nice to see you, Patricia."

"Constance, it has been too long." Patricia approached the large woman and shook her pudgy hand.

"I'm always here," Constance replied.

I believed her.

Constance Hagan looked past Patricia to me. "Who's this with you?"

"Brack Pelton," Patricia said, "a local businessman."

"Pleasure to meet you, ma'am," I said, taking her hand. "And if I'm not being too forward, the Sargent portraits are excellent."

The smile she gave me carried with it something more than an air of superiority. "Can you believe no one else in the family wanted them? It goes to show you can't breed taste." Constance held my hand tighter. "I was sorry to hear about your uncle, Mr. Pelton. I knew him from the old days."

I opened my mouth to ask what she meant by the old days but Patricia cleared her throat.

Constance released my hand and said, "Please sit. Can I interest you all in some coffee?"

"That would be fine," Patricia said.

We chose two chairs facing Constance. The large woman picked up the bell and gave it two jingles. The butler reappeared and received his orders. When she dismissed him with a wave, he moved quickly out of the room, like a pet avoiding the familiar swat of a newspaper.

Constance shifted slightly to get a better angle on her visitors. "So what brings you out to the Manor?"

Patricia said, "We understand your relationship with your brother has been strained for a long time. We'd like to ask you a few questions."

The large woman cooled herself with a small hand fan. "You

think he's connected to your ex-husband's murder?"

"To get right to the point," Patricia said, "yes."

"I wouldn't put it past him. He's turned into a real heel since Daddy died."

The pinging sound of china announced the butler, who came into the room holding a tray with two cups and saucers, an elaborate silver pot, and a plate of cookies. He held the tray with a practiced hand, poured coffee into a cup, and handed the cup and saucer to Patricia before doing the same for me. He set the plate of cookies on a coffee table closer to Constance than to us. I didn't let manners or the distance stop me from reaching and taking one with chocolate chips before the host chose hers.

"Thank you, Charles," Constance said, and the butler left the room. "As I was saying, my brother has declared himself the head of the family. In his pursuit of leaving his mark on our dynasty, I'm afraid he's taking us down the wrong path." Constance examined the tray before choosing an oatmeal raisin cookie. "You should know this, Patricia. Your newspaper has printed more about his enterprises than anyone else."

The corners of Patricia's mouth stretched into a full grin. "He does make good copy."

Constance nibbled on the edge of her cookie. "Frankly, I'm surprised you get away with it."

Patricia crossed her legs. "When it comes to publishing about someone like your brother, we triple-check our facts."

"You'd better," Constance said, "or he'll sue your skinny rear-end off."

Patricia opened her oversized bag and took out a stack of papers. "Are you aware your brother is in the process of trying to purchase one hundred acres of wetlands with the intent of using offset credits to develop them?"

Constance choked on her cookie. "What?"

When Patricia handed her the papers, Constance jerked them out of her hands and scanned them line by line.

"The land is in North Charleston," Patricia said, "on the Ashley River."

Constance shook her head. "It's not possible. The board has to agree before anything like that can happen."

Patricia sat back and re-crossed her legs. "It appears your brother has found a loophole."

Constance reached among many folds of light-blue fabric to a pocket, took out a cell phone, and made a call. "Bill, I found out Michael has acquired the Sawyer Forest property and is going to use it for credits." She listened to the reply. "Yeah, but how was he able to buy it?" Another reply. "But we should have known about it before it happened." Her pale face reddened. "Listen Bill, this is my foundation. My brother—"

She stopped speaking, her eyes narrow with fury. After a few deep breaths, she said, "Bill, do me a favor and find out what's going on."

Ten more seconds and she hit the End button. She put a pudgy hand to her chest as she took several deep breaths.

Patricia managed to get us back to the *Palmetto Pulse* in one piece and without accumulating any speeding tickets. I drove to the beach rental in my Mustang, and taking a cue from Constance, who'd said she was upset and needed to rest, crashed on one of the lounge chairs on the back deck.

The *Ai Ai Ai* woke me up. I hit Accept.

Patricia said, "I got a call from a Craig McAllister."

"I don't know who he is."

"He's one of the few reputable developers in the county. He said he was calling on behalf of Constance."

"She moves faster than she looks."

Patricia ignored my humor. "He'll meet with you tomorrow. I can't make it, but I'm sending my best reporter along."

CHAPTER SEVENTEEN

Darcy and I took a booth in the diner where we were to meet Craig McAllister, Constance's friend. It was Tuesday. The only windows in the small space faced the street by the entrance. Worn hardwood lined the floor. Vinyl and chrome covered the rest. The smell of fifty years of grease hung in the air as thick as the sulfur around a marsh. From the looks of the other patrons, I suspected I wasn't the only one with a concealed weapon.

A waitress came to our table and laid two menus in front of us. "What can I get y'all?"

We ordered milkshakes and waited. When bells tied to the entrance door jingled, I watched our man come in. He slid his sunglasses from the ridge of his nose to the top of his head. His polo shirt had a monogram on it similar to the one Galston's stooges wore and his work boots and khakis showed splattered mud. He was in good shape for what I guessed was sixty, with the deep tan of an offshore fisherman. His eyes scanned the place before they locked on mine. He came and slid into the booth facing us.

The waitress broke the silence. "What can I get you, hon?"

"Black coffee to go, please," McAllister said. His accent sounded more like upstate South Carolina than Charleston low-country.

The waitress left and returned with his coffee. "You wanna see a menu?"

McAllister shook his head and she left.

"You called this meeting," I said. "Want to tell us what this is about?"

"Constance Hagan called this meeting," he said. "I was sorry to hear about your uncle. We were in Vietnam together a long time ago."

I sat back. "No kidding."

"Yeah. Lost touch over the years."

Darcy asked, "You ever been to his bar?"

"Maybe once or twice. My work keeps me busy."

I put enough money on the table to cover our tab. "You want to talk here or somewhere else?"

McAllister led us to a big Ford F450 Dually pickup truck with four doors. It was white and caked in mud like his boots and still had dealer plates. On the front door was stenciled McAllister and Associates. I let Darcy take the front seat. Despite the soiled exterior, the truck had that new-car smell.

McAllister fired up the diesel engine and drove slowly through the small town, easing across railroad tracks and potholes. "Galston uses his companies to buy Superfund sites, and then filters money through them with minimal cleanup."

"How'd you find out about this?" Darcy asked.

"Because I'm one of the few people around here with the capability and experience to do environmental restoration. I know everyone in the business and no one is doing any real work for Galston."

"What are you," Darcy said, "the only ethical contractor in town?"

Watching the rearview mirror, I saw McAllister's mouth form a crooked smile.

"Weirder things have happened."

Darcy turned toward him. "Not that weird."

McAllister veered onto a two-lane and gunned it. "This area is thick with wetlands, which is why it's so dangerous that a Superfund site is here."

Two miles out of town he flicked his left indicator and slowed. A pine forest surrounded us, taking the edge off the sun. He slowed more and steered onto a dirt road. The remains of a rotting sign jutted from the ground. I could barely make out the name.

CHROMICORP

We were in the middle of nowhere and I wondered for more than a few minutes how well Constance knew McAllister. Out the back window, I watched the trail of dust kicked up by the four rear tires and questioned where all the water was if this was wetland.

The road turned sharply around a fallen tree and into a mud hole. McAllister touched a button on the dashboard just before we hit the thick clay, engaging the driveshaft to the front wheels. The nose of the truck dropped a foot or so into the pit and bounced us around the cab.

Darcy grabbed the handle above her door. McAllister revved the diesel, spinning the wheels and powering us through the muck. The front wheels climbed out the other side of the hole, but the mud didn't end there.

Silently I took back what I'd thought about dry soil. I said, "We just having fun mudding in your new truck here or is there a purpose to this?"

"Galston hasn't touched this site since he bought it five years ago," McAllister said. "He's always a few steps ahead of the EPA. Even tried to put me on retainer to cover for him."

A clearing in the middle of the trees opened up. He slowed the truck to a stop and killed the engine. Through the windshield, I saw a small, overgrown gravel parking lot and two buildings; the small one looking like it was used for an office at one time. The other was larger and must have been where the chemical processing took place. Two rats scurried out of a hole in one of the buildings and underneath the broken-down door of another.

"I call this place the rat farm."

Darcy said, "Yuck."

McAllister faced me. "I think your uncle was going to expose Galston."

"Got any proof?" Darcy asked.

"That, little lady, is the tough part. Galston's got more lawyers than sense. As long as he can show due diligence, he's safe."

"But why kill my uncle?" I said it more to myself than to anyone else.

McAllister said, "If he did it—or had it done—it must mean Reggie was close or had something very incriminating. I wish I knew what it was. So does Constance."

"Won't she suffer if her brother goes down?" I asked.

"She's got her own money," he said.

I already knew that, but I wanted to see if he did. Patricia had filled me in on Constance on the way back from Yemassee. The youngest of five siblings and the only daughter, Constance had been wild in her day, which from the looks of her was a good twenty years ago. Arrested at twenty-two for possession of stolen property and cocaine, she had been forced to marry a member of the Hagan family, another wealthy Charleston clan. She accepted her role to avoid jail. The new life didn't kill her, but her husband died at forty-five of a heart attack in the arms of his mistress. Constance became the sole heir to a fortune valued in the mid-nine figures, more than enough to keep her fat in oatmeal raisin cookies and African American servants.

McAllister brought us back to the diner. Darcy went inside to use the restroom and I stood outside with him next to his truck.

He propped a foot on the running board. "If Galston did kill your uncle, I'm surprised he hasn't come after you yet."

I said, "My house was trashed and my car vandalized. I think it was the two dirtbags he's got working for him. We've got a line on someone who can give us an I.D. Apparently the killer likes Asian prostitutes. Young ones."

"Really?" McAllister put his hands in his pockets. "Well, I wouldn't put it past Galston's property managers as he calls them. They act respectable but they're just hired muscle." He paused as if to think. "If you want some revenge, I might be able to help. How can I get in touch with you?"

I gave him my cell number.

Darcy and I stopped by my rental and picked up Shelby. The three of us rode to Patricia's house for a late lunch. When we walked in, Patricia asked me to get the grill ready and proceeded to occupy herself with my dog. The grill was a nice one, a Weber, and it lit easily. As I watched it heat up, Tom Petty sang from my pocket about living like a refugee. I pulled out my phone but didn't recognize the number it displayed.

"Pelton," I answered.

"Hey Brack, it's Ken Graves, EPA. I found out a few things. Had to cut a lot of red tape to do it. Have a minute?"

"I thought you feds carried the red tape dispenser," I said.

"We do, but the departments we report to have got ones of their own. We get a big dose of it ourselves."

"Good to hear we mere civilians aren't the only ones. Hold on a sec." I slid the glass door open and asked Patricia for something to write with. She handed me a purple pad and matching pen. I took them to a garden table with a pedestal umbrella sticking out through a hole in the middle. "All set. Go ahead."

"The owner of the Chemcon site went belly-up this year.

Because that was after the EPA classified it a Superfund site, we acquired the property. Current public opinion aside, the federal government is not in the real estate business. We immediately put the property for sale. It wasn't a private auction. We wanted anything we could get for it, so I'm sure it was advertised."

I took notes. "So, who bid on it?"

"Hold on." I heard the shuffle of papers. "Palmetto Properties."

"What business are they in and do they own any other property in Charleston?"

"You'd have better luck than me. I only have access to information that interests the EPA. Palmetto Properties did not come up anywhere else in our database."

As we ate grilled chicken, couscous, and some sort of vegetable medley, Darcy and I filled Patricia in on everything McAllister said. I added what Ken Graves found out. Patricia leaned forward. "We have a link."

"More than that," Darcy said, swiveling her chair from side to side like a schoolgirl, "we have allies."

"I did a search on McAllister last night," Patricia said. "He's into restoration and conservation and he's given big bucks to Constance's foundation. I think they're more than friends."

"We should let her look at everything we've got," Darcy suggested. "Maybe she can connect more of the dots."

"First," Patricia said, "we have to see how much she hates her brother."

I fed Shelby my chicken scraps, sans bones. "You think she may be lying? She gave us McAllister."

"It sounds far-fetched," Patricia said, "but we need something Galston and all the lawyers he keeps on retainer can't dispute."

Darcy said, "How about murder?"

★　★　★　★　★

From the back deck of my beach rental, I watched the color of the water alternate between many shades of green. Vivid—that's how Jo had described the ocean around Saint Lucia on our honeymoon. The crystal-blue water gave up its secrets when we donned snorkels. Vivid—the bright colors of the schools of fish changing direction at the first hint of our presence in their domain. Vivid—my memory of the first trip to the hospital when she started feeling weak. Vivid—Jo and I seated facing the doctor and hearing him explain the end of Jo's life. Vivid—holding Jo's hand when she took her last breath. Vivid—Uncle Reggie dying in my arms in the alley.

A dark cloud formed over me. One I couldn't shake. I pulled out a cigar and sniffed the Cuban tobacco. It smelled earthy and acerbic. I clipped the end, stuck it in my mouth, and lit up. Shelby slept at my feet. My cell phone rang and I dug it out of my pocket and answered.

Fisher said, "Pelton, I'm in trouble."

CHAPTER EIGHTEEN

The sun was setting when I walked out Folly Beach Pier for the second time, already wishing I'd brought Shelby. At least I'd brought the forty-five. Fisher paced nervously.

"What's up?" I said.

He looked down at the wooden decking as he paced. "I got caught."

"What, like they found you listening with a glass against the door?"

"The senior partner walked in when I was printing more files."

"So, isn't that part of your job?"

"Not these files," he said. "I was stupid."

"What did he say when he saw them?"

Still pacing, he shook his head. "Nothing. But he knew what they were the moment he saw them. I mean, it was so obvious, Cooper River Chemicals letterhead plastered across the screen."

"How many companies do you guys do business with? Hundreds? How's he going to know exactly what you were looking at?"

Fisher stopped pacing and looked at me. "He's the senior partner. He knows everything that goes on in our firm." His eyes lowered to the decking again. "He knows I wasn't handling that particular account."

I spoke before thinking. "What's the worst that could happen to you?"

His eyes shot up to mine.

I raised my hands in surrender. The worst that could happen was exactly what happened to my uncle.

He shook his head and rubbed his eyes. "I can't go home."

"Makes two of us."

"You don't understand," he said.

"I do. They've got their hooks into your boss or he's in cahoots with them. Either way, they found their leak. Whoever got to my uncle is going to come for you."

He grabbed my shirt. "Stop it! Stop saying that!"

I forced his hands off me. "You know I'm right."

"What do I do? I didn't even get the file. After he left my office, I powered down my computer and walked out."

"Look," I said, "I don't know you from Adam, but I'm running out of choices. I've got a place here at the beach. You're welcome to crash there."

"They'll find it. All it takes is a few phone calls and anyone can be tracked down."

"Sure, if they're looking for me. But I rented the house with my uncle's credit card, and I haven't canceled it yet. I don't think they'll be asking around for him."

"But you have the same last name, don't you?"

"No. He's my mother's brother."

Fisher looked at me but wasn't looking at me, more like he was thinking.

I put a hand on the railing and watched the water, letting him make up his mind.

He said, "No one knows?"

"No one I don't trust." I turned and faced him. "Stay there. I've grown to like the couch in my uncle's office anyway. I have one condition."

He stiffened. "What's that?"

"I want you to talk to Patricia Voyels."

Fisher eventually relented. What else could he do? At the beach rental, he relaxed a little. The freezer had a bunch of frozen dinners and the view was, of course, perfect. Dressed in a pair of my shorts, and a T-shirt, Fisher wolfed down two microwave meals in record time and was working on a six-pack of beer. For a little guy, he ate as much as I did.

I called Patricia. She said she couldn't meet with us until eight, which was in four hours. Fisher passed out on one of the chairs on the back deck. Shelby and I left him there and drove to the Pirate's Cove, the gun in the glove box. I wanted my dog with me as I didn't trust Fisher. On the way, I used the hands-free connection and phoned Darcy.

She answered on the first ring. "What's up?"

"I've got the man with all the information on Galston in my hideaway on Folly."

"Great," she said. "As soon as I finish I'll be on my way."

"Hold your horses. The guy's too jumpy. It took some convincing to get him there. Patricia's coming at eight tonight."

"You mean you aren't there now?"

"I'm on my way to the bar."

She said, "Who's watching him?"

"He's sleeping off a six-pack," I said. "He'll be fine as long as he doesn't leave. Meet me at the Cove."

I spent the time before the meeting with Fisher by helping the women wash out the industrial-sized freezer in the kitchen. It was in bad shape. Shelby napped on the lower back deck.

Paige had done a lot to clean the Pirate's Cove. With a few added staff members, she had everyone scrub the wood flooring and walls, and polish the old mismatched brass fixtures my uncle had accumulated over the years. The bathrooms received new coats of paint and a thorough cleansing. Clean enough to maybe raise our inspection score next time around.

In order to see inside the freezer, I had to replace two burned-out light bulbs. The new illumination showed a filthy floor and a lot of past-due food to be pitched—stuff that hadn't been on the menu for a long time. The way my life had been going lately, I half-expected to find a dead body hanging in there. My cell vibrated and I left the freezer to answer it. Fisher's number was on the screen.

He was already talking when I accepted the call. "Pelton, I've got to go."

"What's the matter?"

"Look," he yelled. "Something's come up. They . . . they . . . My family. I gotta go."

"Hold on a minute, Fisher."

Nothing.

"Fisher?"

The call ended. I tried to get him back. No answer. Tried again. Again no answer. I stared at the phone. The urge to throw it against the freezer made me put it back in my pocket.

Patricia and Darcy strolled into the Pirate's Cove at precisely eight o'clock. I'd already told them Fisher was gone, but they decided to come anyway. They took stools in front of me at the bar.

Patricia handed me a sheet of paper. "Here's what I could find on your Mr. Fisher."

It was a letter-sized sheet, handwritten, with Fisher's name at the top.

"He works at the most exclusive accounting firm in Charleston," she said. "Senior associates like him make mid-six figures, easy. More if it's a good year. And it's been a good year."

I said, "No address?"

"I'm working on it," Darcy said. "He's got an unlisted number so I have to up my bribe."

I put my hands on the bar. "What are you waiting for?"

Darcy snapped, "I'm on it!"

"The guy was scared," I said. "Someone got to him."

Darcy's cell rang. She read the caller I.D. and answered, listening for a minute. Her mouth opened slightly and she looked at me.

At four o'clock Wednesday morning, I sat in the main conference room at the *Palmetto Pulse* with Patricia, Darcy, and Shelby. A picture of David Fisher splashed across the front page of the next issue, in color, hot off the press. He was slumped in the driver's seat of his Volvo. Someone had found him in a back alley in North Charleston, not far from crack dealers and prostitutes. He'd been shot in the chest several times. Patricia had a cameraman meet us at the scene and Darcy did takes for the next evening's news.

I crumpled the paper in my hands. "This story sucks."

Shelby raised his head and looked at me.

Darcy propped her feet on a chair. "I didn't realize you'd been promoted to my editor."

"Not your writing," I said. "The whole thing."

The young reporter slipped off her sandals and massaged her feet. By my count, she'd been on the go for more than twenty-four hours.

"The police are filing it as a solicitation attempt gone bad," Patricia said.

I said, "Gunned down by an unhappy hooker. You believe that garbage? I mean, the way they wrapped up the crime scene so fast, you'd think the cops had been paid by the job instead of the hour."

"I've a connection at the bank," Patricia said. "He told me Fisher was up to his eyeballs in debt."

"A lot of people are," I said. "That doesn't tell me anything."

"Most people aren't successful accountants with eighteenth-century mansions on Tradd Street close to foreclosure," Patricia said. "That's probably why he was selling information."

"He did say he was good with numbers."

Shelby and I went to the beach rental to crash for a couple of hours.

I felt a tug at my sleeve and opened my eyes. Daylight made me close them again, fast.

Shelby barked.

"I guess I been neglecting you, huh?"

He barked again and ran to the back door.

I pulled the covers off and got out of bed. "All right, all right. I'm coming."

He scrambled down the steps when I opened the door. While he did his business in the backyard, I looked out at the ocean, thinking David Fisher would never see this again. Shelby barreled up to me, barked, and grabbed his leash with his mouth and dropped it at my feet.

"But I haven't even had my coffee yet."

His next bark told me he didn't care what I needed. I pulled on a pair of shorts, slid on sunglasses, and grabbed my wallet, and we headed out. Near the pier, I found a vendor selling coffee and bought an extra large. It was the way I liked it, sludge. After an hour or so of wandering aimlessly around, we headed back. The message symbol was on the screen of my cell phone and I listened to Darcy tell me to wake up. She was on her way and we were going to see McAllister. I dressed and slid the gun in the small of my back. With Fisher gone, it was not worth the risk going unarmed. Using the same logic, I left Shelby in the safety of the rental.

Darcy turned into the entrance to McAllister's house on John's Island. Posts holding iron gates flanked a driveway half-mooning to the front of the home. The large McMansion stood on twelve-foot stilts covered by lattice. As we swung around the drive, I saw the open garage doors. Taillights from a low-slung sports car peeked out at me in one of the three open bays. The red beauty with white racing stripes brought a whistle of admiration from me.

Darcy pulled us to a stop. "What?"

I pointed. "He's got a ZR1."

Darcy rolled her eyes and opened her door to get out. "So?"

"It's the fastest production Corvette," I said.

Too much like Jo, Darcy ignored my fascination with cars. "I did some checking. Our Mr. McAllister has another home in Mount Pleasant—ocean view. And a helicopter, a McDonnell Douglas 500E five-seater."

Environmental cleanup must be a boom industry.

McAllister answered his own door wearing shorts, a knit shirt with a sports logo on the sleeve, and tennis shoes.

"Glad to see y'all," he said. "I was ready to head to the courts."

A black tennis racket case leaned against a black gym bag on the hardwood floor in front of a carved wooden entrance table. We stepped around the bags and McAllister led us past a great room with a high ceiling to a bar in front of the kitchen counter. He motioned for us to take seats at two tall chairs.

He said, "Can I get you anything? Coffee, OJ?"

"Black coffee," I said.

Darcy passed.

McAllister poured my coffee and refilled his own.

I noticed the logo printed on the cups. "What's Ashley River Recovery?"

"Oh, a business I'm working with," he said. "We're cleaning a site on the river. So, what's up? You sounded a little concerned on the phone."

Darcy flipped open the paper on the counter and turned it so McAllister could read the headline.

He took a drink from his coffee mug. "I saw that this morning."

"He knew my uncle."

McAllister raised his eyebrows. "The accountant did?"

Darcy said, "Did you know him?"

"I use the firm he works—worked for—to handle my taxes."

"Galston used them too," I said.

McAllister set his cup on the counter. "I'm not surprised. It's the best in Charleston. At least the one with the best pedigree."

The same could be said about how people were measured in Charleston. Either you had status or you had to buy it, but it was always there, around the corner of the next question, tucked in a few layers behind an insinuation. I was fortunate enough to carry the double negative of not from around here and not enough money. Darcy, on the other hand . . .

She hooked an arm over the back of her chair. "You know anyone there who would talk to you about what happened? Maybe what he was working on?"

McAllister said, "Being a pretty Channel Nine reporter, you ought to be able to get what you want without my help."

"Maybe," she said to him, "but I always work as many angles as I can."

"Be careful those angles don't have any sharp edges." His mouth formed a slight grin and he took a sip of coffee.

I said, "So can you help us or not?"

He chewed on his lip. "Yeah, I'll see what I can come up

with. Now, if you don't mind I have a tennis match in thirty minutes and need to get going." He walked us to the door. "Give me a call this evening."

I turned to him and offered a hand. "Thanks."

He shook my hand and looked me in the eye. "No problem. Someone's got to make sure things are on the level."

Patricia found a home address for Fisher. After some discussion among the three of us, we decided I should go solo. Mostly, it was me saying I should go in solo. Darcy wasn't giving in so easily. Patricia relented, saying Fisher's wife probably wouldn't want to talk to a reporter about why her dead husband was soliciting prostitutes.

In my bungalow on Sullivan's Island, I buttoned the one white oxford shirt I owned and tucked it into the pants of my one suit, the Italian light wool I'd worn to my wife's funeral. I laced polished black shoes, also made in the boot-shaped country, and added a matching belt around my waist. The dark-blue Hermes tie, a surprise gift from Darcy, knotted a perfect Windsor. I slid into the jacket as I walked into the living room.

Shelby stretched out next to Darcy on the couch, rested his head on her leg, and dangled his paws off the edge. His eyes closed.

Darcy saw me slide my gun down the small of my back. "All you need is a shoulder holster and a fedora and we could call you Bugsy."

Ignoring the reference, I pulled a pen and pad out of a drawer, scribbled something, and placed the note in the inside pocket of my suit jacket. "Take care of Shelby if I don't come back."

"Don't worry," she said. "If you don't come back, I'm taking him and this house."

"How about in the meantime you just take him back to the rental on Folly for me?"

CHAPTER NINETEEN

I followed Seventeen downtown and parked in front of the Fisher home next to a sign.

RESIDENTAL NEIGHBORHOOD
NO PARKING WITHOUT PERMIT

This wasn't just any residential area, either. It was Tradd Street, one of Charleston's oldest. Paved with cobblestone, lined with brick sidewalks, and inhabited by money. Lots of it. And, I guessed, broke accountants.

The front door's antique brass knocker made a loud thump. After a few minutes a black woman opened the door.

I said, "Good afternoon, ma'am. I was wondering if Mrs. Fisher was in."

"She is. And who are you?"

"My name's Brack Pelton. Tell her I knew David."

The woman's eyes dropped at the sound of his name. "Please come in. I'll let Mrs. Fisher know you're here."

The entryway's ceiling was thirty feet high and dressed with elaborate crowning. Wooden chairs flanked a long narrow table holding fresh-cut flowers in a vase. From what I could see, the residence had been furnished with no expense spared. My beach house, on the other hand, had been decorated in late American Goodwill, and much expense had been spared.

A female voice broke the silence. "May I help you?"

I turned and found green eyes staring intently at me framed by a pretty face and red hair trimmed just below her neck.

"Yes, ma'am," I said. "My name's Brack Pelton. I knew your late husband."

She cocked an eyebrow. "*You* knew David?"

"Yes, ma'am. We were sort of business partners, you might say."

"Business partners?"

"Um—"

She folded her arms. "My husband worked in an accounting firm. He never told me about any business he was involved in."

"He located important information for me. I came to pay my respects."

"The funeral's on Sunday," she said. "You could've done that then."

"I also had a few questions for you, ma'am."

"What did you say your name was? Pelton? David never talked about working with anyone by that name. I'm busy with my kids and don't have time for this." She pointed to the door. "It's time for you to go."

"Mrs. Fisher, I'll be straight with you. This information your husband located for me. There's a possibility he got killed over it. I'm not sure."

She let her bottom lip drop a few millimeters, but regained her composure quickly. "I think I better call the police."

I took a seat in one of the wooden chairs next to the table with the flowers. "Ask for Detective Rogers and his partner, Wilson. They're the ones saying your husband was killed by a prostitute he solicited."

It came out as harsh as I wanted it to, and I saw the sting in her eyes.

"What exactly do you want from me? You come in here posing as a friend of my husband's. Then, you insinuate the police are wrong and he might have been killed because of something he gave you."

"Sold me, actually. The cops don't know that, either."

"How much?"

The question came out sharp and caught me off guard. "Huh?"

"Don't play games with me, Mr. Pelton. How much did you supposedly pay him?"

"Twenty grand. In cash. Two bands of hundred-dollar bills."

Her mouth dropped further and she lowered herself onto the other chair. She leaned forward and put her head in her hands.

I said, "Are you all right, Mrs. Fisher?"

She sighed. "Justine."

"Excuse me?"

She lifted her head. "My name is Justine." She stood and walked toward the rear of the house.

"Can I offer you a drink, Mr. Pelton?"

"Iced tea if you have any."

She spoke from down the hall. "I was thinking something a little stronger, but Isata made lemonade for the kids, if that will do."

"That'd be fine," I said, wondering what changed her attitude.

The chandelier suspended above was brass and crystal and big. It hung by a chain and was exactly what I expected in a place like this. I wondered if Justine Fisher had known how broke they were before her husband was killed.

Her nearby voice broke my concentration on the ornate fixture. "Are you going to remain in the parlor, Mr. Pelton?"

She stood at the edge of the hallway holding a tray with two glasses, one filled with lemonade and the other with ice. A bottle of rum completed the tray. I followed her to a sitting area. She sank into a leather sofa and I eased into a chair facing her. She handed me the lemonade, poured an inch of rum in the other glass, and took a long sip. I tasted the lemonade.

"Isata makes the best lemonade, doesn't she?"

"Perfect," I said, noticing she had already finished her drink. "The right amount of bitter and sweet."

She set her empty glass on the tray and poured another. "I found the money in our safe. Two bands of one-hundreds, like you said."

Not what I expected her to say. "Could be a coincidence."

"Something tells me it isn't."

"Did you happen to find anything else?"

"Papers. Our lawyer is looking at them."

I nodded. "Do you have any idea what you are going to do?"

"My parents live in Virginia," she said. "I'm selling this place and heading there." Her mouth formed a frown and she poured a third drink. "My husband was a good father to his kids, but I didn't realize he was so bad with money until I got a look at our finances. Large credit card balances, two expensive car payments, and this place." She gave the drink a rest. "Mr. Pelton, do you know what the upkeep is on a two-hundred-and-fifty-year-old home?"

"No." I barely kept my own place.

"Neither do I, and I'm not sure I want to find out. My Mercedes is up for sale and I have a realtor stopping by tomorrow. The police still have David's Volvo, but no one will want it the way it is." She shrugged. "If I'm lucky, after I pay the bills, I'll have enough left over from the insurance policy to start again and still be able to stay home with the kids."

I stood. "Mrs. Fisher . . . I mean, Justine? I appreciate your time. I think given the seriousness of what's happened to your husband, moving is probably a good idea. I might suggest leaving sooner than later."

It was her turn to nod.

"The only thing I'd ask of you is to see those documents you found with the money."

She stared for a minute, got up, and left the room. Before I could decide what it was about her I liked, she returned carrying a file folder. "I made copies. You can have them. I get the feeling you're not telling me everything, but I'm not going to ask. I'd rather not know."

I handed her the note I'd put in my inside jacket pocket at my house earlier. On it was the number for the Church of Redemption. "If you need someone to talk to, Brother Thomas is a good man. My wife died of cancer three years ago so I know what it's like. Don't try to get through this alone."

Justine said, "Did you have any children?"

"No." I drank the rest of my lemonade.

She held out her hand as if to take the glass from me. "Can I get you some more?"

I found myself counting the few freckles on her cheeks and nose and thinking she was attractive without a lot of makeup. Instead of finishing the thought, I gave her the glass and said, "No thanks. I'd better get going. I am very sorry about your loss."

Tears formed in her eyes. "I'm . . . I'm—"

She collapsed into my chest, buried her head in my shoulder, and shook. I put my arm around her to let her get it out, and there was a lot. I knew because there had been a lot for me to get out when Jo died. But my relief had come in bottles, not tears. I thought about what I'd been through in the past three years and felt very sorry for Mrs. Fisher. If she was strong, she'd make it. If not, she could always sign up for the next war.

After her whimpers faded, she spoke softly. "Thank you."

Her hair smelled like flowers and felt soft as it fell over my hand. She moved away, slowly. I watched her wipe her eyes with a Kleenex from a box on the table and try to regain her composure.

"Take care of yourself," I said. "Your kids need you."

She followed me to the door, not saying anything. I looked at her one last time. She waved goodbye and I walked out, scanning the street as I loosened my tie. Someone had stuck a parking ticket under the wiper of my freshly washed Mustang in the same spot David Fisher had left his message. Even the meter maid knew I didn't belong here.

At my house on Sullivan's Island, I found Darcy had left me a note on the counter saying she'd call me later. I changed out of my suit and was about to head to the Folly Beach rental when my phone rang.

McAllister. He said, "Your boys are at Domingo's this very moment. It might be a good idea to see where they go for dessert. If I'm right, you'll find yourself some payback. Bring a camera."

The Mustang roared to life and I sped off. I thought about calling Darcy but decided against it. This was for me.

At a swing bridge ahead, yellow lights flashed as I approached, signaling it was closing to cars and would rotate to allow boats on the Intracoastal Waterway to pass. I dropped down two gears and floored it to beat the road barrier. Four-hundred-and-twenty horsepower shoved me back into the seat as the speedometer arced into the triple digits. When I crested the bridge I felt the tires leave the pavement. The sensation of levitating above the ground felt surreal for the few seconds I was airborne. The tires chirped back onto the road and the suspension soaked up the impact. I floored it again and the car went into hyperspace.

CHAPTER TWENTY

Downtown, I circled Market Street looking for a black Chrysler 300 and found it parked in front of the Italian restaurant McAllister told me about. Pulling into a spot by a meter where I could watch their car, I got out of the Mustang and ducked into a nearby tourist trap for a can of Coke and a disposable cell phone. While quenching my thirst in the front seat of the Mustang, the only break from the heat was a slight breeze blowing through the open windows. "Brown Sugar" played on the classic rock station, reminding me of Uncle Reggie. He loved the Stones. I remembered the hot summer night when he took me and four friends to an outdoor concert in Columbia. We piled into his Shelby convertible. My friends and I had barely turned thirteen but Uncle Reggie was always good about not treating us like kids.

The next song came on, Crosby, Stills, and Nash's "Southern Cross," and my thoughts drifted farther back. When Uncle Reggie got out of the service and bought the Pirate's Cove, it was like a Deadhead oasis. Hippies everywhere. Uncle Reggie let his hair grow long. He sported a shaggy beard and a tie-dye ensemble, and he sat on his stool at the bar smoking a King Edward cigar with Bonny on his shoulder. Together, they welcomed the disconnected.

My reminiscence ended abruptly when I saw movement in the doorway to the Italian restaurant. Shorty and another man came out and stood, talking for a few minutes. They chuckled and slapped each other on the back. My fingers impatiently tapped the steering wheel. Three more men came out of the place, the man with the goatee being one of them, and they stood around talking and laughing.

Ten minutes passed before Shorty and Goatee got in the 300 and drove off. As soon as the others went inside I followed my targets. The slight delay let me settle in behind several other cars. It wouldn't be pretty if Galston's muscle spotted me. And I'd ruin my chance to get revenge. The 300 drove through the tourist traffic, made a few turns, and ended up in the projects. On Harmon, a side street two blocks from Mutt's bar, I stopped at the curb and watched Shorty and his buddy park across the street and walk into a small, light-colored house. The drapes were pulled. I parked behind an old van and chambered a round in the forty-five. The street had a slight incline to it, which was odd in Charleston.

Half an hour later, the men were still in the house. The Chrysler hadn't moved from under the light on the other side of the street. I wiped sweat from my forehead and dried my hand on my shorts, put my cell on vibrate, and got out of my car. Using the shadow of a vacant shack surrounded by thick weeds for cover, I stretched my neck. Dead leaves crunched under my feet.

Lights inside the house made the closed drapes glow orange. No shadows of figures moved past the windows and I wondered if the men had entered and disappeared. I walked past five or six houses before I crossed the street and reversed direction.

"Hey, there," crooned a female voice from a porch.

I stopped. A single red bulb glowed from somewhere inside the woman's open front door.

"You wanna come in?"

I still couldn't make out what she looked like, but it occurred to me this might be the village that Suzy, the teenage prostitute from the Chinese brothel, had referred to. I pointed to the house next door I was staking out.

"She's busy right now," the voice said. "Be busy for a while."

The long wait in my car for Shorty and Goatee to come out, and McAllister's comment about payback, made sense now.

"You wanna come in or not, handsome?"

I thought she might know something about my targets. At least that was the excuse I gave myself as I stepped onto her porch. The woman got up from a chair, the silhouette of her figure outlined by the glowing red light. Long curly hair, slender arms and stomach, and slightly plump hips and thighs. The scent of vanilla and lust filled the air. Inside the doorway, she turned, and waited. I followed. After closing the door, she pulled the drapes across the front windows and turned toward me, her petite face illuminated by the amber light. The negligee she wore left little to the imagination.

"You nervous, handsome?"

"A little, I guess."

"You're cute," she said.

I tried to figure out how to play this.

"And shy, too," she added. "You like me?"

I nodded, not wanting to scare her with questions yet.

She motioned to a room in the back. "You wanna go in there where it's a little more comfortable?"

I nodded again.

She reached her hand out and I took it. Her mocha skin was soft and warm. She giggled and led me to a small room lit by a tiny "princess" night-light close to the baseboard. I sat on the edge of the mattress.

She stood in front of me. "Why don't you tell me what you like, handsome."

I felt as if I was in a private club where there were no rules.

She walked closer to me and placed a hand on my chest. "I

like you. If you want, you can like me too."

I stopped myself from nodding.

She leaned in and kissed my cheek and whispered in my ear, "All I need from you is a hundred dollars."

I reached for my wallet and handed her the bill. She took it, walked to the dresser, and placed it in a wooden jewelry box.

In the mirror, I caught her eyes. "Can we talk for a minute?"

She turned to face me and leaned against the dresser.

I found the sheerness of her attire distracting and wiped a hand across my forehead again. "I'm following the guys visiting your neighbor. What can you tell me about them?"

She bit her lip as if to consider.

We sat at a small table in the kitchen at the front of the house. Her name was Dora. She said she didn't know why she told me her name. That was against the rules.

I rotated the can of beer she'd given me with my palms. "Rules? I got the impression there weren't any rules."

She raised her dark eyebrows and looked at a clock on the wall. "Of course there are. Like, if you aren't outside in five more minutes, I have to charge you more." She wasn't mean about it. More like matter-of-fact.

I laid another bill on the table. "For the meter."

She looked at it. "And you still don't want to go back there?"

"That's a question with all kinds of answers."

"It's what I'm here for."

I said, "Who would know?"

She put her hand on mine. "No one."

"No, I mean who would know how long I've been in here?"

She took her hand off mine to motion toward the front door. "Temp-a."

"Who?"

She stared at her hands. "Temp-a. He runs the show."

The AC unit in the window blew cool air and the ceiling fan whirring above our heads circulated it around the room.

"He's your pimp?"

She nodded.

I raised the beer to my mouth but stopped. "Is he Chinese?"

"No. He's black."

"How do the Chinese fit in?"

"You mean the girls?"

"No. The ones Temp-a reports to."

Dora shook her head. "I don't know about them."

"What can you tell me about the girl next door?"

"She told me her name was Kim Lee."

"And the men with her?"

"They're regulars. Every Wednesday night. Kim says they're rough but they pay double. Temp-a's scared of them. He says they're connected, whatever that means."

I needed to know where I could be attacked from if this turned bad so I asked, "Where is Temp-a?"

"He stays in the first house across the street. There's someone else in the house at the other end. They have radios and watch everything."

I did a quick calculation. As long as I knew when her pimp would be coming, I had about one minute to prepare for him if it came to that. "I was outside for a while before I walked by."

"I know," she said. "It's a slow night."

"They probably saw me too."

"Don't worry. You looked nervous, like a first-time john."

I smiled and said, "I am a first-time john."

"Not yet." She smiled back.

Because I didn't know how to answer, I rose to leave. On a napkin on her table, I wrote Brother Thomas's church phone number and hoped he appreciated all the exposure I was getting him.

As I walked past the Chrysler, I had an idea—a scene from a movie, actually—that seemed appropriate to replicate. More appropriate was the movie's title—*Payback*. Remembering the pimps at each end of the street, I didn't waste any time. I pulled out my pocket knife, got on my back, and scooted underneath the car behind the rear tire, feeling around until I found the gas line. I shuffled left so I wouldn't get a mouthful of unleaded, reached with the knife, and sliced the rubber line. Gas drained out of the severed hose. Lucky for me the street had the incline. I got to my feet and walked to the rear of the car behind the Chrysler, reaching for my lighter. When the stream of gas exposed itself at my feet, I knelt and lit it.

Then I ran.

I made twenty paces before the explosion knocked me off my feet. Debris rained down like a hailstorm. A loud crash shook the ground, the 300 returning to earth. I jumped up, rushed to my car, and got out of there. A mile away, I spotted an abandoned gas station and stopped. Adrenaline coursed through my veins. I had to take a few minutes and calm down. With the disposable cell phone, I made a call.

"Nine-one-one," the voice said. "What is your emergency?"

"Ye-ah," I said, adding a lazy drawl to my voice. "I want to report two white guys stuck in cracktown with a blown-up car."

"What is your name, sir?"

I thought about the question. "Galston. Michael Galston."

"And your location?"

"Me? I'm fine. It's the two white guys I'm worried about. When they finish with the hooker—Kim Lee I think her name is—they're going to need a ride."

"I don't understand, sir. What is your emergency?"

"It isn't exactly a nice neighborhood they're stuck in, ya know?"

"No, sir. What are you reporting?"

I looked at my watch. "They're probably wrapping things up with Ms. Lee as we speak. I'm guessing the explosion blew their interlude. At least I hope so. It sure blew out the windows of all the houses around."

I gave the operator the street name and the license plate number of the Chrysler and hung up. From where I stood, the hot night air tasted sweet. A minute later, a patrol car cruised by, made a fast U-turn, and accelerated down the street. It headed in the direction I'd come from, roof lights blazing all over the place. I lit a Cuban and leaned against the fender of my car, grinned, and sang, *Happy birthday to me . . .*

Chapter Twenty-One

Another idea popped into my celebratory head. Before I went through with it, I considered how much I could trust Darcy not to turn me in and decided I didn't have any choice. I dug out my personal cell phone from a front pocket and hit speed dial. Darcy answered on the second ring and I told her where I was.

She said, "What are you doing there?"

I told her the story, leaving out the part about giving Dora two hundred dollars. Darcy didn't need to know everything, and I'd spend too much time explaining.

"You blew up their car?"

I exhaled a cloud of smoke. "Yep."

"And called the cops?"

"Yep."

Silence for a few seconds. "And told them you were Galston?"

"I gave them his birth name in case they didn't know."

Another good five seconds of crickets.

"Stay where you are," she said. "I'll be there in twenty minutes."

Fifteen minutes later, a red Infiniti screeched to a halt in front of the abandoned gas station.

Darcy said, "Get in."

I made sure the alarm was on in my Mustang, hopped over

the passenger door of the convertible, and landed in the leather seat.

She accelerated before I could get my seatbelt buckled and busted through a red light. Lucky for us there were no cars because she didn't look. "Get the camera bag from the back-seat."

"Camera?"

"If I'm lucky," she said, "I'll get pictures for the morning edition."

I pointed to the street where the action was. A patrol car had pulled across the entrance, stopping john traffic from entering. Red and blue lights tried to make the street look like an amusement park. It worked—I was amused. The air was thick with the bitter smell of smoldering rubber and plastic.

"Yes!" yelled Darcy. "We might still get a shot."

She pulled onto the next street and parked.

I said, "Are you sure you wanna park your car here?"

"You worry too much." She leapt out and ran.

I followed with the camera and we ran through the backyards and alleys of abandoned houses. At least I hoped they were abandoned. The acrid methane and sulfur smell of decomposing garbage was wrenching.

Seeing the flashing lights ahead, I spoke in a loud whisper, "Hold up."

Darcy stopped.

"You can't push your way in there like Katie Couric," I huffed. "There's a rundown house across from the hooker's. We can huddle there in the shadows and use the zoom."

"Lead the way," she said.

I didn't dwell too long on the fact that she didn't normally give up authority easily.

We maneuvered to the position I had taken earlier when I scoped out the street. I hoped all the police in the area had scared off Temp-a and his buddy. Darcy grabbed the bag from me and took out the camera. Two firemen sprayed aqueous film forming foam onto the remains of the smoldering luxury car. We used AFFF in Afghanistan a lot. And like Afghanistan, I wouldn't be seeing that black menace of a car again. The car behind it was toast as well. Darcy raised the camera and snapped photos. In the flashing lights, I could make out Shorty and the man with the goatee standing twenty feet away from their ride, looking puzzled. After a few minutes Darcy and I snuck out of there. Two streets over, she stopped me.

"I got them all," she said. "The johns and one of the detectives investigating your uncle's murder."

"Who?"

"The clean-cut one. Rogers, right?"

"What would he be doing answering a nine-one-one call?" I asked

"All I know is I saw him in the zoom."

We made it to where Darcy had parked her Infiniti, which, not surprisingly, was gone. Someone had moved it and neglected to tell us where. The police had a term for that—grand theft auto.

In the middle of the projects and without any streetlights, we had a long walk to my car. I couldn't shake the feeling of being a walking target. The last time I'd felt eyes on me, I held a machine gun and plenty of ammo. Darcy and I kept to the shadows. Lucky for us, the Mustang, with the alarm turned on, sat where I'd left it. I opened the passenger door and she got in. When I was seated in the driver's seat, I hit the power door lock button.

"You gotta report your car," I said.

She stared at the camera in her hands. "Later. Let's get to the office and check these out. I think we have a story."

"Stop the presses," I said.

She gave me the same look Jo used to when I was out of line.

I started the engine the Ford engineers code-named Coyote. With the traction control turned off, the only way I rode, I laid two solid tracks of rubber through first and second gears.

At the *Palmetto Pulse,* I made coffee in a nearby kitchenette while Darcy booted up her computer and explained our adventure to Patricia. My uncle's ex-wife stood looking over Darcy's shoulders, her hair pulled back in a ponytail, wearing jeans and a polo shirt. "You mean you woke me up to meet you here because Brack blew up a car belonging to two white guys having sex with a prostitute?"

"Not just any white guys," Darcy said. "They're connected with Galston."

I handed each of them a full cup and placed the sugar and powder creamer on the desk beside them. The one thing I knew for sure about women was they always put cream and sugar in their coffee. Darcy plugged the camera into the USB port of the computer and downloaded the pictures. When the images appeared, she double-clicked on one and enlarged it. Patricia took a sip of black coffee and held the mug close to her face. Darcy did the same. The cream and sugar remained untouched.

We stayed at the *Palmetto Pulse* until three o'clock Friday morning working on the story, holding up the morning edition until the last minute. The printer was not happy. But the excitement level of the staff could be felt as we hammered out the details.

I fell asleep on the couch in the Folly Beach rental, my dog lying on the floor beside me.

Just before lunch, I drove back to my home on Sullivan's Island and worked on my stack of mail, my gun a constant companion now. Sitting in the rocker on the front porch with a glass of iced tea beside me on a small table and the current issue of the *Palmetto Pulse* open on my lap, it felt good reading the words we'd written just hours before. Shelby lay at my feet. The perfect cloudless blue sky intersected with the span of marsh grass bordering the Intracoastal Waterway directly in front of me. A white Toyota Solara convertible cruised by heading for the beach-access parking a block away. The four girls in it wore cutoffs and bikini tops and waved as they passed. I waved back, feeling good about life, for a change. My shorts vibrated, and it took me a moment to realize it was my cell phone. Brother Thomas wanted to meet me at Cassie's for dinner.

Once again I turned my attention to today's *Palmetto Pulse*. The front page was a beautiful enlarged photograph of Shorty and Goatee standing in front of Kim Lee's house. Shirts untucked, hair disheveled, looking guilty as sin. It was pitiful the way they stared at the charred remains of their car. The headline read:

CAR EXPLOSION TRIGGERS POLICE INVESTIGATION INTO SEX CRIMES

Darcy wrote a scathing piece full of anonymous sources divulging what the homes on the street were used for and suggesting the two johns, who could clearly be seen in the photo, might be linked to Charleston high society. She was careful not to print any names, especially Galston's. Patricia had blocked out the ever-present monograms of Galston's company displayed on their shirts as well. Though the truth was stretched to the point of being irrelevant, Patricia didn't want a lawsuit. Besides, this would likely end up in Galston's lap anyway thanks to my phone call and sweet southern drawl.

The only fly in the ointment of my day, so to speak, was the group of mosquitoes nipping at my ankles. The bloodsuckers must have thought the scent of my citronella candles was their dinner bell. I lit a Cuban and hoped the heavy smoke would keep them away.

An unmarked Crown Vic parked in front of my house. Rogers and Wilson climbed out and headed for my porch. Shelby growled at Detective Rogers but let Detective Wilson pat his head.

I said, "You fellas out enjoying the sunshine, too?"

"We gotta talk, Pelton," Wilson said.

Shelby watered the bushes closest to Rogers, causing him to step back.

"Oh yeah?" I said. "I was about to boil some shrimp. Y'all want some?"

Rogers's face squinted like a prune. "You wanna tell us where you were last night?"

Shelby returned and sat by my chair.

I took a drink of iced tea. "Here, mostly."

Rogers pulled a notepad out of his pocket. "What do you mean you were here *mostly*?"

"Can I offer you guys something to drink? Iced tea? Coke?"

Wilson looked at his partner. "We'd love a couple of Cokes, wouldn't we?"

Rogers sucked in a breath and exhaled. "Sure."

Shelby and I went in to get the Cokes. When we returned to the porch, the detectives' attention was fixed on Maxine Schell, who happened to be strolling past my house with her kids. She waved at us and we waved back. Even Shelby. Maxine's short shorts and halter top kept my visitors distracted until she'd gone out of range. Wilson looked like he'd forgotten his own name.

I handed the detectives their drinks. "So, what were we talking about?"

Rogers cleared his throat. "Last night."

I scratched behind Shelby's ears. "What about it?"

The clean-cut detective asked, "You want to tell us what you were doing?"

Shelby circled my feet twice before lying down. I sat in the chair. "What are you concerned I was doing?"

Wilson pointed to the newspaper on the porch. "The story in your aunt's newspaper this morning. Wanna tell us what you know about it?"

I nodded. "Pretty interesting reading."

Sweat beads formed on Wilson's forehead and he gulped a mouthful of Coke. "What else?"

My cigar was still lit and I took a hit. "I'd say the newspaper covered everything as far as I can tell. It was pretty thorough."

Rogers fixed his eyes on mine. "Know anything about a nine-one-one call?"

I worked the rocker back and forth. "What nine-one-one call?"

"Just answer the question," said Rogers.

A mosquito buzzed by and I swatted at it. "I'm not sure I know what you're talking about?"

"We got a recording," said Wilson. "Sounds an awful lot like you."

I exhaled a cloud of smoke.

Wilson hooked a thumb in his belt. "Know anything about it?"

I picked up the *Palmetto Pulse*. "There isn't anything about that in here."

"So," said Rogers, "you didn't make any nine-one-one calls last night?"

I shook my head no. "I didn't have any emergencies last night. I told you, I was here. Minding my own business."

Rogers stopped the rocking of my chair with his foot. "Look Pelton, implicating Galston in a prostitution sting is not a good way to win friends and influence people."

"Sounds like you read books without pictures, Detective." I threw the paper on the table.

Rogers picked a piece of lint from his immaculately pressed slacks. "You better hope we can't place you at the scene."

"You've got to be kidding."

"No, we're not," said Rogers.

Wilson asked, "How do you think that reporter broad happened to be there?"

I shrugged. "She's that good?"

"She'd have to be psychic to be there at that particular time," said Rogers.

"Guys," I said. "The paper said this happened in a bad part of town, right?"

They didn't say answer.

"Do you think a young, pretty blonde without a bad habit would be caught dead in cracktown at night?"

They still said nothing.

"My guess is someone else was there and they fed her the story."

"So," said Rogers, "you take the picture?"

"I took no pictures last night." I tapped ashes into an ashtray. "Truth is I'm getting over a cold."

Wilson said, "Cold?"

"Yeah," I puffed on the Cuban some more. "You know, one of those summer bugs. Really took it out of me."

The detectives shook their heads and walked to their car.

After dropping Shelby off at the Folly Beach rental, I found a parking spot in front of Cassie's and stuck the gun in the glove box. When I got out of my car, a black man about my age walked out the door of the restaurant with a thickset woman and stopped in mid-stride.

He said, "That is one nasty car you got there."

The woman joined in. "It sure is. Pretty, too."

I tapped the roof. "Thanks."

The man shook his head. "Nas-ty."

The woman said, "You here to see Brother Thomas, ain'tcha?"

"Yes ma'am."

She hooked her thumb toward the door. "He inside."

"Thanks."

The man asked, "You the one popped Mutt and took his gat?"

This couldn't be good. "Um, yeah. I'm the one."

He said, "Loudmouth deserve more than that."

The woman swatted at the man's shoulder. "Now stop it, Frank. Hear? Everybody deserve a little forgiveness every now and then."

Not everyone, I thought, as I went inside.

Brother Thomas and Mutt were waiting for me at a booth in the back.

"Gentlemen," I said.

"If it ain't Opie," said Mutt.

Brother Thomas nodded. "Brother Brack."

I took a seat. Cassie came with a pitcher of iced tea dripping with condensation and filled my glass. Her gaze at me stopped somewhere past grandkids and she giggled. Tonight her perfume was cinnamon.

"How you doing, hon?" She put her hand on my shoulder. "You need to come see me more than this. Ain't my cooking good?"

"Yes ma'am," I said. "The brother and I were talking about it this afternoon. I had to come out and get me some more."

Cassie rubbed my cheek and sauntered away, an extra kick in her step. She returned with a tray and set out a large family-sized plate of fried chicken, bowls of smashed potatoes, greens, black-eyed peas, and cornbread. After Brother Thomas said grace, the three of us dove in. Brother Thomas wouldn't let go of the chicken plate until he'd grabbed the two biggest pieces. Gravy oozed over Mutt's potatoes and onto the table. I snatched the vinegar away from Brother Thomas before he could drain the whole bottle on his greens. We ate until there was nothing left.

Cassie set another basket of cornbread on the table and looked at the mess we'd made. "Well, I'll be."

We fought over the squares of cornbread while she cleared the empty bowls and brought more. Something about being the only white face here made me feel at ease. No one looking for me would show up here. I slowed after the second round of food and told them about Darcy and Patricia and our boat ride.

CHAPTER TWENTY-TWO

For the finale, Cassie brought coffee and sweet potato pie. A whole pie. As she cut it into three pieces and dished it out on plates with ice cream, an elderly lady sitting at another table called to her.

Cassie nodded at the woman and touched my cheek. "Enjoy it, handsome." She smiled and left.

Mutt finished eating and burped. "Gawd."

Brother Thomas sat back in his chair and patted his stomach. "Mm-hmm."

I chewed on a toothpick and tipped my chair onto its hind legs. At the moment, I felt content with the best meal I'd had since the last time I'd been here.

Brother Thomas's eyes locked on to mine. "Brother Brack, you know anyone by the name of Dora?"

I popped my chair back on four legs and yanked the toothpick out of my mouth. "Why?"

"She called the church this morning. A stranger gave her the number. A white man."

"Really?"

Brother Thomas gleamed. "This woman was of, shall we say, the oldest profession."

"Hey now," said Mutt.

"And this stranger," Brother Thomas continued, "she invited him in and he paid her."

Mutt's eyes opened wide. "Hold on!"

"Then, Brother Brack, this man proceeded to talk to her."

Mutt said, "Talk? He just talked?"

Brother Thomas ignored the question. "He was following some men who were, um . . . visiting her neighbor. Asked all sorts of questions about them. How long they been coming to see the girl. How long they stayed. Then, he asked Dora about herself."

I said, "And you say she was given your number?"

"Yes." Brother Thomas laced his fingers together over his stomach. "You see, not too long after this man left her house, a car exploded outside her door and the po-lice showed up. I read about it in this morning's paper. The situation gave Dora, shall we say, mo-ti-vation to rethink her life. I invited her to visit with a few of the ladies of the church. They found nice donated clothes her size and we managed to scrape together enough money to purchase a bus ticket."

I scratched my head. "Bus ticket?"

Brother Thomas nodded. "She ran away from home two years ago and been selling herself here in Charleston since. She was a mess when she come to the church. Desperate and lost. We made a phone call to her family and she was on the next bus back home, mm-hmm."

"That's a good story," I said.

The minister of the projects stared at me. "Brother Brack, I'd sure like to thank the man who led her out of the life."

"Brother," I said, "you look at him in the mirror every day."

Brother Thomas smiled and didn't say anything else. I think he wanted to let me know he knew. But I didn't want him to be any more involved. And I certainly didn't want him to get a visit from Rogers and Wilson.

The next time Cassie came by I asked for the check and added a large tip.

★　★　★　★　★

I fell asleep on the couch in the beach rental with Shelby on the floor at my side. In the middle of a dream in which I ran the Mustang flat out, hit curve apexes just right, and snapped flawless redline shifts, Shelby's growl woke me. I opened my eyes in the darkness.

He snarled once more and ran to the back door. I grabbed the forty-five from the coffee table, eased my feet onto the floor, and crept up beside him. Shelby's body was stiff when I patted his head and his eyes looked out between the blinds to the back patio. Darkness stared back.

He growled again, louder. My gut told me Shorty and Goatee had found us and wanted payback. Assuming they were in the backyard, I told Shelby to stay, made my way to the front door, and snuck outside to flank them. The ocean breeze and the crash of the surf covered my approach. Shelby's bark echoed through the thin walls of the house. I tiptoed along the side and peered around the corner to the backyard. Two figures stood on the patio in front of the sliding glass door outside the living room. One of them was short and stocky, the other tall and lanky. The short one pointed something at the glass door, low.

I aimed and fired. The forty-five boomed and the wooden deck chair in my sights splintered into pieces. The figures bolted over the railing, dropped ten feet onto the sand, and vanished. When I went to the sliding door, Shelby grinned at me through the glass and wagged his tail.

They were going to shoot my dog.

My blood boiled.

Down the street, an engine started. I ran to the front of the house. A large SUV passed by at full throttle and I put three rounds through the back window. It shattered and the truck fishtailed around a corner. Rage took over my common sense. I ran to keep up but they were gone. A police siren wailed in the distance.

The Folly Beach cops were real sweethearts. They gave me a disturbing-the-peace citation and took my gun. Whoever reported the shooting did not mention a speeding SUV, and the cops had a hard time believing there was one. Even after I showed them the glass and skid marks from the retreating vehicle.

Shelby and I were packed and gone within the hour. No way would I stay here without a weapon. I wondered how they learned where I was hiding. The digital clock in my car said it was way too early. I pulled my cell out of my pocket and hit speed dial anyway.

A sleepy voice answered.

I hit the hands-free button. "Hello, Chauncey. This is your favorite client."

"Hmm?"

"It's Brack."

"Brack? What time is it?"

As I slowed for a red light, I said, "Five."

His response was not quick, as if he were contemplating something. "Are you in trouble?"

"Not at the moment."

"Can this wait until regular business hours, then?"

"I need a safe place for Shelby," I said in the most desperate voice I could muster. "Two idiots tried to shoot him this morning."

"Shelby? Your dog?"

"Yes. They were after me and found him first."

He coughed. "Where were you?"

"Shooting at them."

"I see."

It sounded like he didn't.

"You told me you and your wife have dogs," I said. "So can he stay with you until this blows over?"

If Chauncey didn't say yes, I'd have to park Shelby at the kennel. He wouldn't like that at all. I pictured Chauncey in paisley pajamas that matched his bow ties, sitting in bed with the receiver in his hand, and staring into space wondering how he got mixed up in this.

"Chauncey?"

I thought I'd lost him until he said, "Okay."

"Great. I appreciate this. One thing, he won't eat unless I feed him."

"What does that mean?"

I said, "I guess it means I'll have to be there at feeding time."

More silence. As if relenting, he gave me directions. I told him I'd make sure I wasn't followed but he didn't seem too concerned.

His subdivision was located on the north side of the Isle of Palms. The security hut at the entrance divided the street and monitored cars entering and exiting. Chauncey had called ahead and told them I was coming. His house sat back from the street, hidden behind tall palm trees and large tropical flowers in full bloom. The middle of three garage doors was open and Chauncey stood in the opening drinking a cup of coffee. Behind him I could see the tail end of his large Audi sedan. The stiff creases in his white oxford shirt and navy suit pants were matched by shiny brown leather shoes with buckles. And of course, the bow tie. He wasn't smiling.

His wife, Trish, came out to greet us. She had long, light-colored hair pulled back in a clip and wore a linen blouse and nice shorts and sandals. Thin and tall, she was twenty years older than me but didn't look it.

Before I could stop him, Shelby ran to her, put his front paws on her thighs, and licked her face. As with all other women within a hundred-foot radius of my dog, Chauncey's wife giggled and hugged him, scratching behind his ears.

"Witchy Woman," the ringtone I'd selected for Darcy, woke me from a not-so-deep slumber in the front seat of my car parked at a partially concealed beach access on Sullivan's Island. Somehow my favorite news girl had learned of my adventure with the dirtbags and wanted the scoop. She suggested meeting at a local diner to discuss a follow-up story detailing their exploits with the Chinese prostitute, Ms. Lee. Sounded like a good way to get more revenge. If I thought Darcy would say yes, I'd have asked her to marry me. But I had an idea of where everything that wasn't part of Darcy's career stood in the pecking order of her priorities, and so decided against proposing. The waitress brought a plate of eggs, bacon, and pancakes to the table as the princess of Charleston news arrived.

She said, "Thanks for waiting."

"Happy Friday to you, too," I said. "Don't worry. I'll probably get something else."

Darcy ordered a veggie omelet and I added two blueberry muffins and a coffee refill to my tab. When her food arrived, Darcy used her knife and fork to eat with. Compared with my bulldozer technique, she was all grace and sophistication.

The big breakfast rejuvenated me. I handed the waiter a credit card for the check and leaned in my chair, suppressing a large belch from getting out of hand.

Darcy looked me over, probably deciding I was a little too rough around the edges.

I said, "How'd you get here? You get your car back?"

"I bought another," she said.

"That was quick. Same model?"

She waved a hand to shrug off the fact she just dumped fifty thousand on a new car and most likely still hadn't reported the other one stolen. "I did a little checking on our buddy, McAllister."

"Oh, yeah?"

"He seems to be legit," she said. "He's got several businesses. Mostly environmental cleanup."

"Chauncey confirmed he was in Vietnam with them."

"Good. And I got a tip on Galston. It might be worth checking out."

The check came and I signed with my left hand.

Darcy said, "I forgot Patricia had told me you were ambidextrous."

"As far as writing and shooting go, anyway," I said. It had come in handy, so to speak, in the war and it was always a fun bar trick.

Darcy had arrangements to make so I drove solo to the Pirate's Cove. Some Charlestonians live at the beaches on weekends. They bring their families out to enjoy the natural beauty of the ocean and soak up vitamin D from the sun. Others acquire their tans in clamshell beds. The appeal of heading to a strip mall and spending time in one of those was lost on me—too much like a coffin. There's no substitute for real sunshine.

Detectives Rogers and Wilson showed up, again, at the bar later that afternoon. They sat at a table shaded by an umbrella on the upper deck overlooking the ocean. The temperature had passed ninety as soon as the sun came up. Sweat beaded on their foreheads.

I took a seat at their table. "How's it going, detectives?"

Wilson said, "Just thought we'd come out and see how the other half lived."

Rogers's skin tone was a little too even. Definitely a tanning-bed bunny.

I said, "Been out in the sun, Rogers?"

He ignored the bait.

A large group of sorority sisters from the University of Minnesota chattered at a nearby table. They had come down for the week on a summer retreat and adopted the Pirate's Cove as their home away from home. Paige delivered a round of tequila shots to them and they toasted their school.

Wilson took in the predominance of females and pulled out a comb. "This is the place to be." He rerouted what strands he had left on his cranium to areas long ago abandoned.

The girls downed their shots, and fifteen glasses hit the table in unison.

Unaffected by the beauty around them, Rogers focused on the lunch menu. "So what do you recommend?"

"The burger's the best on the island," I said. "Get the atomic if you like a little kick."

"Make mine well done," said Wilson, "and a Coke. Get us an order of fried dill pickles while you're at it."

Rogers closed his menu. "I'll have a grilled chicken salad, no dressing. Ice water with lemon."

I put the food order in and had a waiter get the drinks. After checking in with my newfound sorority sisters to make sure they were having a good time, but not so good I'd need to call an ambulance for alcohol poisoning, I rejoined the detectives.

Rogers said, "So, what do you have to say about the shooting on Folly Beach last night?"

"I missed," I said.

Rogers leaned forward. "I think you're seeing things, Pelton. Got that post-traumatic stress disorder."

I knew a lot of men better than me suffering with PTSD. Rogers's little barb skirted past my defenses. Anger pulsed in my head. I took a deep breath and exhaled slowly.

Rogers flashed a grin. "Don't worry, Pelton. We've all got problems."

I inched forward in my seat. "Yeah. My problem is you tried to close the case on my uncle's murder."

"Whoa," said Wilson, his attention on the bar.

My eyes followed his. One of the sorority sisters, a big-busted looker, sauntered over to Paige, who listened to the girl, then held up a wait-a-moment finger. The girl giggled and waved at me.

Paige came over. "Seems your girlfriends over there are requesting we change the music."

Wilson ogled the girls. "Hey Pelton, give 'em whatever they want."

I frowned.

Paige put her hands on her hips. "Frankly, Brack, we'd all like a relief from classic rock. I mean, isn't Joe Walsh dead, yet?"

"He's not, and neither are any of the other Eagles." I stood and walked to the sorority sister at the bar.

She gave me her first-class pouty-lip treatment. "Do you mind?" A foot shorter than me, she had long brown hair and tanned skin.

I stooped to talk to her. "Mind? Yes I mind. What's your name?"

Her eyes grew big. "Br-Brandy."

"Brandy," I said, "you girls have been camped out here for the past four days."

She looked at her sisters and back at me. "Yes?"

"Why didn't you say anything before?"

She blinked.

"Paige had satellite radio installed this week," I said. "We'll change the station on one condition."

Brandy nodded quickly.

I pointed to Rogers and Wilson. "We happen to have two of

Charleston's finest police detectives sitting right over there. What do you say you girls dance with them for a song or two?"

Brandy clapped her hands, let out a squeal, and ran to her friends. A hip-hop variation of a seventies disco song replaced "Life's Been Good." The sisters clapped and squealed and pulled Rogers and Wilson out of their seats.

Along with the satellite radio, Paige had decided on a webcam. I turned it toward the dancing group on the deck to make sure anyone logging in would see what a party it was at the Cove. Then I went inside.

Jason, one of Paige's College of Charleston classmates, sat in my uncle's chair in front of a laptop and nodded at me when I entered. "I just put the finishing touches on the website."

I said, "Pull up the webcam for me, would you?"

Jason clicked the mouse a few times and the dancing group appeared on the monitor in front of him. "Looks like there's a party out there."

"It surely does." I pulled out my cell and the business card Wilson had given me the night my uncle was murdered and dialed the main switchboard of the Charleston Police Station. The dispatch operator answered and I asked to be transferred to the police chief. When his voice came on the line, I told him it might be in his best interest to log into our website. I gave him the URL.

Jason's eyes went from me to the screen and to me again. In the amount of time it would have taken the chief to find us on the Internet, his detectives, surrounded by twenty-one-year-old *I-hoped-for-my-liquor-license* beauties, had gone from reluctant stiffs to willing participants. The girls moved their hips in NC-Seventeen fashion, arms raised in the air, and worked their way toward Unrated. Detective Rogers did the electric slide, pointing at the sky in perfect disco stance. Detective Wilson was another story. Hunched down, butt shaking, one arm extended out and the other folded in, he was doing his version of the garden sprinkler—which included two sisters dancing back-to-back with him. When Brandy jiggled by he grabbed her hand and spun her around. She moved in front of him, joined his boogying harem, and led him like a puppy.

Jason said, "What was that call about?"

"It's time for some new detectives."

Paige walked into the office shaking her head. "You'd think those guys were auditioning for a dance show on TV. What are they doing here?"

"Beats me," I said.

She pointed at the screen. "Hey, you've got the webcam working."

"We're testing it right now."

Jason smiled.

I told Paige I'd see her later, thanked Jason, and snuck out the front door, taking the stairs to the sidewalk two at a time.

CHAPTER TWENTY-THREE

Michael Galston stepped out of his long-wheelbase Cadillac Escalade and stood by the open door, surveying the surroundings. His aviator sunglasses glistened in the late afternoon sun. The wide collar of his triple-XL Hawaiian shirt displayed a gold chain nestled in overgrown chest hair. He spoke briefly to his Mexican driver, who had opened the SUV's door for him, and strolled toward a seedy red brick motel.

Seated inside an inconspicuous Ford Fusion rental, Darcy and I spied on Galston from the back parking lot of the motel. A fluorescent sign tried to spell *vacancy* but stopped a few letters short. The lodging would not have been recommended in any tour book unless the listing was for places that rented by the hour.

I watched through binoculars, wondering why Shorty and Goatee weren't with their boss. "You said he comes here two days a week?"

"That's what the source told me," Darcy said.

Someone had called the paper and left a message on her voicemail saying he knew she was investigating Galston and that he'd be at this location at this time Friday afternoon. The door to the no-tell motel room Galston approached was faded brown. Orange curtains covered a large window. A tall Asian woman answered his knock wearing a silk robe open in the front to show off her thin figure clad in a lace bra and panties. She kissed Galston on the cheek and held the door for him to enter.

When he was inside, she eased the door shut.

Darcy captured it all in digital. The thought of a picture of Galston in a compromising position on the front page of Patricia's paper was too sweet to hope for.

I lowered my binoculars and took in the wider scene. In the seconds it had taken the fat man to go inside, the Escalade had vanished. My spider-sense tingled. It had gotten me out of too many hot spots in Afghanistan to ignore. "Something isn't right."

"You're paranoid," she said.

"We better get out of here."

Gunshots exploded behind us. The back window of the Fusion shattered. Darcy jerked forward and bounced off the steering wheel. Her camera skidded across the dash. Blood sprayed everywhere.

"Darcy!"

The horror of seeing her shot brought out the training the Corps had drilled into me when fired upon.

Return fire. Secure the position. Tend to the wounded. *In that order.*

More shots came from behind and exited out the windshield. Darcy must have bumped the rearview mirror out of place because it was angled toward me. In it I saw two figures approaching from behind with guns aimed at us. Something was familiar about them but I didn't have time to ponder. Darcy's bag had spilled open and my eyes landed on her thirty-two pistol. Grabbing it, I released the clip to make sure it had bullets and shoved it back in. I clicked off the safety, jacked a round in the chamber, and rotated my arms over the seat in one motion, returning fire through the open rear window. My bullets hit one of the men in the chest. He fell against a parked car before crashing to the ground. The other man leapt behind a dumpster. The sun glinted off something metallic around his neck.

My drill sergeant's voice overpowered the commotion. "Don't get your ass pinned down, Soldier!"

I swung the Fusion's door open and the shooter blew the glass out. Two more shots decorated the door panel. Ducking low in my seat, I tried to spot him in the rearview mirror.

He shot it out.

The distant wail of a police siren told me they were too far away to help. More shots thumped into the back of the Fusion. The guy was aiming for the gas tank, which meant our time was about up.

I took Darcy's arm, dragged her out with one hand, and fired at the shooter with the thirty-two in the other hand. My shots clanged on the side of the dumpster he was using for cover until the thirty-two was empty and I'd gotten Darcy safely around the side of the motel building. No more shots came our way.

With the position as secure as I could make it, I dropped the empty thirty-two and tended to the wounded. Darcy was unresponsive, her pulse faint. The front of her dress soaked with blood around her right shoulder. I took out my pocket knife and cut her shirt away from the wound, which gushed blood. Tearing off my shirt, I used it to apply pressure to stop the flow.

The police siren was finally close enough to believe it was headed our way. I scanned the area. No movement behind the dumpster where the shooter had been. Two patrol cars slid to a stop next to us.

I yelled at the gun barrels pointed at me, "She needs an ambulance!"

My one allotted phone call did not go well.

Patricia's voice screamed out of the receiver and echoed around the concrete block walls of the holding cell. "What were you two doing outside that motel?"

Nothing came to mind so nothing came out of my mouth. I

looked down at the dull floor.

"Answer me!"

All I could see was the blood. Darcy's blood. On the dashboard. On the front of her dress. On my hands.

She said, "You don't care about anything but yourself, do you?"

With my free hand I gripped one of the bars from the cell closest to me but still didn't speak.

Something must have clicked inside of Patricia because she began to cry. The quiet sobs were worse than the screaming.

Detective Rogers and the holding-cell guard walked in. The detective said, "I have an update on your friend."

Through the receiver, Patricia said, "Oh, God." She must have heard the detective.

"Ms. Wells lost a lot of blood and is in critical condition," he said. "But she's stable at this time."

The holding-cell guard escorted me to an interrogation room and left me alone with a bad cup of coffee. The police had confiscated my watch and phone when they booked me so I had no idea how long I sat there. The door opened and Chauncey walked in with Detectives Rogers and Wilson. Rogers carried a file folder. Chauncey sat in the chair beside me. The detectives took the seats in front of me, Wilson smiling as if he'd won the lottery. My webcam plan hadn't worked out like I wanted it to.

"Brack," Wilson said, "your file says you were in the Marines."

I looked at my lawyer. He nodded.

"Yes," I said.

Wilson continued, "First of all, thank you for serving the country, and I mean it."

"Thanks," I said, thinking about Rogers's PTSD crack at my bar earlier.

Rogers said, "Says you went in at twenty-nine."

"And?"

Wilson said, "You just made the cutoff."

Rogers said, "Why so old? I mean, most screw-ups join straight out of high school when they figure out college won't be on their agenda."

Chauncey said, "I hope you're not insulting my client for serving his country, Detective."

Rogers said, "Wouldn't dream of it."

I said, "Afghanistan sounded like the place to be."

"Yeah, right." Rogers leaned forward. "You mind going over what your responsibilities were?"

I took a long breath, counting the seconds on the inhale and exhale. The detectives would find it interesting that my self-imposed responsibility was death, whether my own or someone else's. "My duty back then was to the Corps and the safety of my men. Not that you seem to care about duty and things like that."

Rogers asked, "What do you mean?"

"My uncle, a good man and probably my only friend, is dead. Two weeks ago tomorrow some coward gunned him down in cold blood. Three days ago, an accountant was murdered in North Charleston. And today someone shot the Channel Nine News girl. I'm not having a good month, but the safety of the city is not my responsibility. It's yours. And frankly, compared to you guys, I'm golden."

"We're trying to do our jobs," Wilson said, "no thanks to you and that stunt you pulled at your bar."

Chauncey said, "Is there a question coming or are you badgering my client again?"

"I meant to comment on your dancing skills, Detective." I pointed at Rogers. "And the disco duck here."

"Real funny," Rogers said.

Wilson asked, "Do you own a weapon?"

"You already have my pocket knife."

"Don't get smart now, boy." Rogers was looking for a fight. He wanted me to take a swing at him—was daring me to.

"Folly Beach P.D. confiscated my gun early this morning. You can check with them."

Wilson said, "Whose gun was with you when the officers arrived at the scene?"

Chauncey touched my wrist. "My client is declining to answer—"

"I found it in the glove box. Must have come with the rental car." Not sure if Darcy had registered it or if she had a carry permit, I decided to lie.

Rogers pounded fists on the table. "Don't think you're getting away with this."

Chauncey stood. "Enough! Is there a charge here or is this a fishing expedition?"

I stood, too. "Getting away with what? Defending myself?"

"You said there were men with guns at your place on Folly," Rogers said, "but there was no evidence to support it. Earlier today, two patrolmen responded to an emergency call and found your girlfriend with a gunshot wound, you with a pistol, and no one else around."

I folded my arms across my chest. "Like I said, it hasn't been a very good month." I let my anger soak up the emotions I couldn't and wouldn't express.

Chauncey lifted his briefcase. "I'll have my client out of here in two minutes and your badges in three."

I said, "I hit one of them today."

Chauncey said, "Don't say another word."

In for a penny, I thought, and said, "Put at least two rounds in him."

Chauncey yelled, "Brack!"

"Why don't you go looking for someone with a couple thirty-two slugs in him?"

"We found him," Wilson said.

I sat back in the chair. "Then why aren't you giving *him* the good cop, bad cop routine?"

Rogers said, "He's dead."

"That's a real shame," I said, definitely not meaning it. "Where'd you find him?"

"In a dumpster behind a strip mall about an hour ago," Wilson said. "The dishwasher taking out the trash opened the lid and there he was. The vic's name was Johnny."

Chauncey said, "This conversation is over."

"Relax, counselor," Wilson said. "Lucky for your client there was a security camera on the back of the motel. Got most of the shootout on video. We ain't gonna press any charges."

Rogers looked me in the eye. "Yet."

Galston must not know about the video feed. Either that, or he wasn't in it. I said, "So why am I here?"

Wilson said, "Because we're tired of cleaning up your messes."

I had a few choice words ready, but my lawyer guided me out of the interrogation room, down the hall, and through the exit doors. Outside, in the balmy night air of the little slice of paradise we called home, Chauncey didn't say anything about me ignoring every piece of advice he'd tried to give. He had every right to drop me as a client and I wouldn't blame him if he did. Instead, he offered to give me a ride somewhere. His Audi waited by a parking meter.

I shook my head no and walked away. Patricia was right—I didn't care about anything. I hailed a cab and went to the safest place I knew.

The neon sign in front of Mutt's Bar lit the dirty glass and sent yellow and red colors across the cracked sidewalk. A man straddled a backwards-facing metal folding chair underneath the light. His baggy shorts and Nike Air Jordans stuck out from the sides of the chair.

Another man leaned against the side of the building watching me through cheap sunglasses. "You lost, white-bread?"

Ignoring them, I grabbed the handle of the rusty screen door and walked inside. Two men wearing stained wife-beaters shot pool at the worn-out table under a crumpled green lighting fixture. Both had cigarettes hanging out of their mouths. The ever-present window AC unit blew unbearably hot air. It mixed with the thick fog of tobacco smoke inside the place. My forehead dripped with sweat when I pulled out a stool.

Mutt came over. "What's up, Opie?"

"I need a place to crash," I said, "and a double-shot of grain."

Darcy almost died so I wanted a drink.

Mutt lived in one of the two-story shotgun homes with a front porch overlooking the God-awful main street of the projects. After he closed his bar for the night, we sat outside his rental in wobbly rocking chairs on mildewed cushions and sipped clear hooch from unmarked bottles until I passed out.

Jo stood before me in a flowing-white wedding dress, her eyes the green they became whenever she was happy. Her full lips opened with a big grin, showing off white but slightly crooked teeth. The pastor read from his bible. People cheered behind us as I took her in my arms and kissed her. She tasted like the fragrance of roses. I carried her through a doorway into our honeymoon suite. We were naked. The touch of her skin on mine was so real, perfect as always.

Then I was alone, running in a field. I called to Jo but she wasn't there. A white dove flew overhead, contrasting with the blue sky. Night came in like an old-school photographer's darkroom and didn't leave.

CHAPTER TWENTY-FOUR

Daylight revealed surprise. Even for a Saturday morning in the projects. Unlike Mutt's bar, or his front yard, the house was neat, clean, and sparse. Aside from the couch I'd slept on, the only other item in the living room was a small flatscreen TV on a stand.

Mutt walked into the living room where I stood. "Easy there, Opie. I didn't see all that on you last night."

I looked down and saw Darcy's blood on my shorts and undershirt and hands.

He said, "You okay?"

The hooch had been sufficiently potent. It felt as if someone were tattooing a Hawaiian girl doing the hula on my brain. "I'm fine."

"I got coffee or more nitro. Take your pick."

I took the offered mug of coffee. It smelled like burnt motor oil but the jolt was pure electricity.

I said, "You mind if we sit on the front porch?"

"I don't know, Opie. You mind being stared at by every brother on the block?"

"What? You don't want to be the first to integrate Cooper Street?"

"How! You pretty quick for a white boy. Lemme get you another shirt."

Mutt boosted his thick eyebrows as if to reconsider the front porch idea but went into his bedroom. I wondered what kind of

198

shirt I was going to get but he returned with a crisp white T and tossed it to me.

"My daughter loves to run," he said. "This is from that crazy thing they do across the Cooper every year."

"You mean the Bridge Run?"

"Yep. She got this for me when she did it last year. It's an extra large."

I looked at it. "Are you sure you—"

"Take it," he said and handed me the shirt.

"Where is she?"

"With her mother in Atlanta."

It had never occurred to me Mutt might have obligations outside of keeping the men of the projects in cheap booze. I cleared my throat.

"What?" He took a swig of coffee.

"Brother Thomas said my uncle might have been helping you."

Mutt held his cup in both hands. "Yeah?"

"He would want to keep it going. I guess what I'm asking is . . . what can I do for you?"

"You can clean yourself up." He flipped on a light in an adjacent room. "Bathroom's in there." He took his cup of coffee onto the front porch.

Through the front window, I watched him wave at someone on the street and wondered if I'd done something wrong. Patricia had said I could be a real piece of work and I might have just proved her right. Again.

Mutt didn't own a car and mine was at the newspaper office. Cab companies avoided the projects so I had to improvise. A phone call got me the ride I needed.

Brother Thomas pulled to the curb and I opened the door to David Fisher's Volvo, the one he'd been found shot in.

I slid into the passenger seat and closed the door. "Nice ride."

"Mrs. Fisher donated it and a bunch of other stuff to the church. It sure do the job, mm-hmm."

I couldn't tell anything so terrible had happened in it. "Who fixed it up?"

"Some talented boys from the neighborhood. 'Course, I think they're more experienced taking cars apart than fixing 'em."

"Maybe you can give them a reference if they ever decide to shoot straight."

"I do what I can, Brother Brack," he said. "I do what I can."

He wheeled us onto Lockwood, which was a little too far west for heading directly to the newspaper.

"We taking a detour?"

He stared ahead at the road. "I thought you might want to visit your friend . . . that reporter girl, mm-hmm."

I felt the heat build. "I don't like it when people think they know what I want."

At the entrance to the hospital, Brother Thomas put his turn signal on.

"The beauty of this situation," he said, "is I'm driving. And you ain't."

We pulled into visitor parking and found a spot. He turned to me. "You coming in?"

I sat there for a few seconds before unbuckling my seatbelt. "I guess I don't have much of a choice now, do I?"

"Man's always got a choice, mm-hmm. It's the one thing we got, free and clear."

I followed him to the receptionist and waited while he asked which room Darcy was in. I didn't want to be there, didn't want to deal with the fact she'd almost died yesterday.

An overweight white lady behind the desk told us Darcy was on the fifth floor but had not been cleared for visitors. Brother Thomas pulled out his clergy I.D.

She shrugged. "Elevators down the hall on the left."

The ceiling lights by the elevators flickered, threatening to burn out, and my eyes adjusted to the weak illumination as we waited.

I said, "You realize you're putting yourself in danger being seen with me, don't you?"

"If the Lord decides today is my day, I will greet Him with open arms."

The doors opened and the bright light inside the elevator radiated around us.

As we stepped on, I said, "You planned that, didn't you?"

Brother Thomas pushed the button to the fifth floor. "Going up."

Two uniform policemen stood outside Darcy's room. They stopped us at the door. Brother Thomas showed them his I.D. They complained about not being informed we were coming, but let us both in the room. The air cylinder at the top of the door hissed as it closed.

Darcy was stretched out on the hospital bed. Her eyes were closed. A large bandage covering her right shoulder and a sling holding her arm in place protruded out from a sheet covering her. An IV ran from a bag hanging on a post. It was one thing to see fellow soldiers in bad shape, but finding Darcy looking like Jo had on her last day buckled my knees.

A woman sitting beside the bed turned to look at us. She looked like an older version of Darcy, down to the blond curls and thin figure. Had to be Mrs. Wells. She said, "Yes?"

Brother Thomas put his hand on my arm to stop me from putting my foot in my mouth. He showed the woman the same identification and said, "Reverend Thomas Brown, ma'am. Call me Brother Thomas."

"I didn't request any clergy," she said.

"Yes, ma'am. I'm sorry to bother you," he said.

I blurted out, "I was with her when she got shot."

Her eyes became knife slits. "You're that Pelton character, aren't you?"

I nodded.

She yelled, "Security!"

The two officers burst in the room and grabbed us.

Mrs. Wells said, "Get them out of here."

Darcy stirred and coughed. Everyone in the room turned to her. She raised her free arm slightly and beckoned us closer.

Her mother gasped and went to her side. "What is it, dear?"

Darcy pointed at me.

I shook the cops off and walked to her.

"Mmff," she said.

I leaned in to hear her better. When I did, Darcy slapped me. Not hard, but enough to get my attention. Her coy grin said it all.

After Darcy smoothed things over for us with her mother and the cops, she said she needed to rest. Mrs. Wells, Brother Thomas, and I sat at a table in the hospital cafeteria and drank coffee from small Styrofoam cups.

"My daughter always wanted to be a reporter," Mrs. Wells said.

Brother Thomas said, "Yes, ma'am."

"I told her she didn't have to," she continued. "Darcy can do anything she wants, and not because we have money. She really is talented." She sighed. "But she loved the excitement. By the time she was eight, she was reading the paper and watching the news on television. We grounded her when we caught her trying to sneak into the den to catch the eleven o'clock news. An eight-year-old, for God's sake." She shook her head.

"It's my fault she's here," I said.

"No, it isn't," said Mrs. Wells. "If she weren't chasing your story, she'd be chasing someone else's."

"Yeah." I looked at my hands and pictured the blood still on them. "But I got her shot."

"She got herself shot," her mother said. "Though you aren't helping matters."

I glanced at her and nodded. "Yes, ma'am.

An hour later, I sat once again with Brother Thomas in his donated Volvo.

"I tried to ask Mutt how I could help him out. You know, like my uncle was doing?"

Brother Thomas started the car. "What he say?"

"He told me to go clean myself up."

"My guess is he won't be accepting anything from you."

I rubbed my dry eyes, an effect of the lingering hangover. "How's he going to make it?"

"We'll have to work on that, I guess."

"*You're* going to help me figure out how Mutt can keep his bar open?"

The big man chuckled. "Stranger things've happened. Peter walked on water until his faith gave out. I guess I'm shooting a little higher, mm-hmm."

"Yeah, like the ozone layer."

He adjusted the temperature settings on the AC. "That Mrs. Wells is one strong woman. Real cool considering what happened to her daughter."

I said, "You know, if I'd been offered the same free ride as Darcy, I'd've wrapped myself around a live oak with the fastest Porsche I could get my hands on. Or burned out on booze and parties and women."

Brother Thomas put the car in gear and drove out of the parking lot. "Sometimes, we are protected from ourselves by the very circumstances we don't like being in."

I thought about what he said the rest of the way to my car.

Patricia looked up from her desk when I walked in and slumped into one of the chairs facing her. Either there was so much work to warrant her being at the paper on a Saturday or she needed something to keep her mind occupied. With her star reporter in the hospital, I decided on the latter.

She leaned back, tapped a pen on her lips, and pointed it at me. "You don't look so hot."

"I've been getting that a lot, lately."

As if reading my mind and my condition, she went to the kitchenette and returned with two cups of coffee, the *Palmetto Pulse* logo printed on both.

"Thanks." I chose a cup and took a sip. It was good, probably Italian.

She asked, "Been by the hospital?"

The heavy weight of guilt pushed me deeper into the chair. "Just came from there."

"How's our girl?"

"She slapped me."

Patricia lowered her cup. "Mrs. Wells slapped you?"

"No. Darcy did. Shot and crippled. IV's and wires running everywhere. The cops about to haul Brother Thomas and me out the door by our collars. And our poor defenseless blond reporter grunts to get our attention."

Patricia listened, her smile growing by the second.

"Then," I continued, "she waves me over to her bedside. I lean in and she belts me."

"Ha!" Patricia sloshed coffee on her antique mahogany desk and searched for a napkin.

"The worst part was, Darcy managed to give me that trademark smirk of hers," I said. "You know. The one she uses when she's on camera."

Patricia wiped the spill with a tissue. "That's my girl."

"Yeah, a chip off her mother's block."

"So you met Mrs. Wells?" Patricia raised her eyebrows when she said it.

"She was the one having us thrown out."

"And Darcy came to your rescue." She laughed.

"Yeah," I said. "Thanks a lot."

"So what's next?"

I gulped the rest of the coffee and set the empty mug on her desk. "I need a shower and clean clothes."

Patricia waved her hand in front of her nose. "Yes, you do."

"Would you care to put your shower where your mouth is?"

"Excuse me?"

"We both agree I need a shower. And I can't go home or I might end up Darcy's roommate."

She held her hand out, palm up. "So get a hotel."

I shook my head. "Galston's probably got every hotel receptionist in the greater Charleston area on the lookout for a six-foot white guy with a busted lip. Same with the bus station, train station, and the airport. I'm pretty sure it was his two goons who managed to locate my beach hideout yesterday morning. The place wasn't even in my name."

"You're serious, aren't you?"

"As serious as Darcy's gunshot wound."

I met Patricia at her house, an old Victorian six blocks south of Calhoun Street on Montague. It was surrounded by other hundred-and-fifty-year-old homes. Some were rented by College of Charleston students while most had been purchased by young urban professionals. Patricia told me she was one of the first of this new group of yuppies to renovate a home there twenty years ago.

She offered to buy clothes for me. I was afraid of what she'd return with, but I hadn't much choice at the moment. The shower washed away the funk from the jail and the projects, and restored part of my sanity. After toweling off, I sat on a couch in Patricia's living room wearing some sort of silk nightgown with lace she'd loaned me, praying I didn't keel over and give Rogers and Wilson an opportunity to find me in it. To take my mind off dying, I turned on the TV.

Darcy's picture was all over the news. So was mine, but I was in handcuffs being escorted by my favorite detectives into the police station.

The anchorman was saying, *". . . Channel Nine News Correspondent Darcy Wells was involved in a shooting this afternoon at a motel in North Charleston. She's currently in serious condition. Local businessman, Brack Pelton, was taken into police custody for questioning. He is the nephew of Reggie Sails, who was murdered a week ago in downtown Charleston during what the police are calling an attempted robbery. For more information of this breaking story, log onto our website at . . ."*

He rattled off the address and broke for a commercial.

I sat in amazement at how the story was spun. Galston had done his homework. Nowhere was he mentioned and the blame landed on me. Well, this wasn't over. Not by a long shot.

I changed the channel. After a few minutes, I found one of the movie channels and got lost in a comedy about a redneck couple stealing a baby named after the State of Arizona. For the first time in a while, I was able to unwind. Sleep came soon after.

Two hours later, Patricia dropped shopping bags on the floor beside the couch and woke me up.

"Hope these fit," she said.

"Thanks." I peered into the first bag. "I really appreciate it."

I found several nice silk shirts in colors I had no name for, linen shorts, and leather sandals. Even silk boxer shorts. Patricia always did have expensive taste. She walked to a minibar and poured us two Dewar's on the rocks.

I said, "You spent a fortune. I can pay for this, just not at the moment."

"It's on the house," she said into her drink.

Dusk settled over the city. The sky filled with a pink-orange pillow and the colors reflected off the transom.

Patricia stared out the window. "I went to see Darcy."

"How's she doing?"

"Great." Her voice cracked when she said it.

My cell phone rang and I checked the caller I.D. before answering.

Brother Thomas said, "Brother Brack, I was wondering if you might be interested in helping me out this evening?"

"Sure. Doing what?"

"Cassie is turning her restaurant into a soup kitchen tonight and we could use more servers."

"Hold on." To Patricia I said, "How do you feel about joining me in a little volunteer work?"

Patricia didn't turn from the window or respond. She seemed deep in thought.

To Brother Thomas I said, "We're in."

Chapter Twenty-Five

While waiting for Patricia to get ready, I drove her car to Chauncey's, calling him on the way to let him know I was coming. Shelby ran down the driveway to me when I pulled up.

I knelt and scratched his fur. "How's my boy?"

"He's fine." Chauncey wore a white oxford shirt with cufflinks and held a cocktail in his hand. At least the bow tie was gone. "Hasn't eaten since yesterday and won't leave my wife's side. Lucky for you, she's out with girlfriends. You may have a tough time taking him home if she's around."

Home would be nice. To go home and put this behind me. To go back to playing with my dog in the ocean, lighting the useless citronella candles on my front porch, and sitting on my rocker minding my own business. To grieve for my uncle. To stop comparing Darcy to Jo.

Chauncey said something but I missed it.

I looked at my lawyer. "Sorry. I was somewhere else."

"That's all right," he said. "You hanging in there?"

"No," I said. "I was wearing a woman's nightgown this afternoon. The thing was trimmed out in lace."

"That could be good, or bad, depending on the situation."

"I think you mean perspective."

"That too." He rattled the ice in his tumbler. "You want something to drink?"

"No thanks."

When I asked about his dogs, he told me he had put them

upstairs so they wouldn't bother us. He led us inside and excused himself, leaving me alone with my dog. I fed Shelby and we wrestled on the floor, me not caring what it might do to my new expensive clothes. This was the first time I had been apart from him for more than a day since I got him and I didn't like it. The guilt of not feeding him since yesterday weighed heavy. I made a mental note to be here to feed him twice a day until this was over, no matter what.

Brother Thomas stood outside Cassie's restaurant talking to people in line. Patricia parked her Mercedes, which was not exactly the best vehicle to be driving at the moment. We got out and Brother Thomas greeted Patricia by kissing her hand.

She blushed. "Why, thank you."

Brother Thomas said, "I hope Brother Brack's informed you what we're doing, mm-hmm."

I said, "She can handle it."

Patricia looked around for the first time. "What is it we are doing, Brack?"

"We're about to serve the best fried chicken in Charleston," I said.

"In the lowcountry," Brother Thomas added.

Inside, Cassie stood by the front counter next to the cash register, an orange dress flowing over her full figure. When she saw us, she trotted up and took my arm. "How you been, handsome?"

Brother Thomas introduced the women.

Before they could say anything, Mutt yelled across the room. "Opie!" He trotted toward us.

We tapped fists.

He honed in on Patricia like a hawk on his prey. "You look too good to be here. What do you say we skip this? I know a nice place we can go and get to know each other."

Patricia, no mere field mouse, laughed.

Cassie grabbed him by the ear and jerked his head sideways. "You listen here, Clarence Alexander."

He howled.

She continued, "You behave yourself or I'll have your black behind tossed out so fast you won't know what hit you." She let go.

He rubbed his ear, grinned, and blew her a kiss. "I love you too, you sweet thang, you."

Cassie rolled her eyes and went into the kitchen.

Brother Thomas put us to work. When we finished pouring a hundred and twenty iced teas in plastic cups, he let the people come in and sit. Patricia and I were sent to the kitchen to get trays of biscuits and butter. We made rounds, refilling drink cups and carrying trays of chicken, potatoes, and green beans.

Two hours later, Patricia came to me and shook my arm, causing me to miss the cup I was trying to fill. The scraggly man in a dirty Panthers T-shirt, whose cup it was, got up and left, grumbling.

Patricia's complexion paled. "Sorry!" she said to the retreating man.

I asked her, "Everything okay?"

She lowered her voice. "There's a man over there wearing Reggie's necklace."

It was hard to tell that he was a white man because of the oily grease smudged on his face and arms. He had wild hair and a long beard and was eating a piece of chicken with dirty hands. Around his neck was the shell jewelry my uncle had worn since Jo gave it to him ten years ago. I went and found Brother Thomas.

"I'll understand if you want it back," he said, "under the circumstances."

I already had enough reminders of my wife and uncle. Two

storage units full, in fact. One in Charlotte and now one in Charleston.

"No," I said. "I want to know if he found anything else with it."

Brother Thomas nodded and went to the man, stooping to talk to him. I watched to see the man's expression. When Brother Thomas finished speaking, the man looked directly at me. His flashed a smile, showing a mouth of brown teeth.

This man was not my uncle's killer, too wild and ratty, but he might know something about what happened.

Brother Thomas returned. "His name is Gerald. He's been on the street for many years." He scratched his chin.

I said, "And?"

"Gerald said he found the necklace fair and square. Says if you want it back, it'll cost you, mm hmm."

"Didn't you tell him I don't want it back?"

"No, because he said he found a bunch of other stuff and it's all for sale."

"Why do I think I'm about to get scammed?"

Brother Thomas said, "Because you are. Gerald is about to take you for everything you got on you. He's got something you want, or you think you want. Either way, you're gonna pay, mm-hmm."

"Where does he want to make the exchange?" I hoped it wouldn't be a dark alley.

"I told him the only place I'd agree to was in my church," he said. "I trust you're okay with that."

"I appreciate your thoughtfulness," I said.

"Mm-hmm."

Patricia said, "I'll let Cassie know we'll be back in an hour to help clean up."

Before we made it to the church, I checked my wallet. I had about a hundred bucks.

To Patricia, I said, "How much money you got on you?"

She dug into her purse. "How much do you need?"

"Who knows what this guy wants? Give me at least another couple hundred just in case."

Without blinking, she handed me two fifties and ten twenties. I put a fifty in each back pocket and split the twenties between the two front ones. We walked into the front door of the church. The inside was dark, but I suspected Gerald was already here because the acrid smell of body odor hung heavy in the air.

Brother Thomas turned on a light and we found Gerald standing at a table in the front with a dirty green duffle bag on the floor by his feet. The odor did not get any better as we approached the homeless man.

I held out my hand in greeting. "Brack Pelton."

Gerald recoiled. "Get your hand away from me, boy!"

Brother Thomas said, "You want to do business or not?"

Gerald was a little shorter than me and I would guess at least ten years older. Although, considering his life on the street, he could be younger. He wore a gray shirt, long coat, and ripped brown pants, and his leather boots were scuffed and worn through in places. His dirty face could not hide the brown eyes that took in everything all at once. His stare seared through Brother Thomas. When the homeless man spoke, his words came out like a snarl. "Well, well, well. So this is three against one, I see. Ha! Cowards."

I turned to Brother Thomas. "Why don't you show Patricia around the place?"

When I showed no hint of resignation, Brother Thomas held out his arm for Patricia. "Care for a behind-the-scenes tour of our little house of worship?"

"Um," Patricia said.

Brother Thomas opened his mouth to say something.

Before he could I said, "Go ahead." The homeless man was

going to try something, I knew, and it would be better if Patricia were out of harm's way.

Patricia took Brother Thomas's arm and they walked to the hall leading to the offices. At the doorway she cast a glance back at me. Then they were gone.

Gerald sprang on me like a cat. "You're gonna die, rich boy!"

I was ready.

A glint of steel in his hand reflected the light. I jerked back. The knife whipped through the air, missing me by inches. He'd swung wide from his left side to his right, leaving his torso unprotected. I stepped in and delivered a hard uppercut. It went into the soft spot below his diaphragm. A whoosh of air smelling of spoiled eggs escaped his mouth. His eyes bugged out. I wrenched his arm back and twisted his hand. He released the knife. It clanged on the floor and Gerald dropped to his knees. I drew my fist and aimed for his face. All I saw was a pool of blood seeping between the cobblestones in an alley off Chalmers Street. I wanted to end the pain. End the nightmare. End the battle. I felt I could end it all here.

A voice boomed from the corner of the room. "I think you've made your point, Brother Brack."

I looked away from the angry man gasping for breath in front of me to a face of peace, of righteousness. The face of Brother Thomas. Behind him, hanging on the wall, was a cross.

I stepped on Gerald's knife, let go of his arm, and moved back, sliding the knife across the linoleum with my foot. Gerald slumped to the floor, inhaling large gulps of air. When the knife and I were a safe distance from him, I stooped and picked it up. It was a pretty decent survival knife with a six-inch blade, serrated on one side, and a stout guard. The handle was wrapped in leather. Brother Thomas approached, Patricia following. I handed the preacher the knife and lowered my hands to my sides.

Brother Thomas looked at the knife and at Gerald. "I thought we had an understanding, Gerald. You go and disgrace yourself in the Lord's house?"

Some of the fight came back into Gerald's eyes. "You was supposed to leave. I wanted what was mine."

Gerald winced when I moved toward him.

Still unwinding, I said, "What do you think I've got that's yours?"

The fear and hatred painted on his face were deeper than the lines of grease and dirt. "You got money. I can tell it a mile away. It's supposed to be mine."

"You kill my uncle?" I said, knowing he didn't.

Gerald gave me a crooked grin, exposing black and green slime between his rotted teeth. "Maybe."

" 'Maybe' will get you gutted like a fat little pig," I said. "I'll stuff an apple down your throat and throw you on a bed of coals."

"You ain't man enough to do nothing," Gerald muttered.

I took another step forward.

"Brother Brack." The steel in Brother Thomas's voice stopped me.

"You two need to stop acting like children," Patricia said, "and get down to business. That is if you're still interested in money, Gerald."

Gerald showed his slimy teeth again. "I'm always interested in money."

"Good," she said. "Then we're ready for you to show us what you've got."

He said, "You got the cash?"

"Of course we do," she said.

"Prove it."

Part of me wanted to just take the bag and leave. But I knew the man wasn't all there. I pulled out a hundred dollars in twenties from one of my front pockets.

"If that's all you got, you're wasting my time," Gerald said.

"We may be able to get more," Patricia said. "It's your turn. Show us what you've got."

Gerald huffed and grabbed the duffle bag.

I said, "You better open the bag slowly so no one gets the wrong idea."

The homeless man grunted as he unhooked the clasp and reached inside. He dug around like he was looking for something specific, growing angrier by the second, and dumped the contents on the floor. Dirty silverware and empty cans clattered on the linoleum along with filthy clothes and old magazines. A few cockroaches scampered out of the pile and Brother Thomas stepped on them before they could procreate.

Patricia said, "Why don't we start with the necklace?"

" 'Cause I don't wanna sell it," Gerald said. He continued to dig through the mound.

"Now Gerald," Brother Thomas said, "if it wasn't for the necklace, we wouldn't even be here."

"Two hundred," Gerald said.

I laid down forty bucks.

He grabbed the necklace with one hand. "That's not two hundred."

"Take it or leave it," I said.

Gerald looked at the money for a long moment before slipping the necklace over his head and laying it on the floor. He snatched up the money and stuffed it in a pocket.

"Good," Brother Thomas said. "See, that wasn't so bad."

"Let's make this easy," I said. "How much for everything you got?"

"Everything's not for sale," Gerald said.

I thought I saw a hurt look in his eyes, but it didn't stay long. He arranged his junk in piles, talking to himself as he did it. I realized how far gone the poor street bum was when his dialogue turned into a two-sided argument where he played both sides, getting louder and louder with each reply.

Patricia spoke in the sweetest voice I'd ever heard from her mouth. "Gerald, what *is* for sale?"

Her words brought him back to reality. He looked at us as if trying to figure out who we were. His focus landed on the bag. "I got lots of things for sale."

She said, "Like what?"

Gerald picked up a dinged butter knife. "I got the best silverware in Charleston."

Brother Thomas said, "What else?"

"Aluminum cans," Gerald said. "The price of aluminum is at an all-time high these days, you know."

"Sure," I said. "How much?"

"A hundred."

I laid down another two twenties.

Gerald said, "I guess you can't add good."

"How about you show us what else you got before I lose interest," I said.

Gerald stood and lunged at me.

Brother Thomas grabbed him by his collar and shoved him back onto the floor. "How about we finish this up, what do you say, Brother Gerald?"

Gerald sneered at the preacher.

Brother Thomas didn't blink.

Patricia said, "How much for the silverware?"

"Two thousand."

I counted out a hundred dollars. "What else?"

"The knife you took off me."

I gave him another twenty. "Almost out of cash, here, Gerald. Anything else?"

He sifted through pots and pans and dirty rags, talking to

himself again. Then he reached into his pocket and pulled out a change pouch. My uncle's change pouch. Patricia gasped.

He looked at her and held it up. "Five thousand bucks for this."

I pulled out both fifties.

"Not enough," Gerald said. "I want more."

Brother Thomas said, "These people come in good faith."

Gerald pointed at me. "He tried to take my head off. I want more. A lot more."

"That's all I've got," I said.

The homeless man nodded to Patricia. "She ain't coughed up no money yet."

I motioned to the pouch. "Where'd you find that, anyway?"

His beady eyes squinted into a grin. "None of your business."

Patricia showed him two hundreds. "How about now?"

Gerald stared at the money and wiped his mouth with the back of his dirty hand. "By the big parking garage."

My insides tightened. "On Cumberland Street?"

"Yep." Gerald dropped the pouch and snatched the bills.

Brother Thomas was right about Gerald cleaning us out of cash, but it was worth it. Everything I bought from Gerald was junk except for the necklace and coin pouch. Because Uncle Reggie hated wallets, didn't have credit cards, and carried his cash folded in his front pocket, the pouch became the catch-all. I always gave him a hard time about it, but he'd had it since Vietnam.

After Gerald left, I opened the change pouch, not expecting to find any coins. There weren't. Just a few scraps of paper. I unraveled a note scribbled in what I guessed was Gerald's handwriting: *The Lord giveth and the Lord taketh away.*

"Have to agree with him there." I pulled out the next piece of scrap and unfolded it. It took a few seconds to register.

"What is it?" Patricia said.

"I think it's a parking garage ticket."

Later that night I left Patricia's house, thinking a drive alone in my car might clear my head. Since Gerald had cleaned me out, I needed more cash anyway. After a stop at an ATM, I steered my car through the city. As the gas lamps and streetlights on King Street lit my way, I wondered how I was going to get at Galston. The necklace hung from the Mustang's rearview mirror like a noose, reminding me of my murdered uncle, who wore it, and my wife Jo, who bought it for him.

When I'd gotten the offer to race stock cars professionally, Jo had been so excited. We went out and celebrated, getting a nice hotel room after dinner and making love until we exhausted ourselves. If ever I'd felt my life was perfect, it was then. A few days later, her headaches started. She was gone in six months.

I crossed Calhoun and a dark Navigator with a big chrome push bar kept up a little too close. I made a slow right turn. The SUV followed. Two more rights put me back on King, which curved after it crossed Market heading toward the Battery.

A Honda Odyssey ahead of me with New Jersey tags crept along at the speed limit. I downshifted to second, cut around the Yankee-mobile, and four-wheel-drifted onto the first side street on the right. With the accelerator floored, I cranked the wheel and made a tight right-hander onto Beaufort.

I glided into a parking lot and killed the lights but kept the motor running. Wanting to reverse roles, I pulled the emergency brake and took my foot off the pedal so my taillights wouldn't give me away.

A few moments later, the SUV appeared in the street, moving slowly. Sweat poured into my silk shirt. Maybe I was in the clear. The Navigator bounced over the entrance ramp into the parking lot.

I released the parking brake, threw the gearshift into reverse, and smoked the tires out of the tight spot I was in. The lights of the sports utility grew larger in my rearview mirror as I jammed the shifter into first and got on the gas, heading for the exit to the next street.

Bullets blew out my rear window.

Glass, hot air, and lead shot over me. I crashed through the wooden barrier blocking the exit. The motor in the Mustang screamed. I made a turn onto the first side street I found. It was blocked by traffic stopped at a red light. I slammed on the brakes. The antilock system kept me from sliding into a waiting beer truck. I unlatched my seatbelt, opened the door, reached back and snatched the necklace, and dove for safety.

The Navigator plowed into my beautiful, newly painted Mustang. The front of my car embedded into the beer truck. I scrambled to the sidewalk and ran to King Street. Loud footsteps and voices followed me.

King Street didn't have nearly as many people on it as I thought. A neon sign identifying Sharky's Bar illuminated the entrance to the closest watering hole. A linebacker-sized doorman sitting on a barstool in front of the place stiff-armed me. "I.D., pal."

I glanced back. Three men rounded the corner and headed for me, two of them looking familiar—Shorty and Goatee. The third was some Asian punk. I opened my wallet and handed my license to the doorman.

He looked at the I.D. "Five bucks."

I held up a wad of twenties from the ATM proceeds and motioned to Galston's muscle. "I don't think my friends are old enough."

The doorman grinned, took the money, and pointed me in.

Once inside, I watched the three argue with the doorman until he stood up. He had a good six or seven inches on Goatee and the third guy and was a foot taller than Shorty. Probably twice as strong as all of them together. Their mouths gaped open and they backed off. They must have forgotten they had guns.

I hadn't.

The bartender came over and I ordered an iced tea and called the police on my cell. The woman on the line asked me to hold. A minute later, she returned to the line and said officers were already at the scene of the accident and to return to my car. Through the window, I saw the doorman sitting on his stool again. The goons were gone.

I spent an hour with the police, trying to explain why I had run and why I didn't know where the Navigator was. What was left of my ride was being dragged onto a flatbed. I felt nauseous. The front and rear were crunched like an accordion and all four airbags had deployed. I cleaned out my personal items and the shopping bags Patricia had given me, waved goodbye to my once beautiful baby, and took a cab to the airport. At the counter of one of the car rental kiosks, I requested the blandest car they had. The attendant did not disappoint. He handed me the keys to a silver Camry.

CHAPTER TWENTY-SIX

The best news I'd received in a long while came the next morning, Sunday, two weeks since my uncle was killed. Patricia woke me from a deep sleep on her couch and told me Darcy was out of intensive care. While I was having coffee, Brother Thomas called and wanted to know if I was interested in attending David Fisher's funeral later that afternoon. He said Justine Fisher had asked him if I was coming.

I drove to my bungalow on Sullivan's and checked the mail. With time to kill, I put on running shoes and stretched. It had been more than a week since I'd jogged, and I hit the beach at a fast pace. The sun felt hot on my back. The tobacco poison in my lungs from the cigars caused me to hack and cough the first mile before I found my old rhythm.

The surf eroded the shoreline at the tip of the island where I lived. Like most of the untouched land in Charleston County, the beachfront homes were losing ground, not to overzealous developers and retirees but to a more aggressive force, the Atlantic Ocean.

The tide was high and I ran along the sand until I came to a spot where the beach was gone and had to backtrack to a path leading to the street. I passed Fort Moultrie, the location where a haphazard garrison of Patriots had held off a well-armed British naval fleet in the Revolutionary War. The redcoats' cannonballs had done little damage to the palmetto log walls of the original garrison. Half a mile farther, I cut over to Atlantic

Street and circled back.

After the run, a shower and change of clothes left me feeling as near to my old self as possible. I walked out my front door in time to see Detectives Rogers and Wilson park their Crown Vic in my drive.

"Detectives," I said. "Nice to see you this fine, hot Sunday."

Wilson said, "Heading somewhere?"

"As a matter of fact . . ."

"Heard you got into an accident last night, Pelton," said Rogers. "Fled the scene. The news said you were drunk."

I put my sunglasses on. "Ain't life grand."

Rogers pulled his notebook out and flipped through a few pages. "We found out something."

"It's about time."

Rogers said, "The owners of the car that exploded don't want to file a report."

"You guys get promoted out of homicide?"

Wilson said, "A triggered automobile explosion could be considered attempted murder, whether they file a report or not."

I nearly pointed out that no one was in the car when it blew but decided it wouldn't help my case. "Am I a suspect?"

Wilson wiped sweat from his forehead. "It's heading in that direction."

"Then I guess you'll have to speak to my lawyer from now on. If you don't mind, I have another funeral to get to." Actually, I wanted time to feed my dog. And see Darcy. For reasons not obvious to me, that was more pressing than the funeral.

"Who died this time?" asked Wilson.

"A friend of a friend."

Rogers said, "We'll give you a ride to your car."

I started to protest when Wilson interrupted. "It was almost a good idea to leave your rental two streets away. Except the owners of the house you parked in front of called Sullivan's Island P.D. to complain. They had the car towed. Did I mention my cousin works night shift there? He knows I'm on this case and, when they tracked the car to you, gave me a call."

When I walked into her room, Darcy was propped up on her bed reading a magazine. Sheets pulled to her waist exposed a light blue pajama top.

I said, "How're you doing, kiddo?"

She looked at my suit and the bouquet of flowers and gold box of candy I was carrying. "What's this, another date?"

I felt a little stupid and said, "I didn't think you'd be up." Then I felt *really* stupid and put the flowers in a vase that an aide sat on the table. The box of candy went there too. "Where's your mother?"

"She said she'd be here in an hour."

I pulled a chair over. "She doesn't like me."

Darcy closed the magazine. "Actually, she does. What she doesn't like is me being a reporter."

"Gotta do what you love. So where's the fiancé? I was looking forward to meeting him."

"He isn't one for hospitals." She finished with a tight-lipped smile.

Deciding not to push it, I just nodded.

She said, "Is that a box of Godiva?"

I fetched the chocolates, removed the cellophane, and gave her the box.

She selected a starfish-shaped piece and nibbled at it. "I looove Godiva." She held what was left of the piece between two fingers. "So tell me, what do you love?"

I sat in the chair. "My dog. In fact, I had to hide him at Chauncey's until this blows over. I just left there from feeding him."

She finished off the starfish and chose the cherry cordial. "Anything else?"

Something about watching her eat the candy relaxed me.

"The beach. At one time, I loved racing." I also loved Jo and my uncle, but it hurt too much to say.

"I read about your career," she said. "You were some up-and-coming driver on the verge of making it big."

"What do you mean you read about it?"

"I looked you up."

"When?"

"When all this started," she said. "I always do research. I don't like surprises."

I picked a piece of candy from the box. "Neither do I."

She looked at me for a moment and said, "Suzy's dead."

I stopped chewing.

Darcy continued. "My source said she was found in an apartment in North Charleston. What was left of her, anyway."

"What was left of her?"

"Someone used her for target practice. Mostly nine millimeter bullets, which didn't leave a lot for identification."

"The kids in the back room of the Red Curtain brothel all wore holsters and nines. And they seemed more than capable of shooting a defenseless kid like Suzy." Then it hit me. "I think those idiots were the ones that tried to kill us. The detectives told me the one I hit was named Johnny."

"That's pretty thin, Brack."

"The silver chain."

"What silver chain?"

I leaned forward. "Remember the kid that opened the back door and told us where Suzy was?"

"Not really."

"He had a thick chain around his neck. I think I saw it when he dove for cover."

Darcy's eyes met mine. "But it doesn't make any sense."

"It does if the ones managing the Red Curtain figured out who you are."

Darcy bit into a cordial. "So what's our next move?"

I blew out a long breath. "Your next move is to lay low and heal up."

She said, "Are you kidding me? They made a huge mistake. I'm going to put their pictures all over the news."

I propped a foot on the lower rail of her bed. "Your mother said you wouldn't quit."

"It's what makes me the brains of the operation."

"And the looks," I said.

She chose another piece of chocolate. "How perfectly chauvinistic of you."

"So, why don't you tell me about the source who set us up?"

She raised the bed with a remote control. "Not much to tell. It was an anonymous call. A man. My voicemail had only time, place, and that it was for my story on Galston."

"We were set up."

"Yes. And I'm supposed to be released soon. The guards watching the door are more interested in catching me getting a sponge bath than in my well-being. Any chance you can get me out of here in one piece?"

"I'm not sure I'm the best one for that. Galston's crew chased me through downtown last night."

She pointed to the flatscreen hanging on the wall. "I saw it on the news. They showed a clip of the cops interviewing you and suggested alcohol might be involved. You know, you're becoming a celebrity these days."

"Let me guess. They never said I was drunk or that someone had run into my car."

"Of course not."

★ ★ ★ ★ ★

At the funeral service, Justine's inner determination to be strong masked the sorrow in her face. I knew this because I'd been at the same point. Maybe I still was. Like David Fisher, Jo died too young. While Jo and I didn't have children, the Fishers had two and it took a cold-hearted individual to kill a man with a family. The Fisher children, a little boy and girl, sat with their mother and cried.

During the reception Brother Thomas and I were standing by the fruit tray when Justine approached. She wore the prerequisite black dress and simple gold earrings, bracelet, and her wedding band. I'd worn mine through my tour of Afghanistan underneath my uniform gloves, and wondered how long Justine would wear hers.

She patted our arms. "It was so nice of you two to come."

"I am indeed sorry for your loss," Brother Thomas said, setting his plate of hors d'oeuvres on a table and taking her hand in his. "If there is anything I can do for you, don't hesitate to ask, mm-hmm."

Justine squeezed his arm. "You've been a good friend to talk to, Brother. I was wondering if I could borrow Mr. Pelton."

"Of course," Brother Thomas said. "I need another glass of punch, anyway."

He gave me a curt nod and walked away.

Justine said, "Um . . . I wanted to thank you for your kindness the other day."

"It was really generous of you to give Brother Thomas the car and other things," I said. "How are you holding up?"

"One of my neighbors purchased the house," she said, not answering my question.

"That was quick."

"Luck, really. They stopped by to see how I was doing and when they found out I was selling, made an offer. I think they bought it for their daughter. The movers came and packed our things yesterday and I have a room at Charleston Place."

"Nice hotel."

"I had always dreamed of spending a night there," she said. "My parents are taking the kids back to Virginia with them tonight. I'm staying behind for the closing."

I waited for her to say something else but she didn't.

"Justine?"

"Yes?" she said.

"Are you all right?"

She hesitated. "I was wondering if you would have dinner with me tonight."

I didn't answer right away. For the first time in a long time, I felt something other than my own sorrow.

"It's okay if you don't want to," she said. "I understand."

"What do you like to eat?"

After spending time with Shelby, including making sure he ate dinner, I headed downtown. The Charleston Place hotel had marble floors, expensive shops, and high-dollar rates. Justine had given me her room number and I walked past the reception desk to the elevators.

At exactly seven, I knocked on her door. When it opened, the faint scent of Chanel Number Five escaped from the room. Jo had worn it often, and the reminder distracted me until I looked at Justine. She had changed from funeral-black into a yellow sundress. It accentuated the light freckles on her face, chest, and arms, and the wedding ring on her finger. The second attractive female I'd been out with this side of a week, and no future potential with either of them. Something told me I set it up that way on purpose.

We walked to High Cotton on East Bay Street, the restaurant Uncle Reggie wanted to meet me in for my birthday. Justine had made a reservation and we were seated at a table in the back. The waiter brought our drinks.

I squeezed a lemon into my iced tea. "Thanks for inviting me."

"I wasn't very nice when we first met."

"Under the circumstances . . ." I took a drink and didn't finish what I was about to say.

An aura of hurt lingered in the lines of her young face. The waiter returned with a basket of cornbread, told us about the specials, and took our order.

After he left, Justine said, "So how did you cope with losing your wife?"

"I drank."

"You're not drinking now."

I took a piece of cornbread and buttered it. "It didn't help so I joined the Marines and went to Afghanistan."

"Did that help?"

I set the cornbread on my bread plate and wiped my hands with a napkin.

Justine said, "I'm sorry. We can talk about something else."

"No. It's all right. The hard thing is realizing I lost more than three years of my life." I met her eyes and decided to let it all out. "I spent the time trying to kill myself without actually pulling the trigger. The booze was for numbing the pain, but I couldn't bear it any longer. I wanted to die, but I didn't want to do it myself. When I got there, I did everything I could to fulfill my death wish—suicide raids, reconnaissance, escort missions, you name it. Guys were getting killed just walking around the base and there I was hunting for a bullet with my name on it and didn't find it."

"How are you doing with it now?"

I picked up the cornbread. "I'd say I'm better, but then someone murdered my uncle."

"Brother Thomas said you've been trying to find out who did it. You think it's connected to David's death?"

"Yes. I haven't found the right link yet. It's a good thing you're leaving soon because I think this is a dangerous place right now. The other night, a friend of mine got shot."

Justine flushed. "The Channel Nine News girl. I've been following you in the news."

I said, "You seem to be handling all of this pretty well. Either you're a good actress, or you're stronger than I am."

"I don't think it's sunk in yet. I've been cooped up in my house with the TV, my kids, and funeral arrangements. It's nice to be able to talk to someone I don't have to sugarcoat things for."

I watched her eat a scallop. "How is it?"

She nodded, her mouth full. Her manners were much better than mine. I grabbed a piece of shrimp out of the grits on my plate and ate it in one bite, pinching the tail to get all the meat. Our conversation drifted to the lighter side of things. We talked about our favorite parts of Charleston. She described her sorority days at the University of Virginia and laughed when I told her she was one of those girls engineering majors like me dreamed about when they weren't cramming for tests.

She snatched the check before the waiter could hand it to me. "I asked you, remember?"

I raised my hands in surrender.

As we left the restaurant, we encountered a crowd of people meandering along the slab-stone sidewalks of East Bay.

I offered my arm. "Would you like to walk off dinner?"

She accepted and we made our way past tourist shops and bars, the sounds of music escaping from open doors, and stopped at the big pavilion overlooking the Cooper River by Waterfront Park. I rested my hands on the railing. Justine cradled herself in her arms and I could sense a mood shift.

I said, "It feels awkward being out with someone else, doesn't it?"

She closed her eyes and tears came again. "What am I going to do?"

I put my arm around her. "People will tell you to get on with your life. I haven't, so don't use me as a role model."

She rested her head against my shoulder.

I said, "After basic training, my team got a three-day pass. The best thing I can say about those days is I don't remember a lot. The worst thing I can say is I remember enough. Like waking one morning in bed next to a woman I didn't know and couldn't recall meeting. Cigarette butts and empty liquor bottles littered the floor. A shirt with the name of the bar I'd been in the night before hung off a vanity mirror. I barely made it to the bathroom before I threw up. The sleeping beauty in the bed snored away. I told myself she was a bandage on loneliness. I mean, she meant nothing to me, right? Just someone to use. In my mind, the pain of losing my wife justified everything. And I truly believed it. Until a little boy walked into the room—which turned out to be the master bedroom in the back of a mobile home in some God-awful trailer park. The little boy seemed used to strange men in his mother's bed."

I felt Justine's breath on my neck and found it distracting.

"I guess I told you all this to say it might be in your own children's best interests if you didn't end up in a trailer park after a three-day bender merely because the world isn't fair."

Our return trek to Charleston Place was quiet, neither of us saying much. We wandered over the broken and cracked sidewalk and avoided crunching palmetto bugs under our feet in front of the U.S. Custom House building. At her hotel, a black Escalade pulled to the curb and stopped. Galston got out. His bald head shone in the streetlights. And I didn't have a gun.

I turned to Justine. "You better get inside. I don't want you to be part of this."

She said, "Is it about your uncle?"

"Yes." I looked at Galston and felt my insides burn.

She kissed me on the cheek and was gone.

Shorty and Goatee flanked Galston.

I said, "You think three of you are enough? Where's your Asian backup? You know, the ones who do the dirty work."

"Easy, now," said the tall man with the goatee.

I took a step toward them. "I'm afraid I've got to turn down your offer."

Galston wiped his forehead with a handkerchief and fixed his gaze on me. "Just like that?"

"That's what the cops asked me when I repeated my uncle's last words before he bled to death."

The bald man said, "I didn't have anything to do with that."

"Sure you didn't. And your boys here didn't try to run me down the other night, either."

Galston jerked his head toward Shorty, looking like he wanted to ask him a question.

Goatee said, "It doesn't have to go like this."

I shook my head. "You set me and Darcy up at the motel. You're going to pay for all of it."

They were less than ten feet away. I planned my next moves. Shorty would have to go first because he had something to prove and would fight dirty. Goatee was next because he was as cautious as Shorty was eager. Galston would fight like a girl. We stood in front of the five-star hotel staring at each other. Shorty made a move. Goatee was a split-second behind. And a split-second too late.

I drove my fist hard into Shorty's gut. He dropped to his knees. Goatee pulled something out of his pocket. I caught him with a right hook to the jaw and he fell backwards. Galston stepped out of the way as Goatee hit the ground. The short Latino driving the Escalade stood on the running board, extending his arms over the roof. I saw the pistol in his hand and ducked around the corner before he could fire. Police sirens echoed off the buildings, getting louder. I kept on running.

Chapter Twenty-Seven

After a restless night at Patricia's, I drove my rental Camry to the Isle of Palms. The security guards at the gated entrance to Chauncey's neighborhood stopped me long enough to get clearance. Chauncey must not get many visitors on Monday mornings. I parked in the drive. When I got out of the car I felt something poke my leg.

"Hey, boy," I said.

Shelby barked.

I sat on the concrete and let him lick my face. "I missed you, too, buddy."

He smelled like coconut and his coat was trimmed and shiny.

Chauncey walked out of the garage, hands in his pockets.

I scratched behind Shelby's ears. "Thanks, um, for cleaning him up."

"Don't worry. I'm adding it to your bill."

Trish stood next to Chauncey. "You aren't coming to take him away, are you?"

"No, ma'am," I said. "I came by to see how he was doing and to feed him."

"He keeps me company," she said. "We have our dogs groomed every month. The groomers were going to be here anyway and his fur was a little matted. I had his claws trimmed too. I hope you don't mind."

At least she didn't have them painted pink while she was at it. "He looks good and probably feels better, too."

"Oh, he's such a pretty dog," she said. "You should keep him like this."

My dog, my companion, the one I rescued from the shelter, brought home, and fed and took care of for the past six months, left my side and went to Trish.

Sitting on the driveway by myself, I said, "He's always been a sucker for the ladies."

Trish leaned down, let him lick her face, and walked into the house. Shelby gave me a quick glance and trotted along after her like the dog he was. I watched the four-legged freeloader go inside.

Chauncey said, "Why didn't you call me after you had your accident?"

I stood up. "It wasn't my fault. They chased me."

"That's not what I saw on the news," he said.

"They shot out the rear window of my car," I said. "I tried to get away and they rammed me into a delivery truck. I'm not sure why the news got the story wrong."

He took out a pipe and stuck it in his mouth. "I see."

"No, I don't think you do see, Chauncey. Galston is out of control. He needs to be stopped. He and his goons tried again last night. Four against one."

Chauncey put his hands up. "So what can I do to help?"

I thought about the detectives finding me yesterday through my rental car.

"For starters, I need another set of wheels," I said. "Not in my name and the faster the better."

Brother Thomas sat in his office behind the massive, cluttered desk. The captain's chair creaked under his massive girth as he leaned back.

"Let me get this straight," he said, his arms folded across his ample stomach. "You want me to escort Ms. Wells out of the hospital?"

"Not just you," I said. "You and some of your church members. Mutt, too."

"And she was admitted because someone shot her." He gave me the same look I was getting from a lot of people lately. The one suggesting my faculties were not fully operational.

I leaned forward and gestured with open palms. "I can't be sure they weren't aiming for me."

He laced his fingers together as if in prayer. "Mm-hmm."

"Besides, I don't want her to be recognized when she leaves."

"And you think a white girl being surrounded by a bunch of Negroes is camouflaged?"

"We could disguise her."

He opened his hands. "As what, a black girl? That'd take a lot of work."

"I was thinking of a big hat and long sleeves."

His hands came to rest on his desk. "Mm-hmm."

I took a sip of takeout coffee I'd purchased at a convenience store and winced at how bad it was. "Look, Brother. I don't have a lot of options, here."

"Why is she your cross to bear?"

I sat the coffee cup on the edge of his desk. "Like I said, I'm not sure who the shooter was aiming for. Darcy did the spin piece on the men with the prostitute. They worked for Galston."

Brother Thomas raised his eyebrows.

I could read the doubt on his face. "I'm the one who blew up their car and put her on the story."

"You can't save everyone, Brother Brack." His voice had the same tone the headshrinker used on me after Jo died. It didn't work then either.

"I'm not trying to save everyone," I said. "I'm trying to

protect one woman."

"By endangering members of my congregation."

"This man, Galston, buys properties like the one you showed me. He buys them and sits on them, collecting federal money and not doing any cleanup. And I think he had something to do with shooting my uncle."

"If you know so much, how come you haven't informed the po-lice?"

I folded my arms. "They closed the case on my uncle once already. I wouldn't be surprised if they try and do it again."

"Young black men die here all the time. Think the police come around and ask why, much less open a case?"

"So you're not going to help Darcy because she's white?"

The venom in my words showed in the way Brother Thomas's face hung in mid-contortion. He started to say something else but stopped himself.

I got up to leave.

He cleared his throat. "Wait."

Channel Nine News ran a special segment on Darcy during the six o'clock broadcast. They reviewed her career and how she ended up in the hospital, and showed pictures of her with balloons and flowers scattered around her room. They casually announced in the course of the story she would be released in the morning and asked her what she was going to do once she got out. What a beautiful setup.

While the news was on, a group of parishioners entered the hospital and spread out over the fifth floor. Darcy's room number at the time happened to be five-twenty-one. The parishioners, members of the Church of Redemption, donned their Sunday best. The women wore bright dresses and big hats. The men had slick suits, dazzling ties, and shiny shoes. Everyone was black and Brother Thomas was in charge.

The faithful went room to room greeting each patient and giving away bibles purchased with part of the cash Patricia, Darcy, and I had found in the crab pots. Before *Wheel of Fortune* came on at seven, the group had made the rounds and left. And room five-twenty-one was empty.

Chauncey called and said he had a car waiting for me in the parking garage close to his office. I said goodbye to the Camry at the airport's rental car return and took a cab downtown. What I found was a used Audi, a charcoal gray four-door bomber with twin turbos and a six-speed transmission. It looked like a thousand other yuppie-mobiles trolling the streets of our fair city, perfect for stealth cruising. I pressed the unlock button, opened the door, and eased into the driver's seat. The bolsters held me firmly in place and I shut the door. The key fob went into the ignition and a chime greeted me. I pushed in the clutch and pressed the Start button. The engine fired to life with a snarl. I backed out of the spot and headed to the exit. Two blocks over, I hung a left onto East Bay Street and took the entrance ramp onto the new bridge over the Cooper River.

"Let's see what you've got." I floored the loud pedal in third gear. The turbos spooled up and pushed me back into the seat. I let off the gas before it hit the triple digits. Not as fast as my Mustang, but Chauncey had done well.

CHAPTER TWENTY-EIGHT

Since I needed another gun and didn't want a record of it, I went to the library, signed for a computer, and found on the Internet a local gun show in North Charleston. Suspicious people, and those of us with citations for discharging a weapon in a residential neighborhood, could still exercise our right to bear arms. I just had to be sneaky about it. And lucky for me, Big Al had a booth at the show.

"Back for another watch?" he joked when I strolled up.

"Afraid not," I said.

"Stereo, right?"

"I need another piece."

"I saw you on the news," he said. "You switching to moving targets?"

I tried to read him but he didn't have a tell.

His eyes went to the money clip I took from my pocket. He said, "I happen to have come across another forty-five in. It's nickel-plated."

"I'll take it," I said. "And something for a backup."

"Backup? What are you going to do, settle the score with the federal army?"

"Something like that."

He rummaged through a box. "Let's see . . . I got a small twenty-two caliber. It'll fit in your pocket. Of course, I wouldn't put it there. Be afraid of shooting off the family jewels." His huge body moved in waves as he guffawed.

"Sold."

The transaction was done in cash, no records. I walked out lighter by six hundred-dollar-bills.

My favorite gun range had all the bullets I could ask for. And it was open late. I spent a lot of money on shells so the wrinkled old man let me use one of his lanes for free. While he set the target, I loaded clips for the twenty-two. The small pistol popped in my hand and had little recoil. Then I pulled out the cannon.

The forty-five boomed. I took a black marker I'd purchased at a drug store, drew Galston's melon head on the target, and practiced blowing the seeds out between his ears until the clips were empty. Before leaving, I bought more shells and reloaded the clips.

Lastly, I stopped at Chauncey's to thank him for the car and to feed Shelby.

I spent the night at my bungalow on Sullivan's with both pistols close by. The Audi sat in the driveway of a vacant house for sale down the street. The next morning, Tuesday, Patricia woke me early by calling to say she'd meet me at my uncle's bar.

After another stop to feed Shelby breakfast, which did not go well because he barely looked at me as he ate, and went to Trish when he was done, I drove to my bar. In case anyone was watching, I parked at a beach access half a mile away from the Cove and walked to it along the surf, my sandals swinging from my hand. Low tide widened the shoreline. Several volleyball nets were set up for the day and in full use. Two-man teams played barefoot in the fine-grained sand. I stayed close to the tide and let the water cool my feet.

The sun was bright in the cloudless sky and reflected off the gentle surf. The water and the ocean air created a peace unique in its ability to erase the stresses of the world. I climbed the wooden steps on the backside of the Pirate's Cove, stopping halfway to put on my sandals. The superheated wood burned the bottom of my feet. The Cove didn't open for another fifteen minutes and the back door was still locked. I pulled out a set of keys and let myself in. The alarm should have been on but it wasn't. I reached for the forty-five. "Paige?"

Paige poked her head out of the office door. "Brack?"

As I got closer, I saw she had a baseball bat in her hands.

I said, "You okay?"

"No, I'm not," she said. "It's really tough to run this business when I have to worry about when I'm going to see you on the news again."

I nodded.

She leaned the bat against the wall beside the door. "What am I supposed to do if something happens to you?"

I had no will and no heirs. All my stuff—everything of Uncle Reggie's in one storage locker, and Jo's personal things I couldn't bring myself to give away in another unit—would be auctioned off to the highest bidder. "I'll make a will if it'll make you feel better."

She stomped over and smacked me on the shoulder. "I don't want you to make a will, you stupid oaf. I want you to stop being so careless with your life. You may not think you have anyone left who cares about you, but you do. I do. You're the only family Simon and I have left."

She was right, of course. I had all but stopped caring about anything when Jo died. What little compassion I had left vanished with Uncle Reggie in the alley. I was a train wreck looking for a busy intersection. Paige showed her stress in the dark circles around her eyes.

"I'm sorry," I said.

"You should be," she said. "I've been left in the background seeing you every other day on the news after some gun fight or car wreck. It's got to stop."

"You want to close up the bar and take time to rest?"

"Are you even listening to me? I'm not asking for a vacation. I'm asking you to think about what you're doing. For once, think about something besides yourself, Brack."

"I can't let his death go. The thought of someone getting away with killing him is too much. I'm not sleeping well. I'm not eating well. Basically, I'm a mess. But I'm onto them, Paige."

"And when you find them what are you going to do? Have you thought that far ahead?"

I didn't say anything.

"Just as I thought," she said. "You're planning to kill them, aren't you?"

I muttered something.

"I didn't hear you."

"Yes."

"Then everyone loses. Don't you see? Reggie's dead. You'll go to jail. And none of that is going to bring him back."

Brother Thomas's words came to mind. *Man doesn't have the right to avoid reaping what he sows.* My eyes moved past Paige to my uncle's barstool.

"Look at me," she said.

I did.

She put her arms on my shoulders and faced me. "You think you're onto them and I believe you. You are the smartest person I know. Smarter than your uncle. He said so. The problem is you're too smart for your own good." She wiped tears from her cheeks. "I believe you will catch whoever did this awful thing. That isn't the issue. The issue is they will kill you when you do. You might get a few of them, but how many close calls have you had already? No one is that lucky forever."

A knock at the front door made her jump. I went to the door to let Patricia in. It was time to open so I left the door unlocked.

She followed me into the bar area where Paige stood with her arms cradled across her chest.

Patricia gave me a *What did you do now?* face. "Is everything alright, Paige?"

"Sure," Paige said, snapping out of her trance. "Everything's grand. Can I get you something, Patricia? How about coffee?"

Patricia nodded. "That would be nice, thank you."

Paige set three cups of coffee on one of the tables and we sat. Vivaldi's *Four Seasons* chimed in Patricia's purse and she answered her phone. I sipped my coffee and tried to enjoy the taste. The habits of my mind wanted to take me to the dark places where the ghosts of my life haunted me whenever I gave them the chance. I struggled to stay in the light and keep it together.

Patricia ended her call.

I didn't say anything.

"You haven't asked me what I want to talk to you about," she said.

"You're right. What have you got?"

She pulled out a sheet of paper. "It took digging, but I found information about the owners of the three sites listed on the memory stick. I found out which law firm brokered all the deals, anyway. I should have known."

I said, "Known what?"

"There isn't much in this town I don't know," Patricia said. "As soon as the thumb drive led us to land acquisitions, I should have known whom to call. Only a few firms handle real estate law here—the big-ticket properties in particular. I found out when the current owners purchased each property. After I saw which law firm was on the first one, I should have made the connection."

Paige said, "What connection?"

"When outside companies come in and buy land, they have

their own lawyers. But in each of these cases, a local firm was used. The same local firm, Ketting, Fowler, and Reid. One that caters exclusively to the Charleston elite."

I sat back in my chair, still fidgeting with my cup.

Patricia said, "See what I'm saying? It's someone lo—"

"Someone local," I said. "Someone like Galston."

Patricia nodded.

I said, "But why? Why would someone like him, with old family money and connections all over the state, buy them? If he did, which we haven't proven yet. And why is he sending his goon squad after me?"

"That I don't know." The *Four Seasons* chimed again. Patricia answered the call and listened. "What? Why aren't you at home resting?" A pause. "Where are you?" Her eyes opened wide. "We're on our way." She pressed the End button. "Detective Rogers was found dead from a gunshot wound."

Darcy stood outside a taped-off barrier the police had strung around an abandoned warehouse in the old port district. A group of people stood with her. Everyone's attention focused on the open door of the warehouse. Police cruisers and an ambulance were parked inside the tape line and several officers and crime-scene technicians kept busy.

Darcy's arm was in a sling, but otherwise she looked healthy, in fact ruddy, like she'd recently spent time in the sun. She waved Patricia and me over with her free arm. I found it hard to believe four days ago she was listed in critical condition. Aside from the visible changes in her appearance like the bandages and sling, what changed the most were her eyes. Gone was the gleam of childlike inquisitiveness. In its place I saw a hardness I'd seen men get in war. After the first shelling, idealistic fun and games were over.

Darcy held a notebook. "They found him this morning. From

what I can gather, he was alone. Camera crew's on the way."

Patricia used a hand to shield her eyes from the sun's glare off the upper windows of the warehouse. "Are they calling it murder or suicide?"

"They haven't made any official statements," Darcy said, "but it looks like murder."

Wilson emerged from the entrance and spoke with a uniform.

I called out to him and he saw me. He turned to say something more to the uniformed officer and joined us.

"Good news travels fast, I see." He spoke with no humor in his voice or expression. "What are you doing here, Pelton?"

Darcy said, "Detective Wilson, can you confirm the identity of the victim?"

"No comment." Wilson stuck a finger in my chest. "What's up with you bringing the press?"

"They brought me," I said.

"Well, since you're here, it will save me the trouble of having to track you down. Stay put. I've got something for you to look at."

He turned and walked inside the building. After a few minutes, two uniformed officers came out and escorted me into the roped-off area.

Just inside the open door, one of the officers said, "Hold on."

I stopped, my eyes adjusting to the darkness. Wilson held out several evidence bags in his gloved hands. "Recognize any of these items?"

Ms. July stared at me through the clear plastic of one bag. The spreadsheet pages were in another. All taken from my home when it was broken into. And my fingerprints were probably still on them.

"Wilson, what would make you think I'd know what these are?"

He pointed to Ms. July. "Your birthday is marked on the

calendar, unless you know anyone else with the name Brack. The spreadsheets were found with it. I figured they might be connected."

"They're my uncle's," I said, remembering I shouldn't let on I'd had them. "They must have been taken when his place got trashed. Maybe now you'll believe he was killed for a reason."

He thrust the bags at one of the officers and grabbed me by the shirt. "Are you telling me how to do my job?"

I let him vent. It wouldn't get me anywhere to provoke him further.

The other uniformed officer came up beside him. "Easy there, Detective."

Wilson gripped my shirt for a second longer, let go, and walked away.

The other men working the scene—I counted five of them—had stopped what they were doing to watch us.

Patricia and Darcy spent the rest of the day composing the story for the evening news. I stayed at the Cove until seven, both guns close at hand, and went to Chauncey's to feed Shelby before crashing at Patricia's house.

CHAPTER TWENTY-NINE

Wednesday at three-forty-three in the morning, a neighbor of mine on Sullivan's Island called nine-one-one emergency to report a loud boom and a bright flame coming from a window of my bungalow. By the time the fire department organized, which was within five minutes, the wooden structure built a century ago was completely engulfed. After realizing I wasn't trapped inside, the firefighters made the wise decision to protect the other homes nearby from the flames. My house burned to the ground, taking my Jeep parked in the backyard with it. Sullivan's Island P.D. phoned my cell, waking me from a deep sleep in Patricia's guest bedroom to give me the good news.

As the sun came up, Patricia and I stared silently at the charcoal remains of my bachelor-pad bungalow. Charred footings jutted out of the ground like an artist's interpretation of Armageddon. I supposed this was Galston's way of getting my attention, as if shooting at me wasn't enough. Unless someone was trying to help with the termite problem I'd been fighting since I bought the place. My homeowner's insurance company, the ones that promised to always be there for me in trying times, decided to initiate an arson investigation. I told the agent no investigation was needed. It was arson.

He wasn't amused and mentioned something about me being upgraded to high risk. I suppose that was because they also covered my car insurance. A new paint job followed by a total loss on a brand-new car might have had something to do with his need to recoup the claim costs.

A couple hours later, once my unhappy dog had been fed his breakfast, I sat in a beach chair on the upper deck of the Pirate's Cove staring at the ocean and the whitecaps relentlessly pursuing the shore. A layer of SPF 8 sunscreen covered my back while sunglasses hid my eyes. I chewed on a Cuban cigar, nursed an iced tea, and thought it had been a stupid idea to leave my guns in the Audi. At least Chauncey had been smart enough to pull strings and register the car under a fictitious company.

"Stand up slowly, Pelton," a loud voice behind me said. "You're under arrest."

I turned in time to see two officers in uniform rush me and grab my arms.

"What's the charge this time? Trying to enjoy the day?"

Chauncey sat beside me in the interrogation room. He'd advised me not to say anything and I was inclined to go along with it this time. The door to the room opened and Detective Wilson came in holding a clear evidence bag, one with a Glock semiautomatic pistol showing through. He turned on the recording equipment and poked the evidence bag in front of me. "Recognize this?"

"Mr. Pelton doesn't wish to make a statement at this time," Chauncey said.

"On the hook for three murders, one of them a cop," Wilson said. "He better start talking."

I watched the bag with the gun dangle in the detective's hand before he set it in the middle of the table.

"Maybe you can help us out," Chauncey said.

Wilson sat in one of the chairs facing us. "How's that, counselor?"

Chauncey placed his elbows on the table. "What makes you think my client committed three murders?"

Detective Wilson lifted the bag again. "Ballistics shows that bullets fired from this weapon killed Reginald Sails, David Fisher, and Detective Hamilton Rogers."

It took me a few seconds to comprehend what he'd just said. "So you're finally going to call my uncle's death a murder. It's about time."

"The gun was discovered at your residence, Mr. Pelton. 315 Osceda Street, Sullivan's Island."

"Yeah, right," I said.

"The firemen found it among the charred rubble." Wilson set the bag on the table. "Unfortunately, no fingerprints were located on the weapon and it's unregistered."

Chauncey said, "My client has no knowledge of any weapon found in his house."

Wilson raised his eyebrows. "Your client has already been charged with firing a weapon in a residential neighborhood."

"That is under appeal," Chauncey said.

"Haven't you figured out yet that I'm being set up?" I asked Wilson. "That whoever murdered my uncle also trashed his house and my bungalow looking for something or trying to get me to quit looking for him, killed David Fisher, shot Darcy Wells, wrecked my car, and shot your partner?"

Chauncey put his hand on my arm as if to stop me but I shook him off.

"You really think I killed my own uncle?"

Wilson assumed his favorite position—he folded his arms across his paunch. "You were in the alley with him. Makes sense to me."

Chauncey stood. "We'll see you in court."

"I was at the Pirate's Cove when Fisher was killed," I said. "I've got the whole wait staff as my alibi."

The frown left Wilson's face. "How do you know when it happened?"

"I've got a good idea," I said. "Check the cell phone records. His and mine. They'll tell you I talked to him a few times. You'll be able to track which towers my signal bounced from. If that's not good enough, there are a bunch of witnesses who saw me at the bar."

Still standing, Chauncey tapped the table. "I'll definitely see you in court, Detective Wilson. Not just for these outlandish allegations, either. I plan on filing a harassment suit against the Charleston Police Department."

Wilson held up a hand. "Hold on a minute."

A knock at the door caused us to turn our heads. Wilson walked out of the room, closing the door behind him.

"Ten to one we're out of here in fifteen minutes," Chauncey said.

"That's nice and all," I said, "but someone killed my uncle and two others—one a cop. This isn't over yet."

Chauncey was right, of course. Wilson came in the room and kicked me loose.

"You know," Chauncey said on our way out the door, "you're more than welcome to come and stay with Trish and me."

"I appreciate it," I said.

We stopped in a corridor.

He said, "You going to be all right?"

I nodded.

"I've got a court appearance to make this morning so I have to say goodbye for now."

"Thanks Chauncey—for everything."

"Don't thank me yet."

I watched him walk away.

Wilson came up to me. "If I find out you had a hand in Rogers's shooting," he said, poking me in the chest again, "I'm going to feed you to the sharks."

I held his glare. "Don't blame me. Your Rolex-wearing partner was dirt and you know it."

I saw him swing his fist but chose not to stop it. The impact was harder than I expected. Real hard. Like my head was a bell and his fist the gong. I hit the floor hard, too. When the ringing stopped, I lifted myself up and waited for the cobwebs to clear.

"That all you got?" I slurred.

Wilson wore the pain of his partner's dishonesty like a badge. His fists were clenched, ready for the next round. Two men jumped in and restrained his arms.

"Come on, Wilson," said one of them. "Let's take a walk."

Wilson's gaze stayed fixed on me as the men guided him into another room.

A uniformed man said, "Are you okay?"

I spit blood onto the floor of the police station and grinned and felt a welt forming on the side of my face. "Tops."

Sometimes, the only way to feel alive is to feel pain.

I didn't press charges against Wilson. How could I? My uncle kept a lot from me. I guessed Wilson got a good taste of the same thing from his partner. I was tired of mooching from friends and found an old motor court north of Mount Pleasant on Seventeen, renting a room under an alias and paying in cash. If Galston wanted to come and get me, he'd have to work for it. The woman behind the counter barely looked away from a soap opera on the television when she handed me a form to fill out and the key. I decided my new name was Cary Bogart, a tribute to two classic tough guys. She stuck the form in a folder without a glance. I took the key and left.

My luggage consisted of shopping bags full of clothes Patricia had bought me and toiletries I'd picked up at a drugstore on the way. Other than my dog, the Pirate's Cove, and two storage units of stuff I didn't want to deal with, it was all I had left.

The bruise from Wilson's sucker punch wasn't bad. After a hot shower, I donned a new silk shirt, linen shorts, and cologne—all of them Patricia's choices—and felt like a new man. I invited Darcy over.

"How you feeling, kiddo?" I asked when I answered the door.

"Better than you look." Her eyes wandered over my room. "You sure have interesting taste. This place is a bigger dump than the last one. At least that dump had a beach view to make up for it. This place doesn't have anything except a trailer park."

"I know. It's perfect, isn't it?"

"If you say so."

We sat in front of my small cottage in the motor court and drank iced tea from sweating glasses. Worn-out lawn chairs were included with the room. I treated myself to one of the Cuban cigars. The bug zapper hanging on the side of the office a hundred feet away popped and snapped as another mosquito met its end. Aside from three junkers on the opposite end of the lot, one of them on blocks, we had the place to ourselves. A slight breeze blew through and took the edge off the heat rising from the asphalt under our feet.

Darcy said one of her sources told her Detective Wilson had gotten suspended and after an hour, she left, saying something about having to film a news clip.

The Tom Petty ringtone woke me. It was four in the afternoon and I'd fallen asleep watching TV. I didn't recognize the number but risked answering it. "Hello?"

The first sound from the other end of the connection was someone clearing their throat. "Yeah, this is Detec . . . this is Wilson, James Wilson."

"I'm full up on limp-wristed beatings at the moment, Detective."

"Real funny, Pelton."

I waited for him to say something else and heard a long inhale followed by a longer exhale.

He said, "Look, I'm sorry I popped you. I was wrong."

I smiled to myself. "I'll bet that hurt to say."

"Not as bad as being asked to take a few days off to think things over."

"I heard you're on vacation," I said. "That wasn't my doing."

"I know."

"Next time," I said, "don't do anything stupid around witnesses. I learned that in Afghanistan."

"Are you finished with the lecture?"

I was beginning to enjoy this. "Since it's getting to you, no. But how about I buy you dinner while I'm at it?"

"That's a start."

"Meet me at the Cove in an hour."

"You got it."

"Oh, and hey, Wilson?"

"Yeah?"

"You hit like a girl." I pressed End and rolled out of the creaky bed. It was a good thing Wilson called and woke me up. I needed to get to Chauncey's and feed Shelby.

The bartender was a kid with short hair parted on the side and no visible tats—too clean-cut to work at an island bar. He must've been one of Paige's new hires because I didn't recognize him. He said, "You guys want shots or something?"

Wilson said, "How about a couple cherry Cokes?"

The kid frowned and walked away.

Wilson stuck a toothpick in his mouth. "I guess he thinks we're gonna stiff him on the tip."

I tapped my fingers on the bar. "He doesn't know I own it. Don't tell him. It might spoil his day."

"Whatever." Wilson reached into the pocket of his bright orange Bermuda shorts that were the hottest thing in 1986 and pulled out a key chain with two keys. "I found these in Rogers's locker."

"What're they to?"

"A condo in the Caribbean."

I smiled. "Not bad. I don't suppose you found any bank account numbers to go with them."

"No such luck." He turned toward me and locked his eyes on mine. "How could I not have known my partner was dirt?"

"Same reason I didn't know my uncle was a renegade field agent for the EPA. He let me know only what he wanted to. I was too self-absorbed to see what was going on. The thing bugging me the most is the feeling that if I'd known what was going on, I could have helped him been his backup—taken the bullet. I don't know. Something, you know?"

"At least your uncle was clean. I can't imagine what I would've done if I'd known about Rogers. I guess . . . maybe after I kicked him around the block, I would've thrown him in jail." Wilson took the toothpick out of his mouth and bent it with his thumb and index finger a few times. "Some partner, huh?"

"I don't know about that," I said, "but I'm glad you called." I opened my wallet and handed him the parking garage ticket from my uncle's change pouch.

He said, "This what I think it is?"

I nodded. "A loose end."

"You know I'm off the case."

"Look at it," I said. "He parked at seven o'clock."

"So?"

"So, he wasn't meeting me until eight. He was early. My uncle wasn't early for anything in his life."

"Okay," he said. "I'll bite. Why was he early?"

"Considering everything he had going on at the time, I figure he was meeting someone."

"And you think it was the same someone who shot him."

"Yes."

Wilson put an arm on my shoulder and was about to speak when a well-built young blonde walked by, catching his attention. The see-through wrap failed to cover her bright orange bikini.

He threw the old toothpick on the bar and selected a new one. "I could get used to this."

The bartender finally brought our Cokes.

Wilson said, "Where's the little plastic umbrellas?"

The bartender stared at him. "Huh?"

Wilson tilted his drink slightly so the bartender was looking at the top of it. "The plastic umbrellas. Everyone else around here's got one. Where're ours?"

The kid smirked. "You didn't order a mixed drink."

"Oh, I get it," said Wilson. "We ain't worthy of an umbrella."

The kid turned to help another customer.

"Hey kid," said Wilson.

The bartender stopped.

"Look, I was only joking." Wilson motioned to me. "We're kind of having a rough day here."

"Join the club," he said.

Bonny the Macaw chose that moment to leave her perch and fly to my shoulder.

"Hey girl," I said.

She nibbled my ear. "Hi, Brack. *Squawk!*"

The bartender's face registered shock. He reached toward her.

I didn't know what he was about to attempt, but whatever it was it wouldn't end up good for him.

I said, "Don't come any closer unless you want her to bite

your hand."

He jerked his arm back.

"And if she doesn't," I said, "I will."

"She's supposed to be a good bird. I'll get the manager."

"It's okay," I said. "We haven't met. I'm the owner."

The kid opened his mouth but didn't say anything.

"First rule of employment, kid," Wilson said. "Know who signs your paychecks."

Paige joined the kid behind the bar. "I see you met Grant."

"Bonny and I were giving him pointers," I said.

Bonny flew to her perch above the bar.

I excused myself and headed for the restroom. On the wall above the urinal, I had written a familiar phrase as a reminder to myself and other miscreants: *"Man cannot avoid reaping what he sows."*

When I walked back to the bar, I said, "Someone's gotta pay for all this."

Wilson flicked the toothpick to the other side of his mouth with his tongue. "Someone's cleaned us out of witnesses."

"What do you know about a brothel in North Charleston called the Red Curtain?"

Wilson's face lit up. "Every cop on the beat knows about that place. They shortchange you?"

"They're involved."

As soon as I sat on the stool, my cell phone rang. It was my EPA contact, Graves.

I answered. "What's up, Ken?"

"Brack," he said, "wanted to let you know I sent a couple auditors down to check out the properties you mentioned. They reported back to me that the conditions of all three sites are far worse than we thought. Palmetto Properties is in a lot of trouble."

I said, "How much trouble?"

"Of course there are all the fines we are going to heap on them. Then there's the IRS."

"Great news." I said it but didn't feel it.

Graves said, "Do you know of a Michael Galston?"

I gave Wilson the thumbs up. "I might have heard the name before."

Graves said, "He is the primary shareholder in the properties. And it appears he has disappeared."

"Huh?"

"The local law enforcement went to his home this morning and he was gone. They checked with family members and his place of business. Nothing."

I rested a hand on the bar. "Not good."

"The reason I'm calling, and this is an unorthodox request, I was wondering if you had any ideas where he might be? I mentioned your name to the police and, well, they said you were not a credible source, which I personally find hard to believe."

I said, "Me too."

"Anyway, you mentioned you had someone there who knew a lot about the city. I wondered if you might be able to locate Mr. Galston. We have already flagged his passport so if he tries to get on a plane, we've got him."

I winked at Wilson and said, "Ken, you just made my day. I'll see what I can dig up."

After Graves ended the call, I relayed the story to Wilson.

He said, "Any ideas?"

"Remember the Chrysler that exploded?"

Chapter Thirty

Dusk settled in as we pulled in front of the familiar row of houses on Harmon Street. I parked in the same spot as before across from Dora's place.

Wilson looked around, "Gee, Pelton, we sure don't stick out driving this yuppie-mobile or anything."

The single red bulbs on each porch were lit up like Christmas. Windows were covered with plywood thanks to the car explosion. But apparently business was still booming. Maybe it was all the free press. A man left one of the houses and got into a Chevrolet pickup.

"I'll be," Wilson said.

"What?"

"You know who that is?"

I tried to get a look at the driver as he passed us. He wore a ball cap and the collar of his shirt was turned up. It was too hard to tell. "No, who is he?"

"Ted Watkins."

I think I blinked.

"That's right," Wilson said. "Mr. 'I'm gonna clean up the city.' The eager senator must be doing it door-to-door."

Another man walked to one of the shacks and was led inside by a woman.

Wilson looked at the door to Kim Lee's house, which was still closed, along with the drapes. He said, "You know I can't get anywhere near them, right? They'll make me for a cop before

I step out of the car."

Just like the senator, I slipped on a ball cap to hide my face in case the pimps running the street remembered me from the night of the car explosion. "I need you for something else."

"What?"

"I need you to watch my car."

He shook his head. "Fifteen years on the job and I'm bumped down to parking lot attendant."

Kim's door opened.

"Blow the horn if you see anyone coming." I got out of the car and waited until the john left before I approached. Kim sat in a chair on the porch in a negligee and lit a cigarette.

"Hey, honey." She made a motion like she was going to stub out the cigarette.

I leaned against the railing. "Take your time."

She said, "Time is money, honey."

"I got plenty of both."

In the light of the red bulb, she studied my face. "I like you already." The cherry of her cigarette glowed as she inhaled. She let out a steady stream of smoke. "I haven't seen you before, honey. I'd remember."

I recognized her as the girl in the trench coat Galston had visited when Darcy and I got set up. When she finished her cigarette, I followed her inside. She shut the door and pulled the drapes.

"Time is money," she said. "A hundred gets you thirty minutes. Two if you want it kinky."

I flashed a money roll I'd put together from the funds found in the crab pots, peeled off two hundreds, and handed them to her.

She started to pull her negligee off.

"I'm into something different," I said.

She stopped and looked at me.

I said, "Conversation."

She tilted her head. "You want me to talk dirty to you?"

"Not exactly. I want to know about the two guys with the car that blew up."

The shape her face contorted into had more wrinkles than anyone her age should have. "You five-oh. Get out."

I tried to hand her another fifty. "I'm not a cop."

"You something," she said. "Get out!" She pressed a button on the kitchen counter. "You got two minutes, big boy. Temp-a gonna come blow you away."

I pushed past her, pulled the forty-five, and headed for the back of the house. The knob was missing from the back door. I kicked hard. The rusty hinges groaned but didn't give. I kicked it again. The jamb splintered open. Formosan termites, dirt, and sawdust peppered the floor. The Audi's horn trumpeted a warning.

Moments later a man yelled from the front room, "Where is he?"

I jumped through the open door and crashed into cans of rotting garbage. Coated with slime, I made it to the corner of the house. Bullets sprayed from a machine gun behind me. As I rounded the house heading toward the street, light mounted somewhere over my head showed someone running toward me. He must have been blinded by the light behind me and couldn't see me coming. I lifted the pistol in my hand and smashed it sideways into the runner's face. Legs went out from under him and he landed on his back with a thud. I crouched, turned, and shot out the light a second before the man with the machine gun came around the corner of the house. Still crouching, I held the forty-five steady in my hands and let my eyes adjust to the darkness. The machine gun sprayed over my head and the outline of the shooter came into focus. I exhaled, aimed, and put a round in his upper right torso. The force of the forty-five jerked him backwards. His shoulder wouldn't do him any good for a while, but I didn't care. I turned and ran to the street.

Wilson crouched behind my car, his arms extended over the roof and a Glock aimed squarely at me. "Freeze!"

I held up my hands. "It's me. We gotta get out of here."

He pointed his pistol to the sky.

"Come on," I said. "Time is money. We can call a meat wagon from the road. They aren't dead, but they might have friends."

We jumped in the car and I got us out of there. With the disposable cell, I called it in but didn't give my name. When I hung up, Wilson was looking at me.

"What?"

He said, "If I run the number, is it going to be the same one you used when you blew up the Chrysler?"

"Who says I blew up anything?"

"Right. What—" Wilson stopped. "You smell like—"

"Don't say it."

At Wilson's house, I took a shower and tossed my garbage-smeared clothes. Wilson let me borrow his, which were a size or two big and a decade or two out of style. He made a few calls to find out what he could about the "trouble on Harmon Street," or as he put it to me, the "new mess you made."

We sat on his back patio with glasses of iced tea. Darcy called to say she heard about a shooting in the red light district and thought it might be me. I lit a cigar and filled her in on how far I didn't get with the unhappy hooker. Darcy said she and Patricia were finishing the story of the EPA and IRS crackdown on Galston and would keep me informed if they found anything new.

I ended the call and looked at Wilson. "You find out how the pimps are doing?"

Wilson flipped open a pad I'd seen him take notes in when he was on the job. "The one you clubbed, name is Anton Henry

Smith, has a concussion but is otherwise in stable condition. His partner, a Randall Jackson Clay, calls himself Temp-a, with a hyphen before the 'a.' I'm guessing it's slang for temper, or the guy can't spell, or both. Thirty years old. This guy should play the lottery he's so lucky. Either you're a bad shot or you aimed high. His shoulder is wrecked but you missed his lung by inches." He looked up from the notebook. "Both have sheets and are being held for questioning. The machine guns they carried guarantee jail time."

"It is a beautiful world we live in." I took a drag from the cigar.

"Maybe you should play the lottery, too," he continued. "The hooker said she didn't remember what the perpetrator looked like."

"Huh?"

"Yeah," he said. "She gave you a free pass."

"Know what that means?"

"We take another shot at her."

"So to speak." I got up. "This time you drive. My car smells."

Around ten PM we returned to the red light district in Wilson's unmarked cruiser whose keys he'd conveniently forgotten to hand in when they suspended him. He monitored the police radio as he drove to make sure his Brothers in Blue had vacated the scene. I enjoyed riding up front for a change. Every other time I'd been shackled in the back. One street over from Harmon, he pulled to the curb under what had to be the last functioning streetlamp around. I wondered how it was spared when the others had been used for target practice. I put a fresh clip in the forty-five and slid it down the waistband of the extra-large shorts Wilson had loaned me.

Wilson said, "I'm gonna pretend I didn't see that since my fellow officers are looking for the gun that shot the forty-five-caliber bullet that went through Temp-a and ended up in a tree."

"Good, and I won't mention you drive like an old lady."

The sound of a car coming up from behind made us duck into the shadows. An American sedan from the seventies rolled by on huge chromed wheels, its bass system shaking the ground. It looked like something out of the comics.

After it passed, Wilson whispered, "What are you gonna say to the Chinese squeeze?"

"That's really clever, Wilson," I whispered back. "I was planning on kicking the door in and dragging her out by her hair."

"As a detective, I always found knocking first worked pretty well."

We turned the corner and headed up the street where Kim Lee worked. With the two guys who usually watched the street in the hospital, we didn't bother trying to be sneaky. As if to pay his respects, Wilson stopped by the spot where the Chrysler went up in flames.

"I can't believe you blew up their car."

"You can't prove I did anything."

A female voice came from across the street. "You bring big money with you, honey?" The end of a cigarette glowed in the darkness.

Inside Kim Lee's hot pad, Wilson watched her bend over to get two beers out of the refrigerator. I pulled the curtain open to peer out. With no illumination on the street, the darkness was heavy.

Kim Lee set the beers in front of us. "So, you guys want same deal as the ones you asked about, honey?"

I turned away from the window to look at her. "Depends. What'd you have to do for them?"

She took a seat at the table between us. "Why don't you tell me what you like, honey."

I took out my gangster roll, unfolded two more hundreds, and laid them on the table. "I like lots of things."

She reached for the bills but Wilson put his hand over them.

"What I'd like right now," I said, "is information."

She moved her hand back and looked at the button on the counter she'd pressed the last time I was here.

"Temp-a's in the hospital," Wilson said. "The other one's in jail. What's his name? Anton?"

"So it's just us," I added.

In the weak glow from the fixture in her kitchen, I saw Kim Lee sigh and drop her eyes. "Am I in trouble?"

"You could be," I said, "if you don't answer our questions."

Wilson picked up the can of beer with one hand and opened a leather badge holder on the table with the other. I guessed it was Rogers's badge because Wilson had to surrender his own to the police captain.

Wilson raised the can to his lips, took a swallow, and said, "It's your choice."

Kim Lee glanced at the badge.

Wilson snapped it shut and put it in his pocket.

"If I talk, they'll hurt me," she said.

I leaned in close to Kim. "Ten days ago, I saw one of your career sisters. She was sucking down opium as fast as she could get it, scared to death because someone's idea of foreplay was assault and battery. The john paid Temp-a's handlers so he could hurt her. Maybe it's the same someone we're after. He might come here next to tie up any loose ends."

The frown on her face told me she wasn't impressed. Like she ran across those types of johns every day. And she probably did.

"Did I mention the girl was found with a bunch of nine millimeter holes in her?" I asked. "She was only sixteen."

Kim Lee focused on her hands resting on the table. "What do you want?"

"Remember the morning you wore the trench coat when you opened a motel door to the big fat man?"

She took her time and eventually nodded.

I slammed my hand on the table. Kim Lee flinched.

"They shot my friend there," I said. "Who set it up?"

Kim Lee whimpered.

I pounded the table again. "I want to know everything. Get yourself together and spill it."

Tears welled in her eyes. "Th-they pay me. They say I don't have to do anything except answer the door and look sexy. The fat man, he come inside the room and leave through the back door. They give me a hundred bucks and take me back here."

I said, "You don't know anything else about that day?"

She shook her head no.

Wilson said, "You didn't hear any gunfire?"

She nodded. "I hear something, but I leave out the back door after the fat man."

Wilson finished his beer. "Is that the only time you met the fat man?"

"Yes," she said. "He didn't want anything to do with me. He has his own girl."

I gathered my thoughts.

She said, "The fat man said something when we heard the pops. Something like: 'that should take care of it.' "

"All right," I said. "Tell us about your Thursday night regulars. The ones with the blown-up car."

"They come every week," she said. "I think they like each other more than me."

Wilson chuckled. I would have too if I hadn't been so mad Galston got the drop on me and Darcy.

I said, "You know the names for your Thursday night action?"

"Besides john," Wilson said.

Between sobs, she said, "Freddy. Freddy and Chad. That's all I know."

I said, "Which one's the young one?"

"Chad."

Wilson said, "Who is the fat man's girl?"

"Alexus," she said. "Like the car. The other girls say he keeps her in an apartment. No other johns can touch her."

Wilson made a notation in his pad. "You know where the apartment is?"

Kim Lee shook her head again.

CHAPTER THIRTY-ONE

From the front seat of Wilson's car, I called Darcy and Patricia and had them start digging up anything they could find on an Alexus. Patricia said she'd tried to call Constance but couldn't get through. On a hunch, I called McAllister.

"I hear our boy's on the run," he said.

"Yep," I said. "You were a big help before."

"I read about the car blowing up. Nice work."

I said, "The prostitute they got busted with said Galston's girl's name is Alexus. He's got her up in an apartment but she couldn't tell us where. Any ideas?"

"What's the name, again?"

"Alexus. Like the car, so I'm told."

"I don't think I know that one. I can check around, call in a few favors."

"I'd appreciate it. So would the government." I hung up.

Wilson and I were on Seventeen heading toward West Ashley when McAllister called back.

"I got something," he said, "but I'm not sure how good it is."

"I'll take it, whatever it is."

"Galston knows everybody's looking for him. I was told he was packing as we speak. He's got a boat waiting in the City Marina."

"Thanks." I ended the call.

Wilson looked at me. "What?"

"City Marina," I said. "And we better hurry. We might be too late."

Wilson's car was at a stretch where Seventeen became a divided four-lane. At the next light, he blasted his siren and cut ahead of a line of cars waiting to turn left, made a screeching U-turn around them, and headed back the way we came. He radioed it in and was told there were no units in the area.

The police captain patched through. "I hope you aren't working a case on suspension, Detective Wilson. I thought I made it perfectly clear you were to take time off. If you continue, I will have no choice but to proceed with termination."

Wilson held the radio in his hands but didn't press the button to respond.

"He sounds like one of my commanding officers," I said.

"He's a real peach." Wilson slalomed through the traffic with one hand on the wheel. He brought the radio to his mouth. "The suspect is on the run and there are no units in the area, sir. I can make it in fifteen minutes. The feds want this guy. He—"

"I know who he is, Detective Wilson," the captain said. "But the fact remains you cannot pursue a suspect while under suspension. I am ordering you to stand down."

Wilson threw the radio in the backseat and punched the accelerator harder.

"We're not stopping?" I asked.

"We're not stopping."

Charleston Harbor was full of boats. The parking lot was well lit and virtually empty. Parked in a handicapped spot was a black Escalade with the vanity plate MLG ONE. The tailgate was open. I got out of Wilson's car and ran toward the yachts. Wilson went to find someone who worked there.

Floodlights illuminated the dock. With no triple-extra-large shapes in sight, I turned and headed to the parking lot. As I passed one of the boats, a life preserver flew at me at the speed of light and tagged me in the face. I lost my footing and fell, sliding across the rough wood surface. Splinters tore my knees and hands. Galston jumped from a boat and kicked me hard in the stomach. The wind blew out my lungs.

A woman yelled, "What are you doing, Mike?"

The decking vibrated underneath me. The fat man rushed down the dock like an elephant on the loose. I got to my feet, gasping for air, and stumbled, losing sight of him when he left the main dock. Wilson was nowhere to be seen. I staggered toward the parking lot. My stomach throbbed where I'd been kicked. The black SUV appeared when I turned the corner. Galston headed toward it. I aimed my gun and fired. The front tire went flat.

"Stop running . . ." I gasped, "or the next one . . . will be in you."

Galston did what I asked. I closed the distance between us to less than ten feet. He turned around.

"You gonna kill me, kid?"

I cocked the hammer, my breath returning. "You set me and Darcy up. She almost died."

"You can't shoot me. You'll never get away with it. I got too many friends."

I sighted on his melon head. "You killed my uncle. Why?"

"Listen," he said, staring at my gun. "Take it easy. I didn't kill anybody."

"I count at least three dead and one with a hole in her shoulder, and you're telling me you didn't kill anybody." My finger tightened against the trigger. I thought of my uncle dying in the alley. "Man doesn't have the right to avoid reaping what he sows."

Sweat beaded on my forehead and I brushed it off with my

free hand. I could taste blood. I wanted blood. But something clicked inside me and I lowered my gun. "I'm thinking I'll like you better in jail."

Galston raised his right hand. In a tenth of a second, I registered he was holding something metallic and shiny. I jerked my gun up. The blast came quick. Galston's face exploded and blood sprayed everywhere. He slumped and fell forward. A silver, two-shot Derringer dropped from his right hand. Behind him and to the left stood Wilson, legs spread apart, his pistol locked in both hands. I realized I hadn't gotten a shot off.

The police captain came to the docks and personally escorted Detective Wilson away. I sat in the back of an ambulance swabbing Galston's brains and blood from my face with alcohol wipes. His funeral would not be open casket. A paramedic cleaned my wounds and removed the splinters in my hands and knees.

An Infiniti pulled in close and Darcy's mouth dropped when she saw me. "Yikes. You all right?"

"Better than Galston."

She scratched the bandage over her wound. "I guess he got what he deserved."

I said, "I would have preferred to watch him and his empire go down, but I guess it will go down without him. How'd you find out about this so fast?"

Darcy winked. "I told you I was good. Mind if we get shots for the paper?"

"Do I have to smile?"

"I'd rather you didn't," she said. "In fact, I'd prefer if you stretched out on the gurney and let them stick IVs in. You know, play to the dramatic."

"Fat chance of that," I said.

"Where's Detective Wilson?" Darcy asked.

I threw blood-soaked wipes into a biohazard bin. "His boss took him away. I get the feeling he might not be a detective much longer."

With Galston out of the picture, I thought it might be safe to find a more permanent residence. Since mine no longer existed, Shelby and I were moving into Uncle Reggie's old house. Thursday morning, when I called about picking my dog up, Chauncey's wife asked if I could wait until the afternoon. Apparently she was giving him a special grooming treatment. It sounded like a stall tactic but I relented. She also informed me he was letting her feed him.

Just great.

I decided to spend the time at the Pirate's Cove before I went to get him.

About two o'clock Darcy strolled onto the back deck. I was making drinks for a couple on holiday from Australia.

She took a seat in front of me at the bar. Her arm was still in a sling. "I got an interesting call from a friend of yours."

"I don't have any friends so that kind of narrows it down, don't you think?"

She ignored what I said. "Be a good sport and fix me a bloody; extra Tabasco. You might want to pour yourself one as well before I tell you what I found out."

I mixed two Bloody Marys, one with a shot of Ketel One, the other a virgin, and both with a lot of hot sauce. In honor of ex-detective Wilson, I put miniature plastic umbrellas in them along with celery sticks and straws and handed the one with vodka to Darcy.

"On the wagon again, I see." She took a long drag on the straw. "Not bad. You might have found your calling."

"Mixing drinks for pretty celebrities in paradise is easy. Throwing those same celebrities out when they get too drunk is icing on the cake." I took a drink from my glass and added pepper from a shaker. "So who called?"

"A guy named Chad. Said you and he are old acquaintances. I think he's one of the guys with the car you blew up. Am I right?"

Bonny flew from her perch and landed on my shoulder. I propped a foot on the shelf underneath the bar and leaned forward. "Yep. What does he want with you?"

She took another drink. "Says he's got evidence showing he and his coworker, Freddy, were in Daytona with their boss when Fisher was killed."

"He just wants a get-out-of-jail card. Like I can give him one."

Bonny gave me a kiss and flew back inside.

"Either way," Darcy said, "I'm going to see what he's got."

I lit a cigar. "You're not going alone."

She stirred her drink. "Why do you think I'm sitting here in front of you making nice in the thong, Einstein?"

After another pull from my drink, I said, "I thought you didn't wear thongs."

Darcy gave me her trademark grin, the one she reserved for TV audiences and me when she felt like it.

I told Paige I was leaving and walked Darcy to the Audi. I'd had to pay serious money to a detailer to get the garbage smell out if it.

As I held the door open for her, she said, "This car is not you."

"I know."

We shot up the Isle of Palms Connector to the city of Mount Pleasant and onto I-526 to Daniel Island. I parked in the empty back lot of a marina where Shorty—aka Chad—had told Darcy he'd meet her. While we waited, she called Patricia. I checked my twenty-two, the one I'd bought from Big Al. From a distance, it looked like a bigger caliber semiautomatic. The cops had taken my other guns and it was all I had left.

Within five minutes of our arrival, a jacked-up Nissan Titan pickup with oversized off-road tires pulled into the lot and parked next to us. Chad climbed from the truck. He wore wraparound sunglasses, a pink muscle shirt hanging loosely, showing off his arms and pectorals, and white gym shorts.

Darcy and I got out of the Audi.

Chad pointed to me. "What's he doing here?"

I said, "I came to see what I can blow up next. This is a nice truck you got here, Shorty."

Chad said, "Whatever. Thanks to you, I can't go home. The police are looking for me."

I said, "Gee, that sounds familiar."

Darcy had her purse looped around her good shoulder. She opened it and took out a miniature recorder. "You mind if I record this, Chad?"

Chad wiped sweat from his forehead and shrugged. "Naw. It's probably better if you did."

She said, "You called me. What have you got?"

Chad reached into his pocket. I pulled the gun and pointed it at him, hoping he didn't know what caliber it really was. "You better just be scratching your jock."

He held up crumpled paper. "Easy, man. I got receipts that show we wasn't even here when that accountant was killed."

"Where were you?" I asked.

"Daytona. Mr. Galston took us down there for a long week-end."

Darcy walked to him. "Can I see those?"

He handed them to her slowly.

She unfolded the papers and read.

Still holding the gun on him, I said, "Where's your buddy? Freddy, right?"

Chad didn't move. "He left when Galston went down and the cops connected us to them people dying."

Darcy waved the papers. "How do I know these are real?"

"Call the rental agency and the boat charter. They got records."

"If they don't," I said, "I'm coming after you."

Chad swung himself into the cab of his truck. "You're gonna have to get in line."

I watched him drive away and wondered if he was thinking about all the wrong turns he made to end up here.

Darcy and I headed to the bar. On the way, she called the places the receipts were from and found them legit. The boat charter had a picture of Galston and his boys with their catch.

Reluctantly, I called Trish and asked her to hold onto Shelby a little while longer. She could not mask the joy in her voice over the phone. I wondered if I shouldn't pull him out of there and put him in a kennel before she filled out adoption papers.

Bonny kept me company as I went through my uncle's emails when someone rapped on the door. We turned to see who it was. Detective Wilson waved his right hand in greeting. In his left hand was a large envelope.

Bonny said, "Hey kid, know who signs your paycheck. *Squawk!*"

Wilson came in and sat on the couch. "You got that right, little lady."

I said, "How you holding up?"

"They're trying to decide what to do with me so I'm still on unpaid holiday."

I said, "I've got not-so-good news."

He stuck a toothpick in his mouth. "Well, boy, spit it out."

"When Fisher was killed," I said, "Galston and his crew were deep sea fishing down in Daytona."

He plopped on the couch and propped a foot up. "We got the wrong guy?"

"I don't think so. He wouldn't have pulled the gun if he was innocent."

"Figures. Dumb bastard. Wanna hear something funny?"

"What's that?"

He clapped his hands together, obviously not concerned about Galston's demise. "His girlfriend, what's her name . . . Alexus? She split. The executors of Galston's will think she walked away with several million in cash because it's gone, too. Guess she finally got her payday."

"That is pretty funny. So how about dinner on the house?"

"Now you're talking. But that's not why I came."

I dropped a paper I was holding on the desk. "Well, boy, spit it out."

"Remember the parking garage ticket you gave me?"

"Yes."

"I know the owner of the garage and asked him if he'd get me a list of the credit card numbers used after eight PM the night your uncle was killed. It's what we call a long shot because the guy could have paid in cash or used another parking garage or parked in one of the lots."

"And?" I said.

Wilson leaned forward on the couch. "My buddy did me one better. He had his secretary take the list of numbers and get names. Thanks to all this identity theft going around, businesses can call and run a check on a number. She typed out a list of forty names for me."

"For you? I thought you said *he* had her do it."

His face reddened. "You're missing the point, here." He handed me the list. "Recognize any names on it?"

The secretary had added the time of entry and exit to each line. Eleven names down, between a Mr. Carl Long and Ms.

Jacqueline Carman, was the name of a company. Ashley River Recovery clocked in at six forty-five and out at eight fifteen.

He said, "You find something?"

CHAPTER THIRTY-TWO

The Supremes were playing on the juke when I walked into Mutt's. With no customers to serve, Mutt sat at the bar. Reading glasses perched on his nose, an open newspaper in front of him. Smoke trailed toward the ceiling from a burning cigarette in an ashtray to his right.

I laid the T-shirt he loaned me on the bar, pulled out a barstool, and sat. "Thanks for letting me borrow this."

"No problem, Opie," he said. "What's up?"

Resting my elbows on the bar, I looked straight ahead and laced my fingers together. "You got an extra pistol? Something bigger than a twenty-two?"

In my periphery, I saw him straighten slowly and remove his glasses. "What you want with a gat? Opie didn't carry no gat."

"The police took all the big ones I had. I need another."

"What for?"

I told him about Galston and his crew being on a fishing trip when Fisher was killed and about Ashley River Recovery.

The gates to McAllister's house were open when I eased to a stop.

"Nice house," Mutt said.

From where we parked in the drive, through the windshield of my secondhand Audi I could see the front door ajar and two of the three garage doors raised. I pulled out the thirty-eight police special Mutt lent me. "Ready?"

Mutt carried an identical gun. "You sure this the cracker killed Reggie?"

"We're going to find out. You know, we could go to jail for this."

"If he killed Reggie, he gonna get what he deserve. Outside of that, I don't care."

As Mutt and I started to get out of the Audi, we heard the sound of a powerful engine fire up. McAllister's red ZR1 shot out of the garage, down the drive past us, and onto the road. I slammed my door shut and put the Audi in gear. Mutt barely closed his door when I accelerated and went after the sports car.

"I guess he the one," Mutt said. "Let's get him!"

I pushed the accelerator to the floor. The Audi was fast, but I knew it was no match for the supercharged Corvette.

Mutt said, "What are we gonna do when we catch him?"

"*If* we catch him." I shifted gears. "I haven't planned it out that far."

Two sets of stoplights ahead turned yellow at the same time. The rear end of the ZR1 squatted as the car catapulted forward. The Audi was already giving us all she had. We were at the mercy of the timing of the lights. Both of us made the first set. McAllister clipped the second. Mutt and I barreled through a very red light a few car lengths behind. The cars waiting on the cross-street light had moved forward. I laid on the horn and shot through a gap with nothing to spare.

Mutt looked back. "You crazy!"

McAllister turned right at the next intersection.

"He's going for the highway," I said. "If there's no traffic, he'll lose us."

Mutt yelled, "Get me close enough to take out a tire!"

McAllister's car bucked over a dip in the road and he caught it before it spun on him. I hit the same dip a second later. The

Audi bottomed out hard but kept going. When the tachometer hit the red zone, I shifted into the next gear. McAllister turned onto the entrance ramp and blasted up to the interstate. I wrenched the Audi's steering wheel. With the traction control off, all four wheels slid through the ninety-degree transition. The curb came up fast. Less than a foot away, the tires bit and we made the rest of the turn. At the same time, the ZR1, still pulling ahead of us, merged with the other cars. I glanced at the dash and saw we were past eighty MPH and heading toward ninety in a hurry. The bright red sports car ahead zigzagged between the other vehicles like a possessed dog. I did my best to keep up. As if in answer to a prayer, two eighteen-wheelers running side by side loomed in the distance, backing up a line of cars ahead of us. A perfect rolling roadblock.

"We might be in luck," Mutt said.

Brake lights on the ZR1 lit up. McAllister must have seen the trucks too. Mutt hit the button to lower the window and stuck his head and arm out, aiming his gun. I trained the front bumper of the Audi on the rear end of the sports car and plotted a collision course. If Mutt's bullets missed, I wouldn't.

McAllister swerved into the emergency lane and gunned it, passing the line of cars. I did the same. The powerful ZR1 pulled away from us again. The road narrowed ahead and the emergency lane disappeared at a bridge crossing. Stiff guard rails prohibited further progress. I watched in disbelief as the ZR1 ignored the yellow warning signs and cut in front of the trucks with what must have been the slimmest of margins. We were still on a collision course, but with the guard rail, not McAllister. Mutt saw it at the same time and pulled his arm back inside. I slammed on the brakes as hard as I could.

When the tire smoke and dust cleared, we sat in our seats staring at a guard rail inches from the front bumper. The yellow warning signs with black slashes laughed at us.

Mutt slapped the dash hard and took a deep breath. After a moment, he turned and watched the passing cars. "There's a break in the traffic coming up."

My knuckles had turned white on the steering wheel and I tried to relax my grip. When my hands loosened, I put the car in reverse and eased us back a few car lengths from the barrier. I turned my indicator on and, when the break in traffic appeared, merged onto the highway and accelerated to cruising speed. We passed the trucks and found a clear road ahead. No sign of the ZR1.

Mutt said, "Any idea where he went?"

"Nope. And now he knows we're on to him."

Mutt and I walked into the *Palmetto Pulse* and interrupted a meeting in Patricia's office.

She looked up from the three eager reporters in front of her. "What's wrong now?"

"A change of plans," I said.

She dismissed the twenty-somethings. The pretty brunette and two Biff-type males stared at Mutt and me like we were illegal immigrant busboys taking their dinner plates before they'd finished eating. Mutt and I returned their glares and they hurried from the room. When the youngsters were gone, I told Patricia about the garage receipt. "We went to have a little talk with McAllister and he ran."

Patricia's hand flew to her mouth. "Oh my God."

"Sure enough," Mutt said.

"I think he left his house open," I said. "Care for a little breaking and entering without the breaking?"

Patricia said, "The door's wide open?"

I turned and headed for the exit. "It was when we left. Where's your star talent? She'd want in on this."

Grabbing her handbag, Patricia said, "She's looking into something. Said she'd check in later."

Mutt pointed at the three rookies who'd vacated the office. "Why don't you bring them? Especially the fox. Break them in right."

"They aren't ready for this," she said.

"You know it!" Mutt cackled. "How!"

Patricia followed in her Mercedes as I led the way to McAllister's house. We parked a block away and the three of us crept through the gate on foot. The front door was, in fact, still open. So were the two garage doors. The ZR1 was not there. Everything was quiet. Mutt entered first, pistol drawn, and went to the left. I followed him in, stepping right. Patricia stayed behind.

The military had taught Mutt and me how to clear buildings, so we walked McAllister's house room by room and floor by floor. My hunger for blood returned but there was no sign of anyone. I found Patricia in the entryway holding a framed photo of McAllister and an old woman.

Patricia held it out so I could see it. "Recognize her?"

I realized I had seen that rich old bat before. Sitting in Patricia's office just a few days ago, in fact.

"Mrs. Calhoun," I said.

"Hey!" Mutt yelled from the top of the stairs. "He got a bunch of pictures up here and we in them."

A stack of photos in a study area off the master bedroom lay on a desk. Each of us had been photographed—Patricia, Darcy, Chauncey, Brother Thomas, David Fisher and his wife, Justine, Galston, Shorty, Goatee, and me. Even Mutt. Distance shots of Uncle Reggie and the Pirate's Cove. All of them haunting. McAllister had been playing me the whole time.

Patricia flipped through the stack. "You know who's not in these?"

I shrugged and searched through the desk drawers.

She dug out her cell phone and punched speed dial. After a moment, she said, "Constance, are you all right?"

After talking for a few minutes, Patricia ended the call. "She's fine. Oblivious. Doesn't know where McAllister is."

Mutt started on the bedroom and searched through the dresser drawers.

An hour later we stood in the kitchen trying to decide what to do next. We had gone through McAllister's entire house and found nothing but the photos. I went upstairs and grabbed them to go over one more time. When we'd found them, they were scattered on top of the desk. The neat pile Patricia made of them exposed the rest of the desktop. Across most of it lay a blueprint of a plot of land next to the Ashley River. Something about the shape of the river at that particular point was familiar. I pulled the map clear.

"Hey, Patricia," I called.

I heard her hurry up the stairs, her sandals slapping against the hardwood treads. When she entered the room, I held out the map by its top two corners. "This look familiar?"

She moved closer and picked up the bottom corners so the map became horizontal. "Sumter Point. He's been lying to us from the start."

Chauncey warned me against doing anything stupid when I called to tell him of what we'd learned. I neglected to tell him how we found it. It was an illegal search, after all. I said I didn't know what he was talking about.

Patricia's Mercedes followed my Audi to the Pirate's Cove, where the three of us discussed our next course of action. Patricia and I decided we needed to talk to Mrs. Calhoun. Mutt

agreed to watch the Pirate's Cove to make sure it wasn't vandalized—or torched. "Weren't nothing going on at my place,
anyhow," he said from a stool at the end of the bar. "It's the
end of the month. Everyone's waiting on their checks to come
in."

I tossed him the keys to the Audi. "You sure you know what
McAllister looks like?"

"Patricia showed me pictures. Don't worry. I got it covered."

A full-figured college girl in a bikini ordered a drink from the
bartender.

Mutt's eyes roamed over her like a metal detector at the
airport. "I could get used to this."

That was the same thing Wilson said. The only weapon
McAllister would need to take over my bar was a bimbo in a
two-piece.

Patricia texted Darcy and we cruised away in her Mercedes.

Mrs. Calhoun opened the door of her ocean-front mansion on
the Isle of Palms. One look at Patricia and me and the old
woman said in a monotone, "Oh, it's you."

Patricia said, "Mind if we come in and talk to you a minute,
Josephine?"

"Yes, I do," the rich old bat said. "I will not be treated rudely
in my own home by that smart-mouthed hooligan."

For some reason, she was pointing at me. She must have
been holding a grudge from our first meeting in Patricia's office
when I accused her of being an environmentalist hypocrite.

I raised the framed picture of her and McAllister. "We were
wondering what your connection was to Ashley River Recovery."

Instead of answering, she asked, "Why do you have my
nephew's photo?"

Patricia said, "That's your nephew in the picture?"

Mrs. Calhoun grabbed the picture. "Yes it is. This is his

property. I recognize the frame and I'm taking it back." She slammed the door in our faces.

"I guess we know the connection," I said.

"Yes, and once we expose McAllister and mention her relationship to him, she won't have any influence left in this town."

We walked to the car.

"And I was looking forward to seeing the Cove turned into Dolphin Swimmer. Darcy's not going to like missing this."

Patricia took out her iPhone. "She should have checked in by now."

I stopped. "Checked in? What are you talking about?"

"We have an agreement," Patricia said. "She checks in every hour. No longer than two hours."

"You run a tight ship."

"She's young, pretty, and aggressive, and men are men. And, she's still healing."

"When was the last time you heard from her?"

"Three hours ago."

"What did she say?"

"It was a text." Patricia scrolled. *"At Red Curtain."* She looked at me. "I wasn't sure what that meant. Do you know?"

I had an image of Chinese hoods with nine millimeters and cigarettes hanging out of their mouths shooting holes in Suzy, the teenage live target. The instant pressure of my mind racing made my chin droop. I put my hands on the sides of my head and squeezed.

Patricia said, "What is it?"

Patricia threw me the keyed remote to her Mercedes. We jumped in and slammed the doors. I had to move the seat back and adjust the wheel.

"Hurry up Brack!" She searched her cell phone for something. "What is that place, anyway?"

I pushed the Start button and the engine grumbled to life. "An underground brothel Darcy's been scamming to get a story on."

"Scamming?"

I gave her the ten-second version as I floored it.

Patricia listened and made a call. "Get me Ron. Now."

I said, "Call Mutt while you're at it. Let him know where we're headed."

We rocketed onto I-526, the interstate that looped to North Charleston. The Benz scooted into triple digits with ease. Patricia talked faster and more directly with each mile-per-hour increase.

The convertible top was down, but with the windows up and the windscreen behind us, there was little buffeting inside the cabin. The speedometer crested a hundred and ten. I blew by a cop heading in the other direction and hoped none of his buddies would be waiting for us ahead. We had to save Darcy.

The Mercedes engine raced like a stock car V-8. We shot between clusters of cars as if they were parked on the road. I felt the floor resist my foot as I pressed the accelerator hard, squeezing a few more thousandths of an inch out of it. The fuel cutoff was supposed to be around a hundred and fifty-five miles per hour and we'd be there shortly.

"No, I am not joking," Patricia yelled at someone on the phone. "I need every available officer." Another pause and it sounded as if she cut the person off when she said, "Look Ron, if you don't think my calling you directly rates on your radar as an emergency you can find someone else to manage your campaign." She ended the call. "If the good mayor doesn't come through, he won't be getting my support come next election."

The last call she made was to the Pirate's Cove. I half-listened as she waited for Mutt to come on the line and explained where we were headed, hearing only her half of the conversation.

"What do you mean you have an idea?" After a pause, she lowered the phone from her ear.

I could feel her eyes looking at me. "What was that about?"

"He said to hold up and wait. That he had an idea."

"We don't have time."

"You're right. Now move it!"

My hands locked at ten and two o'clock on the wheel and my eyes focused on the road ahead. The suspension absorbed the expansion joints and rough seams in the pavement with the solidarity befitting a hundred-thousand-dollar German car.

And then traffic came to an abrupt halt.

CHAPTER THIRTY-THREE

Forty-five minutes later, thanks to a wreck that had brought the interstate to a standstill, we entered the downward descent of the exit ramp. I let up on the gas and coasted. During our wait, we'd tried to call Mutt at the Cove but he'd left. At the strip mall where the brothel operated, Darcy's car sat where she had watched me attack the geriatric Ohio man in his black Chrysler 300.

Patricia said, "Oh, God."

I parked next to the Infiniti convertible. There were other cars around. But no police.

"The mayor is going to pay for this," Patricia said.

"I don't want you going in," I said.

"What? Why?"

I opened the car door and grabbed the top of the windshield to lift myself out. "If you hear shots . . . if it gets bad, I want you to get out of here and call Wilson."

"This is crazy, Brack. You can't go in alone. It's suicide."

"Suicide missions are my specialty." I closed the door, pulled the thirty-eight, and walked toward the back-door entrance Darcy and I had used before. In the heat, I could feel my heart racing. My fingers tingled around the pistol. Just like war.

I raised my hand to knock.

A horn honked and a familiar voice boomed, "Brother Brack! Mind if we join you?"

Lowering my hand from the door, I turned to face Brother

Thomas, who drove a large white van with blue smoke coming out the tailpipe. With him were a group of about ten people, men and women.

I said, "Y'all shouldn't be here."

He parked the van and everyone got out.

"Funny thing," Brother Thomas said. "We was having a prayer meeting asking the good Lord what He wanted from us and Brother Mutt barged in, mm-hmm."

They must have used I-26 and missed the traffic jam.

One of the men in the group, stocky, about my age, said, "From what we hear, you shouldn't be here, either."

I couldn't argue the point.

My fear kicked into overdrive. "Darcy could be inside being held by my uncle's killer and five kids with guns. I need to go in and get her and I don't need this distraction."

Brother Thomas said, "Sister Wells been our responsibility since we escorted her out of the hospital, mm-hmm." He stepped to the door and knocked. "We going in." The group gathered around him.

A lady with a pink dress and matching hat turned to me. "We all prayed up, chile. How 'bout you?"

Crystal answered the door in her negligee. Brother Thomas and the horde of his congregation stormed the fort, pushing past me and Crystal. I barely heard her say, "You can't come in here!"

I pulled my pistol and followed the group inside, expecting the five guns in the back to start firing any second. What I found I did not expect. Four Chinese goons, hands bound and mouths gagged, were being led into the room by a second group of Brother Thomas's parishioners. And Mutt. The only gun I saw was the one in my own hand.

"Opie!" Mutt said. "How ya doin'?"

"What the . . . ?" I didn't finish. Something was wrong. The goon with the necklace who'd shot Darcy wasn't tied up with the other four. "There's one missing."

Mutt lit a cigarette. "Slippery little sucker peeled away in a Trans Am."

The Madame screamed at Brother Thomas in Chinese. The teenaged working girls, six of them in various forms of negligee, sat in the reception area with heads bowed. Female members of the church congregation found sheets and wrapped them around the girls.

Three of the four johns in the place, older white guys, stood in their boxer shorts and jockeys, hands covering their privates in shame. The fourth, a black man, wore nothing but a white towel. Men from the church gave the johns sheets to cover themselves as well.

The black john shook his head slowly. "Oh, Jesus. Jesus, Jesus, Jesus." He put his face in his hands and cried.

Patricia came up beside me, taking in the sight. "Well I'll be . . ."

Brother Thomas said, "Brother Brack, it appears as if our friend isn't here at present."

Mutt said, "He right. I checked the whole place out."

Patricia pointed a finger in the Madame's face. "You have five seconds to tell me where Darcy is."

The Madame screeched more in her native tongue.

"Look," Patricia said, "I know you speak English. You have two choices." She held up a finger. "One, either you tell me where Darcy is and I let you walk out of here before I call the police . . ." She held up a second finger, ". . . or two, I have you tied up with the rest and deported."

Two of the goons on the floor jerked and thrashed around, hatred in their eyes.

Mutt said, "You guys behave. Or I'll use ya as shark bait."

Brother Thomas addressed the group. "First one of y'all that tells us what we wanna know walks out the do'. The rest will be takin' the slow boat back to China, mm-hmm."

A bald white guy clutching his sheet said, "But I'm an American."

I said, "Those girls aren't old enough to drive and you want to talk semantics?"

One of the teenagers, a tall beauty with slumped shoulders, stepped forward. The Madame berated the scared girl. Patricia took an extra gag from one of the men in the congregation who had subdued the goons and used it to shut her up.

The girl, now shaking, said, "I think I know, but I have no passport and no money. I tell you and you let me go, I get sent back like the others."

Patricia led the girl away from the group. Brother Thomas and I followed.

My ex-aunt said, "You tell us where Darcy is and I will do everything I can to get you asylum." She put her arms around Brother Thomas and me. "These are powerful men. They will make sure nothing happens to you."

The girl raised her head and her eyes met mine. "You came here before with the woman, the one you ask about. To talk to Suzy."

I said, "Yes."

She looked at the floor. "Suzy is gone."

Patricia looked at me.

I nodded. "She's right."

The girl said, "Suzy's trick, the one who beat her up. He took the woman."

Patricia spoke in a soothing voice. "Where?"

"I-I don't know. He say he going to feed her to the rats."

Rats. One place came to mind. McAllister had shown it to

Darcy and me. Chromicorp.

I turned and ran out the door, Patricia on my heels.

North of the town limits, I slowed Patricia's Mercedes and made a sharp left onto the dirt road. The mudhole McAllister's truck had no problem going through appeared like a lake in the windshield. Patricia's Mercedes would not fare as well if I tried the same stunt. With the thick underbrush and trees lining the road, there was no room to go around the water. I stopped short of the small pond.

Patricia snapped. "What are you doing?"

"The puddle's too deep. We have to go on foot from here." I unbuckled my seatbelt and got out.

"Oh, for heaven's sake!" She hopped from the passenger seat to the driver's, started the car, and drove forward.

The front end of her Mercedes hit the water and bounced a few feet. The rear tires dropped in. For a second it looked like Patricia might make it. But the car sank. She tried to rev it but the traction control system I hadn't had time to turn off prevented the wheels from spinning. The engine clogged with water and shut off.

A voice behind me said, "She should have listened to you."

I spun around, reaching for the thirty-eight stuck in the small of my back.

McAllister shot me.

It felt like I'd been steamrolled by an NFL linebacker. I hit the ground hard. Electric lava fried every nerve synapse in my body and I couldn't move my right arm.

Patricia yelled, "Brack!"

McAllister walked over, reached down, and picked up the pistol I'd dropped, sticking it inside his waistband. In my pain, I noticed he wore rugged boots and long pants and a long-sleeved shirt—good protection from the mosquitoes and vegetation.

He trained his Glock on me. "I should have known the Chinks in the whorehouse would talk."

My arm ached like someone had hacked it off with a dull pocket knife. I took off my belt and tightened it above the wound to stop the blood flow.

Patricia screamed, "You won't get away with this!"

McAllister said, "I expected something more original than that from the queen of Charleston news. Now, get out of the car or the next one goes between his eyes."

"Where's Darcy?" she asked.

McAllister fired another shot. The bullet hit the ground inches from my head. "I told you to get out of the car, not ask questions."

The only other weapon I had, if it could be called that, was the Swiss Army knife. McAllister had at least two guns, knowledge of the terrain, and the right clothes. I had shorts, sandals, and a nine millimeter hole in my bicep. Patricia wore pumps and a dress. She got out of the car and waded out of the puddle.

McAllister waved his Glock. "Start walking."

Patricia helped me to my feet. I kept pressure above the wound as we skirted the puddle and followed the path to the condemned site, our captor walking behind us.

Patricia said, "I can't believe Constance actually bought your act."

"Constance believes what she wants to believe. It's not like she gets out much."

The smell of my blood drew every mosquito within a five-mile radius and they feasted on Patricia and me. McAllister must have been under a layer of repellant.

I slipped on the muddy road and regained my balance. "Constance probably doesn't want to be seen with a douchebag like you, anyway."

"More like she couldn't get off the couch," McAllister said.

"You set up Galston real good," I said. "I'm sure his siblings won't mind you got the family cash-cow killed."

"As far as they know it was you and that idiot detective who shot him. Saved me from having to do it myself."

Between swats at the insects, Patricia said, "The Galston family has good attorneys. They'll figure out the truth."

We approached the rundown structure.

McAllister said, "We use the same firm. It's in our lawyers' best interest to make sure it all looks legit."

A side door had been wedged open. Patricia stopped and turned around to face our captor.

McAllister said, "I didn't tell you to stop."

She folded her arms across her chest. "I'm not going in there until you tell me where Darcy is."

Not the smartest play she could have made, I thought.

He pointed his gun at her. I was an equidistant ten feet between them, to McAllister's right. Patricia didn't move.

McAllister closed his finger around the trigger. I let go of the belt tourniquet on my arm and dove for him. He swung the pistol to me just as I grabbed for it. With my good arm I wrenched the gun up. It fired and hit somewhere on the second floor of the building. He bashed me in the face with Mutt's gun and I fell to the ground.

Patricia yelled, "Stop!"

McAllister said, "Try that again and I'll blow your head off."

As I got to my knees, he kicked me hard in the gut, the same place Galston had tagged me.

I doubled over. My chest tightened around what felt like bruised, if not cracked, ribs. Sucking in consecutive breaths, each one more difficult than the last, I tried to think what to do next.

Nothing came to mind directly.

Patricia knelt next to me. To McAllister, she said, "If you're going to kill us anyway, why all the drama?"

The sound of a helicopter getting close caused us all to look up. Patricia stuck something in the left pocket of my shorts as she helped me to my feet. By the weight and feel against my leg, I knew it was a pistol.

McAllister turned to us. "My ride's here. Get moving."

My arm throbbed. My chest throbbed. I was losing blood. Patricia looked into my eyes. She knew I was a better shot one-handed and delirious than she was uninjured. At least, I hoped that's what she thought. From somewhere inside the building came a muffled scream. I'd made it through three years of hell on earth and wasn't about to die in some backwater South Carolina waste dump. We were getting out of this. My drill sergeant screamed, "Snap to it, Soldier!"

McAllister cocked the hammer on Mutt's thirty-eight.

The helicopter's spinning rotors pulsed through my shoes. I faced the open door. "Okay. We're going in."

A musty smell wafted out of the structure. No light exited with it. I moved slowly and stepped inside. As my eyes adjusted to the dimness, I could hear the sound of creatures scurrying around—the rats we'd seen before, most likely. We stood in a large open room. Darcy sat in a chair, tied and gagged. She was dirty but alert.

Patricia gasped and ran to her.

McAllister said, "One big happy family. Get over there with them, Brack." He shoved me and I fell beside the women, pain shooting through my body again. Rats darted away from us.

We were out of options. McAllister was far from out of bullets. My arm pulsated like the bass in a gangbanger's Impala. Injured ribs reminded me of their presence with every breath. I teetered on the edge of a blackout. Darcy was tied up and Patricia had lost her bravado.

The only loose end McAllister had left was us.

I said, "Why'd you kill my uncle?"

McAllister aimed Mutt's pistol and shot one of the rats. The blast echoed in the large brick room. Patricia and Darcy both flinched.

"Nice shot." I sat up, recoiling at the pain in my body.

He said, "I hate rats."

I stood, feeling nauseous and light-headed. I'd pass out any minute. Willing my mind to keep working, I said, "You couldn't buy my uncle off. That's why you killed him."

He spit on the concrete floor. "Reggie wasn't going to look the other way. Not after that two-timing rat Fisher tipped him off. Both of them had to go."

"And Rogers?"

The helicopter's rotors slowed. It must have landed.

McAllister's smile showed off his bleached teeth despite the dim lighting. "You're a smart boy. Why do you think?"

I took two more steps. My only thought was to separate his targets, make him take his focus off the women. "Well, he was dirty. Probably figured you were involved and wanted money. After you killed him, you torched my house and planted the gun. I guess you used him to set me up."

"Bingo."

Standing over the dead rat, five feet from the women and ten feet from the man with two guns, I said, "So many deaths."

McAllister cocked the hammer back again. "There's about to be three more."

The room began to spin. I hunched over and threw up bile, my hand resting on my thigh. My chest burned and the sensation kept me from slipping into shock. After a few shallow breaths because deep ones caused enough pain to knock out an elephant, I regained strength.

McAllister said, "I expected you to be tougher than this, Soldier."

He wiped a bead of sweat from his brow.

I summoned enough strength to kick the dead rat at McAllister, who swatted at the flying rodent with the gun. I reached into my pocket for Patricia's pistol and fired four rounds into McAllister. From ten feet away, I easily hit my mark. The man's knees buckled and he fell, the nine millimeter and Mutt's thirty-eight he held clamored to the concrete floor.

I staggered to the door and aimed the pistol outside just as the helicopter's back door opened and Goatee stepped out. Sweat dripped into my eyes as I pulled the trigger and my shot went wide. Goatee tried to jump back into the helicopter but missed and fell to the ground as the pilot lifted off.

I sighted him in.

The man who had helped set Darcy and me up stood and raised his hands in surrender.

"It's over, Brack," Patricia said from behind me. "You don't have to shoot him, too."

CHAPTER THIRTY-FOUR

After we bound Goatee with the twine we removed from Darcy, Patricia knotted my shirt tight above my gunshot wound. Thankfully, McAllister had done nothing to Darcy other than tie her up.

Patricia stood next to me, her face and clothes caked in mud.

"Thanks for the gun," I said.

"I knew you'd hit him." She took out her phone and called the police. The mayor received the next call and it was not pretty. Needless to say, he would not be getting her support in the next election.

McAllister had kept Darcy alive to find out how much she knew. Patricia and I had interrupted him when we showed up. Help arrived in the form of police cruisers. They got blocked in behind Patricia's Mercedes. Two four-wheel-drive ambulances, one for McAllister and one for Darcy and me, got in past the lot of them. Patricia sat in the back with us.

Chauncey had caught a ride in one of the ambulances through the mud and watched the medics treat our injuries. "Everyone going to survive?"

Patricia took Darcy's hand and mine. "I think we're going to be just fine."

"Good," Chauncey said. "Detective Wilson asked me to give you a message." He took a piece of paper out of his pocket, unfolded it, and read. "An Asian-American male, Lo Chong, was apprehended an hour ago when the Trans Am he was driving collided with a tanker truck carrying septic-tank waste. The police estimate his speed in excess of ninety miles an hour. The driver and passenger in the truck were injured but in stable condition. Mr. Chong was not so lucky. The police are not sure if he will make it."

I didn't say anything. Justice was served.

Chauncey said, "This wouldn't have anything to do with the citizen's arrest at the underground brothel, would it?"

None of us replied.

McAllister was strapped onto a gurney and lifted into the back of the other ambulance. Somehow the bastard was still breathing.

Chauncey sighed and waved. "So long, Radar."

I sat up, gritting my teeth against the pain. "Radar?"

"McAllister," Chauncey said. "We called him Radar in Vietnam because the glasses he wore made him look like the guy from *M.A.S.H.* The movie came out while we were over there."

My ache subsided ever so slightly. "I thought Uncle Reggie said Ray shot him. I guess he was trying to say 'Radar.' "

Two police officers slammed the doors to the ambulance after McAllister had been loaded.

"We got him," Patricia said. She looked at Darcy, her eyebrows pinched. "Did you call in a camera crew?"

Chapter Thirty-Five

Charged with the murders of Reggie Sails, David Fisher, and Detective Rogers, along with kidnapping and fraud, McAllister lawyered up faster than a mosquito on a Yankee tourist. Based on documentation found by investigating officers, he was also revealed as the silent partner pushing to purchase Sumter Point. Galston had lied when he said he wanted to preserve the land and use offset credits to make an eco-friendly neighborhood. Sumter Point would itself be the ultimate offset credit, which would have preserved it at the expense of somewhere else in the state. And he would have made millions.

The senior partners in the accounting firm McAllister and Galston used—David Fisher's employers—were indicted for cooking the books and getting rich.

McAllister's aunt, Mrs. Calhoun, wanted my uncle out of the picture so she could bulldoze the Cove. Apparently murder was an acceptable solution to her distaste for seedy bars. The police could not establish whether or not she had been involved in planning the scheme, but the connection ruined her reputation. As the saying went, "There's a mighty big turd in the punchbowl."

Darcy had recognized McAllister's ZR1 from when I pointed it out to her. No one else in Charleston had a red one. She spotted it at the Chinese brothel but McAllister caught her entering, realized she could expose the whole operation, and told the Madame who she really was.

Darcy's mother set up a trust to take care of the fourteen-year-old prostitute who came forward in the brothel and helped Patricia and me find Darcy. The trust provided for her care and included a provision for college if she wanted to go.

The District Attorney called Darcy and Shorty as star witnesses. Shorty had neglected to tell me McAllister put him up to trashing my car after I blew his Chrysler to smithereens. Chauncey was the one to share that tidbit. I decided since the little freak was cooperating, I wouldn't pursue it. That's what my insurance company and the police were for.

After the doctors stitched up my arm, they prescribed an antibiotic, had me changing bandages daily, and recommended physical therapy. For a little while, Darcy and I wore matching slings.

Chauncey's wife cried when I came to get Shelby. I think my dog didn't want to leave Trish's constant presence and attention. On our way out of the driveway, she flagged us down and handed me the purple leash she'd gotten him, along with a fragranced spray. She told me I needed to put it on him every night.

Yeah, right. I threw it on the passenger side floorboard and sped away.

Constance Hagan and the Charleston Conservation Society held several events and raised money to buy Sumter Point. I was positive Constance fronted most of the money, which was okay with me. I received a cool million for the land and the commitment to preserve it forever, as my uncle had wanted.

After I paid the taxes and received the money the police finally unfroze from my uncle's accounts, I cleared the note on the bar and still had a lot left over. The Pirate's Cove was doing well under Paige's management and I would make sure she had everything she needed to run it and be secure for her and her boy. Uncle Reggie would come back to haunt me if I sold it, though that's what I did with Sumter Point to the C.C.S. I decided I wanted him to be resting in peace.

The Church of Redemption found an anonymous cash donation on its doorstep—just under two-hundred and fifty thousand dollars in fresh crisp bricks of hundreds. The same amount Darcy, Patricia, and I had found in the crab pots, minus a few expenses. When Chauncey determined the money couldn't be traced and gave legal council about how to handle it, Brother Thomas had no excuse but to accept it.

The church also found it had two new attendees—me and Mutt. We looked like a rough version of Paul McCartney and Stevie Wonder singing a gospel rendering of "Ebony and Ivory," but the congregation didn't seem to mind.

Ever concerned about my mental state, Paige handed over a letter from Justine Fisher, who'd sent it to the bar. Paige held onto it for two days before coming clean. Justine wanted me to know she and the kids were adapting well in Virginia. Her closing paragraph contained a surprise—an open invitation to visit.

I considered it for all of two seconds. One thing I definitely learned: leave the past where it is.

On Uncle Reggie's birthday, a month after he was killed, we held a small memorial service at the surf below the Pirate's Cove. Chauncey and Trish, Paige and Simon, Patricia, Darcy, Mutt, the former Detective Wilson, Shelby, and I listened as Brother Thomas spoke about life and death and salvation. Afterwards, the group watched as I carried the urn into knee-high water, with Shelby following behind. Patricia kicked off her shoes and waded out in what looked like an expensive black dress. I handed her the top of the canister.

"Brother said you were in a better place." My eyes watered and my voice broke.

Patricia put her arm around me.

"You always loved the water, Uncle Reggie," I said. "Now you can ride the waves all you want." I tilted the container and let the ashes pour out. Patricia rested her head on my shoulder. Shelby paddled around the ashes, whimpering, as if he knew what was going on.

ABOUT THE AUTHOR

David Burnsworth became fascinated with the Deep South at a young age. After a degree in Mechanical Engineering from the University of Tennessee and fifteen years in the corporate world, he made the decision to write a novel. *Southern Heat* is his first mystery. Having lived in Charleston on Sullivan's Island for five years, the setting was a foregone conclusion. He and his wife along with their dog call South Carolina home.